You really do want him. Right here, right now.

Regret assailed Lyn. Her alarmed expression, her body language…it must have felt like a slap in the face to Joe.

The thought that anything so strong, so overwhelming, could be anything but induced…

She couldn't. Not with this man. Not with a Sentinel gone dark.

A Sentinel who just left himself open to a painful surge of power to save four people…

That didn't mean he hadn't gotten himself into trouble. Troubled men could mean well…could even be admirable. And a troubled man could damn well drag her down into the dark with him, if she let him.

Books by Doranna Durgin

Silhouette Nocturne

*Sentinels: Jaguar Night #64
*Sentinels: Lion Heart #70

*Sentinels

DORANNA DURGIN

responded to all early injunctions to "put down that book/notebook and go outside to play" by climbing trees so that she'd have the freedom to read and write. Such a quirkiness of spirit has led to an eclectic publishing journey that has spanned genres and forms and resulted in twenty-five novels, which include mystery, science fiction and fantasy, action romance, paranormal, and a slew of essays and short stories. But she still prefers to hang around outside her southwestern home with the animals, riding dressage on her Lipizzan and training for performance sports with the dogs. She doesn't believe so much in mastering the beast within, but in channeling its power. For good or bad has yet to be decided....

You can find her online at www.doranna.net, where she keeps a picture collection of gorgeous high desert sunsets, lots of silly photos, the scoop on new projects and her contact info.

SENTINELS:
Lion Heart
DORANNA DURGIN

Silhouette Books

nocturne™

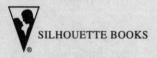 SILHOUETTE BOOKS

ISBN-13: 978-0-373-61817-0

Recycling programs
for this product may
not exist in your area.

SENTINELS: LION HEART

Dear Reader,

For eight years, I've lived in the shadow of the San Francisco Peaks. Their impact on me—from their visual beauty to the way they control the weather patterns to the way I measure the year by the position of the sun and moon along the distinctive ridges—was immediate. Over the years I learned more about their history and their role in the lives of the first peoples to live in this land.

When it came time to ponder settings for *Sentinels: Lion Heart,* there wasn't much question. Joe Ryan, too, loves this land—but unlike me, he has the means to protect it. A little vicarious wistfulness on my part! And while Lyn Maines enters the high country without any particular awareness of the impact it will have on her, soon enough she's caught up in the power it carries… and the power Joe Ryan has over *her.* All for the good, of course.

At least, I think so. I hope you do, too!

Doranna Durgin

Prologue

Dark Sentinel

Lyn Maines stared at the image of Joe Ryan, big as life—much *bigger* than life—as it splashed across the high-definition plasma screen of the sleek Sentinel conference room in Tucson, Arizona. Both Joe Ryans, actually—the man and his beast. On the left, tawny mountain lion, heavy masculine head with black tracings and jaw dropped in a snarl as the animal stalked the camera, clearly aware of and annoyed by the photographer's presence. On the right, Joe Ryan the man, caught unaware, leaning over a railing before an enormous high desert panoramic vista of pines and sere ocher plains, head turned three-quarters to the camera, wind lifting his tawny hair with its dark tracings at the nape of his neck and temple, features clean and strong.

Not always did the human form reflect the Sentinel

form. Her own didn't, aside from a certain something around the eyes. But there in Joe Ryan, the mountain lion lurked out loud—the sinuous authority, the simmering power. All of it.

Too bad that striking exterior covered a corrupt interior.

Joe Ryan was as dirty as they came—a dark Sentinel. He'd killed his partner for cold hard cash, and he'd done it cleverly enough so that the Sentinel's brevis region consul and his echelon hadn't been able to pin him down. Cleverly enough so that Ryan had gone on to a new assignment, a new home at the base of Arizona's San Francisco Peaks, to start a brand-new scheme—acquiring power on top of his money. Still on the Sentinel payroll, still roaming free in his powerful form. Still playing with power itself. And Lyn...

Lyn would prove it.

We think the Atrum Core drozhar might have fled there after the battle near Sonoita, the consul's grim adjutant had said moments earlier, a warning. *He'll know you if he makes contact with you. He'll target you.*

Then she simply wouldn't let herself be seen. "Send me there," she said, flexing her fingers slightly as if she could feel her sharp claws while in this form. Ocelot, small and quick, with a knack for following power traces that had served her well against the Atrum Core this past spring—well enough so that the consul owed her one, if any such thing could ever be said. "I can be on his trail by nightfall."

Yes. Lyn was the one who would finally prove it.

Chapter 1

Joe Ryan took a heady breath of hot, pine-scented air, basking in it—the scents so much stronger to the cougar, so subtly layered. Dirt and fallen pine needles and the scrub oak beside him, tangy and sharp as he barely brushed against it…each scent heated by the rising afternoon temperature and intensified by the moisture in the gathering monsoon clouds.

The humans he followed through this national forest probably noticed none of it, just as they'd missed the red-backed Abert's squirrel shooting away from their blundering dog and the birds gone quiet overhead.

Joe noticed them all—but it was the humans he stalked.

The humans and their dog.

Joe loved dogs. He'd had one in Nevada, a big lunky hound mix who'd been bitten by a rattlesnake shortly before everything else went so bad. So much loss…

This was his turf now—the western slopes of the San Francisco Peaks. From peripheral Vegas to high-altitude desert. He couldn't say he regretted the move. But the circumstances? Oh, yeah.

Still, he protected the area as best he could. Today, that meant ghosting along beside this chattering, trail-bound couple and their loose dog, unseen until he was good and ready to show himself.

There. Up ahead. He trotted a few rangy strides, big paws silent against the ground. He fought that ever-present instinct to *hunt,* to play with the dog like the prey it could be—

Down, boy-o. Dean's voice in his head—or the memory of it. He slipped out through a sun-dappled spot between two oaks, crouching down tight behind the base of a giant old Ponderosa. He could shift in an instant if he had to.

The couple had stopped. "Did you see—?" asked the man.

"I'm not sure what I saw," the woman said, alarm in her voice. "Bunky-Dog, come here."

"Yeah," the man agreed. "Let's get him on the leash."

Joe squeezed his eyes half-shut in practiced patience as the couple cajoled and chased and finally lured the oblivious Bunky-Dog with a treat. If he'd been a wild cougar drawn by the noisy, gamboling canine, they'd be good and mauled by now.

Finally. Their voices faded as they headed down the trail with haste. Mission accomplished. He'd work on saving the world tomorrow.

Joe stood and stretched, yawning hugely and letting his claws slide in and out of the soil, allowing himself some satisfaction. Now he could turn his attention to the power surge he'd felt on his way out—just like the one he'd felt yesterday, and a week earlier, when he'd been so felled by a cold that he hadn't been certain he'd perceived it at all. The Peaks, turning and grumbling and rolling off power in disgruntled waves. Not a good thing.

He couldn't let things go wrong on his watch. Not again.

He turned to cross the trail—and froze.

Not alone.

Ocelot. Cleverly upwind, as silent as he could ever be. She sat, stiff and offended, her tail tucked around her front legs, rich black lining her chained rosettes and striping her legs and that thickly furred tail. She sported black-tipped ears and a pink nose, with black lines defining her delicate face along the inside corner of each eye. In comparison to his tawny cougar's bulk, she was little more than dog-sized house cat.

A house cat who didn't belong here—and whose intelligence shone from her eyes with an intensity that made him wince. Now that he'd seen her, she dropped the wards concealing her etheric presence; her power flowed over him, smooth as weightless silk.

Smooth as…

He fought the startling impulse to lean into the sensation, to let it trickle over his whiskers and ruffle his fur. And yet his ears flicked forward…back…indecisive. She was Sentinel; he knew that much. Those eyes gave her away, that indignant posture…the silky power. That she was here at all, an ocelot out of place and time.

Decision made. He flicked a shake down his spine, quick and sharp, and shed the cougar—sleek and efficient, blurring from one form of tawny and lean to another and assuming the organically made clothes that came with him. Faded jeans and a cotton flannel shirt, moccasin-like ankle boots, his knives enclosed in treated, warded fabric pockets.

Quite a few of those, when it came right down to it.

He stood beside the tree and waited. She gave him a flat up-and-down stare and obliged with her own shift to stand with quick grace, wearing undyed linen summer pants and a scoop-necked, cap-sleeved shirt of some fine mesh weave.

He realized that his gaze had lingered on her body—like the ocelot, it was petite and understated and yet lithe and perfectly balanced—and stared at her face instead. Her hair was black, her eyes deep brown—neither reflected her Sentinel form. But the ocelot was there, in the sharp nature of her chin, her strikingly large eyes…and he would bet that was a natural smudge of darkness around her lashes, and not mineral makeup applied before she'd shifted. There was intensity in those eyes…purpose. It spoke to him.

She stared back without welcome. "Have you no sense at all, putting us to the change out in the open?"

Joe bit down on irritation, knowing his nostrils flared anyway, catlike, and that his eyes narrowed. Of course she didn't like him. She was a Sentinel with a mission…and that mission was probably *him.*

So he kept his voice even when he said, "There's no one here to see us." And he squashed his regret, that he'd never had any control over his heart. Foolish thing, heart.

She was oblivious to it. "I can't imagine what you were thinking, exposing yourself to those hikers."

He leaned a shoulder against the tree, as relaxed on the outside as he wasn't on the inside. Cat-lazy. "When loose dogs lure cougars into human contact, it's the cougar who usually ends up dead in the end. A little reminder that they're not the only ones here generally straightens them up." Training humans, that's what he was doing.

And he'd been doing it since he got here, without incident. He thought about saying that, too, but he'd learned the hard way that vigorous self-defense only made things worse. Made it seem as though there was indeed something to be guilty over.

Especially if someone already believed that you were.

"I'm Joe Ryan," he said. "But I suspect you already know that."

"Yes." She made no apology for it, or for the other things she already knew. "Lyn Maines. Can we talk?" As if he had any choice.

"Sure." He took the short drop to the trail with loose-limbed grace, hesitated long enough for her to join him, and headed up a narrow dirt path littered with volcanic cinders large and small. Raucous Steller's jays followed them through the trees, unheeding of the bright, building clouds above the trees and the heat.

He moved just as she'd imagined he would—balanced, easy, holding himself with authority. But she also sensed a hint of restraint in his movement, and she didn't blame him. He might have gone dark, but he was no fool. He knew she was there for him.

Even if that wasn't the whole of it. Not with the mountain surging power, or the Atrum Core prince—this region's drozhar—retreating here after losing a confrontation with Sentinels at the southern edge of the state. *Retreating, or just moving on to the next greedy, wreck-the-world-along-the-way scheme?*

"It can't be a surprise that I'm here," she told him.

"You must know about the power surges in the area…
even though you've said nothing to the brevis consul."

He stopped short, clearly impatient with the hardly
veiled accusation. In the gathering humidity of the afternoon storm, sweat darkened the tracings at his nape
and temple. "That's worth a phone call, not a personal
visit. And not worth finding me in the woods when you
could have waited for me at my place."

"I—" She gathered herself. Of course he wouldn't
mince words…of course he'd be blunt. Maybe she
should have hidden her bias when she'd met him.

Or maybe she shouldn't have spent so much time fa-
miliarizing herself with his file on the flight from
Tucson to Flagstaff, looking at those photos until she
found her fingers brushing over his image, there with
the wilds of the high desert reflected in his eyes.

Then she would have had the distance she needed,
and not had to create it with her own frank, hard words.

Take a breath. Do this right. *Stop the power drains,
nail the dark Sentinel.* So she said simply, "I wanted to
stretch my legs."

At that understandable truth, he relaxed slightly.
When he spoke, she couldn't read his voice at first, or
his expression. "Thirteen tribes revere this mountain,"
he said, looking up the incline where aspens now
mingled with the pines. "Not so much these lower
slopes, but the Peaks. The Navajo call them
Dook'o'oslííd—Shining on Top—for the snow pack.
The Hopi Katsinas live there. The Havasupai used to
live on the northwest slopes." She heard it, then. Anger.
Not at her, this time. At…

The situation. Because what *had been* wasn't any
longer.

It startled her. She hadn't expected the depth of his

feelings. She held her silence, simply keeping up with him for a moment, watching the whimsical roll of cinders beneath her soft, laced black-leather flats. This trail was more suited to the ocelot than to her travel outfit.

He slowed without comment, just enough to ease her way. It gave her the breath to say, as neutrally as possible, "Are we still talking about the power surges?"

He glanced at her, his dusky hazel eyes an exact match for those of his cougar self. "The Tucson office should have known better than to give you a Caucasian-only assessment of this area."

"Should have," she repeated in agreement. "Didn't. There was some rush." An understatement. For all the relief over the victory near Sonoita, it had been a close thing—Dolan Treviño's victory more than anything. No, the consul did not take this particular drozhar lightly.

"There's been a power struggle in place on this mountain for years," he said. "The tribes didn't want the Snowbowl ski area built. It was. Now they don't want recycled wastewater used to create artificial snow…but the courts are stomping all over the American Indian Religious Freedom Act." His tone made it obvious where he stood on the matter. How he felt about this land.

Maybe how he felt about the power here. *Wanting it.* But she didn't go so far as to say those words out loud. "Maybe I don't yet understand the nuances of the situation—"

He gave a short laugh, turning from a short, steep section of barely a trail to offer his hand; she took it without thinking. "Of course you don't. How can any of us? How can white man's courts make judgments on the validity of religions they can't possibly understand?"

She topped the rocky section and released his hand…or thought she had. She could still feel it, warm and calloused, against hers. She shook out her fingers. "You feel strongly about it, for someone who can't possibly understand."

Something flashed in his eyes, darkened them. "I understand being stomped on."

Point to him. Supposing he hadn't *deserved* being stomped on. Supposing he didn't deserve it again. *Way to play the wounded innocent.*

Except if she'd been that easy, the brevis consul office wouldn't have sent her. "Still not getting your point here, with the local interest story."

"The point," he said, as easily as if he hadn't just thrown such intensity at her, "is that if you listen to the mountain, you'll know that there's just as much power in those ancient religions as the tribes believe there to be. It's what drives this place." He glanced up at the sky gone suddenly, truly threatening, and increased his pace. "I don't think it's any coincidence that the push to expand Snowbowl has escalated. The Atrum Core knows what's here. They want it—they're probably looking for a way to convert it. And they're stirring things up on one front to obscure what they've been doing on another."

Lyn pulled a suede ribbon from her pocket and tied back her hair, feeling it gone curly with the humidity of the building storm. "Apparently the Atrum Core isn't the only one with a reason to go after that power. Or didn't you think we'd notice your trace on the power fluctuations?"

He stopped short, one hand on the huge granite rock

beside their path. *"No,"* he said, just as surprised as she'd meant him to be. Full of reaction, a swell of power she felt against her skin as if it were heat added to the storm. "It's not—they're twisting—"

And then, as if he realized he'd said too much even in those incomplete thoughts, he shut down, his jaw working, the defined nature of his lower lip going hard for a moment.

For it was the same excuse he'd used in Las Vegas over the body of his dead partner. *They're framing me. I didn't do it. It wasn't me.*

Except it had been.

The Sentinels had enough proof to believe it…and not enough to pronounce judgment. Not through Sentinel Justice, not through the mundane justice system which had released him. So the Sentinels—wary of him, yet unwilling to waste his remarkable ability to monitor and manipulate subtle power flows—had sent him here, where the brooding power of the Peaks kept things stable.

Or used to.

"Storm's coming in," he said shortly, turning away from her. "I'm going cougar to beat it home—the strikes come down thick around here." Everything about his body language suggested that she could stay human and get soaked if she wanted. The scathing look he threw over his shoulder confirmed it. Scathing and… something else. Something dark and powerful and warning. She blinked as the impact hit home, sending her a literal step backward.

"If you're going to walk," he informed her, his voice gone flat, "then be prepared to duck the lightning."

Whoa. Way too late for that.

Chapter 2

They ran through the rugged terrain, four legs and fur, easing downslope. He loped along with rangy strides that made Lyn hunt vertical shortcuts. Lightning flickered above them in regular strokes; thunder shook the pines.

A sudden sweep of wind roared through the trees; Lyn flattened her ears, crouching against it. He tipped his head in a gesture she interpreted as encouragement and she squirted forward in an unhappy slink of a run, already ducking against anticipated rain and the next crash of thunder. Thin, dry soil beneath her paws, thick pine-needle patches, abrasive cinders…this was rugged terrain, with rough, unpredictable rocky outcrops that changed the nature of the ground with little warning.

The cougar hesitated at the lip of one of these, looking down over a shallow swale of land. On the slope opposite them sat the back of a log house with a second-story porch cradled in the center and a variety of roof levels. With her ocelot's washed-out color vision, Lyn spotted his small SUV beside the house and her green rental car behind it.

Just in time. Intense, double-pronged lightning stabbed the sky not far from them, teamed with an instantaneous explosion of thunder. The cougar sprang into motion. Lyn followed at top speed, hyperaware of the large rain-drops splatting off her head and back. Another strobing flash of lightning, another explosion of thunder so loud it rattled her body, and then the rain swept in for real and she was running blind, depending on her surefooted nature and the flickering black tail tip before her.

Together they crashed into the space beneath the porch, brushing through wards and giving Lyn a brief glimpse of yard tools and a wheelbarrow before the world lit up again and blinded her; she lost her bearings, paws slipping on the flagstone, and slammed into warm, musky wet fur.

The cougar shook off, short and sharp, and water flew. Lyn, following suit in a tidier fashion, caught the panting laughter in his expression. *He loves this.* The dash through the weather, the exhilaration of the run… right there in those dancing eyes, as if he'd forgotten who she was and why she was there, as if they were no more than two companions who'd outraced a storm.

She saw it the moment he remembered. His eyes shuttered; he shifted his weight away from her. And she saw in his posture the moment he decided to change; she scooted back, her long, full tail sweeping between them.

That's when she felt it. As inevitable as the storm itself, as intertwined with the moment and the place. The deep, thrumming power of the mountain, a basso so profound that it put the rolling thunder to shame.

And dammit, woven in it all was the distinct trace of the very Sentinel who crouched before her—a smooth and corduroy-edged baritone trace, a beguiling brush of sensation even as he entered the change: a quick shake from shoulders up, a flicking twitch of skin down along his back, that elegant rise to his feet—

Except he faltered, and he fell. He crumpled down to his knees and elbows as the storm raged around them and the bass surge of the mountain's power made Lyn's bones hum, and his expression held astonishment and betrayal and pain.

Lyn flicked herself out of the ocelot. She went to him, crouching. "What is it?" She reached out, trying to find something identifiable other than Ryan's trace, other than the wards around this space and those protecting the house.

Dead end.

She looked into his face and saw a dead end there, too. Hazel eyes gone into shadow, body language gone stiff and wary. He sat back on his heels, some part of his expression still lingering on surprise. "It's nothing," he said. "Got something in my eye."

"That's the most—" *pathetic lie I ever heard.* It made her wonder if it wasn't an act, if Vegas had actually broken him, leaving him scrabbling in this last desperate bid for power without the chops to bring it off.

Or maybe he thought she was just that gullible.

Let him think it. No point in giving away the least advantage, even if he wasn't all he'd been made out to be.

What the hell was that?

Good God, he'd almost lost control of the shifting, right in front of her. That hadn't happened since…

Since *puberty,* when it happened to them all. Joe lingered there, sitting on his heels, knowing she was thinking about it, too—seeing the wariness hovering around her.

As if it mattered. She'd had her mind made up long before she'd met him. She had an intensity about her, a burn… Before this was over, he'd find out what had lit that fire. It might be focused on him, but it hadn't started with him. Way too much momentum there. Alluring, shimmering intensity…

He lifted his face to the fine spray of water reflecting off the edge of the porch, let it mist over skin that felt hot. "If you're so sure it's me," he said, "why not trail me instead of coming to me?"

She snorted, but the question did what he'd wanted—took her mind off his shifting stutter. She sat, bringing her knees up and wrapping her arms around them. "I couldn't trail you here without your knowledge, and you know it."

Ah. In this, at least, she was sensible enough. She'd hidden her power from him at first, but no one could keep that up for long. Perceiving power shifts was what he *did.*

"Besides," she said, still sensible, "whether you're innocent or guilty, you want to prove me wrong, right? The best way to do that is by helping me. Or pretending to help me."

Joe laughed. "So you're betting you're smarter than I am."

"Yes," she said, and shivered. The cleverly layered open weave of her shirt wasn't much for keeping in the heat. Nor for obscuring the tightening of cold nipples, when it came to that. "It's just a matter of which of us plays the game better."

She shivered again. The storm—already moving eastward over the Peaks—had dropped the temperature by a good twenty degrees. Typical. Joe climbed to his feet. "C'mon," he said. "Let's go get warmed up."

In response, he received a skeptical look. Eloquently skeptical, with one winged brow arching upward.

He shook his head. "I don't care about your games. I just want to keep this mountain safe." If they'd decided he was guilty of something, he'd be considered guilty whether they could prove it or not. If anyone knew the meaning of *inevitable,* it was Joe Ryan. No point in turning himself inside out over it.

"Keep the mountain safe," she repeated flatly. And then she nodded, rising gracefully to her feet in spite of her shivers. "Okay. We'll play it that way. Especially if it means coffee."

Joe gave her coffee. He offered her a down-filled lap quilt, which she pulled over her shoulders, and he stopped short of offering her dry clothes. He'd long since dispersed of his sister's clothing. No point in hanging on to it, now that she was gone. And thank God she had passed before they'd used her illness to ruin his life; thank God she'd never known.

Not that he'd much cared at the time. Too busy grieving and all that. By the time he started thinking straight again, the Sentinels had tried him in absentia, declared him not guilty but not innocent, and packed him off to this mountain where the deep, stable power was supposed to be big enough to keep him busy— taking advantage of his ability to influence slow swells of deep power—yet too big for him to mess with.

Apparently they'd changed their minds on that last part. He supposed he should feel flattered.

Instead he made coffee for a woman he didn't know

but who was already his enemy. Damn shame, that. Those eyes—

Don't go there, boy-o.

Besides, he'd be in real trouble if they found out just how wrong they were when it came to his limits.

"We just have time to make it to Snowbowl," he said, words she didn't quite seem to absorb as she wandered the most public parts of the house—the entryway with its skylights, the soaring space of the great room with its cathedral ceiling and the wood stove set neatly in the corner. She'd spooked three of his four cats into brief appearance and now she drifted back to the kitchen, an area defined by half walls and countertops and otherwise completely open to the great room. "I can't believe you have cats."

"I don't *have* them. They just live here." He shrugged. "It amuses them." In fact, cat number four, a little black shorthair, wound between his ankles as he pulled coffee mugs from the cupboard, her tail high and quivering. They'd all chosen him…followed him home, refused to go away, and now lived under his protection, indoors and safe from the predators of the area. "But four," he admitted, "is the absolute limit."

"Four," she repeated, looking bemused. And then, finally registering his words, "Why Snowbowl?"

Coffee gurgled in the background, his sleek little one-cup coffeemaker valiantly churning out a dark French blend, the very aroma of which ought to be enough to warm her right on the spot. "Because the Skyride is the fastest way to the top. Because one way or the other, that area is at the root of this problem." He shrugged, and added almost against his will, "Because I want you to see the view. To see what this place really is."

That stopped her. She hesitated, a moment in which

he couldn't read her at all. Even that whisper of silken power faded. And then she seemed to shake it off, and she moved in as he pulled the first mug from the brewer and pushed it across the polished charcoal granite counter. "I'd planned to do some tracking today."

"So do I." Different kinds, no doubt—she was a trace sniffer, someone who could find and follow specific individuals. It wasn't even a guess. Only someone with those skills could have found him on the trail today. Joe himself felt the deeper power, could nudge it around to a point, detour it on occasion, follow it if the flow was sustained. Officially, anyway.

He was perfectly willing to take advantage of her complimentary skills while he was at it.

Chapter 3

*A*gassiz Peak. Lyn squinted upward into a bright sky;
the rising mountain filled half of it. It didn't look like
all that much from here.

Ryan gave her a look. "You haven't really seen it
yet."

Had she said that out loud? She couldn't be certain.
Standing here at the modest ski lodge and gift shop, the
tortuously winding drive up Schultz Pass behind them
and nothing but pines and bare volcanic cinder slopes
up ahead, she'd let something of herself get lost in the
thrumming of the mountain. No wonder the Atrum
Core wanted this place. No wonder *Ryan* wanted it.

Although, as she left the solid-plank porch of the lower
lodge and stepped out onto sparse native grasses, it
occurred to her that he already had it, just by living here.

No. Wrong thinking. He was what he was; she
couldn't forget it. If he'd once made his trade-offs for

his sister's life, now he made them simply for power. For that desperate attempt to balance his life. It wasn't as though he had anything to lose.

After all, he'd already lost his sister even after he'd paid her bills with blood money.

He came up behind her. His solidity made her feel weightless, as though she stayed grounded only because he stood behind her. Over her shoulder, he gestured toward an open space and its ski lift—the barely green grass of a natural meadow, sloping sharply upward and lined by woods. "Hart Prairie," he said. "We can access a number of trails right here. But there are too many people for shifting, and you're not dressed for hiking."

At least she was dry, her wet clothes barely more than a memory in the resurging heat. As was he, in a basic T-shirt and jeans, a black leather vest completing the look in a way that should have been pathetically poser but instead looked perfectly natural. He looked up the slope, and even then she could have sworn he was drinking in the view. Drinking in the feel of the power, too—although it felt stable to her limited perception, and reassuring…like being held in the palm of some giant being.

He gave the slightest of nods as two hikers emerged from the trees. "We'll take the Skyride. Half an hour and we're there."

She didn't mind following his lead. Following blind…that was another thing. "And then?"

He grinned. "Then we see what we can see. And hope it doesn't brew up another storm." He offered his jacket—a lined canvas work jacket, strictly nonkosher when it came to shifting. "It'll be a lot colder up there."

"No, thanks," she said. The last thing she needed— to be surrounded by the scent of him.

He opened his mouth as though to say something—some argument, no doubt—and closed it again, offering a shrug instead. In this light, his hazel eyes looked distinctly green, and the short black edging at his nape and temple stood out sharply from tawny hair.

Nothing about his demeanor made her think of someone who could kill his boyhood friend and Sentinel partner. Nothing about his stance. A big guy, a strong guy, an exceptionally charismatic guy…but not edgy. Not that gritty.

He turned abruptly away from the prairie ski area bunny slopes and headed across the parking lot with assured strides. She caught up in short order, and soon enough caught a glimpse of another ski lift—this one moving steadily, chairs filled with people pointing out the sights to one another.

"From the top, you can see the Grand Canyon."

"I'm not here to see the Grand Canyon."

He gave her a sharp look. "I think maybe you are." He veered toward the upper of the two lodges, bought them both lift tickets, and returned with the conversation still on his tongue. "Thing is, you have to *look*. You have to *see*."

"I've already seen more than you want me to," she said, a deliberate and sharp reminder of her twofold purpose here.

He caught her gaze with a flash of green and held it. Quietly, he said, "If you think I've forgotten, you'd be very much mistaken." And then he left her behind, heading directly for the mechanical clank of the lift.

They'd almost reached it when his long stride faltered. An instant later, she felt it—felt the surge of *him* and the turbulent rapids of power that followed,

saw him stumble—and then they both froze at a shriek
of fear from the ski lift.

They hadn't been the only ones to feel the disruption—to react to it. A teenaged girl in skimpy shorts
dangled from the lift behind a half-engaged safety bar,
crop top riding high with her entanglement. Even as
they watched, one of her flip-flops fell to the rocky
grass below.

The lift wrangler was already on it, easing the cable
to a stop—but so was Ryan. From easygoing to distinctly feral, from stumbling to smooth, poetic movement. He sprinted past the gasping crowd, past the lift
wrangler and his incoherent yell of protest, and up the
hill with no slack in his powerful sprint.

There's no way. That chair had to be twice his
height. *Had to be—*

That's when she realized she was running, too,
right behind him, scooping up the jacket he'd dropped
and ready to…

What? Even drawing on an ocelot's strength, she
couldn't reach that lift….

And then she stuttered to a halt in amazement as
Ryan sprang from the ground, every bit of big-cat
strength in play, latching on to the footrest while the car
swung in reaction. There he hung a distinct moment
while he spoke to the terrified girl.

Lyn wouldn't have thought he could do it, not so
smoothly—not without jarring the girl from her precarious perch. But he did. He swiftly pulled himself up,
swung a leg up to hook around the seat, and slithered
into a position from which he could haul the girl into
the chair, flailing in fear until the moment she flung her
arms around him.

He jerked the safety bar down; the wild edges of her

sobs trickled unevenly down to Lyn, to the crowd. The silence exploded into relief and wonder and excited conversation. *Did you see—? How did he—?*

Lyn whirled around to jump into the next chair. The lift wrangler cried a knee-jerk protest and then he gave up and nudged the cable back up to speed, reaching for the radio at his side.

Lyn engaged her own safety bar, and then—already aware of the rising breeze and dropping temperatures as the lift swooped her up over the trees—tucked Ryan's jacket around her shoulders.

Alone on a half-hour ski lift ride to the top of the tall peak, with nothing to do but contemplate the broad strength of the shoulders that had so easily pulled Ryan into the chair…Lyn thought of the sudden change of his presence when he'd focused himself on the girl's lift chair, gone for it and caught it as resoundingly as prey in powerful cougar paws.

To think, only moments ago she'd been wondering if really he had the grit to go dark.

She laughed out loud, and if the man in the seat ahead with the girl clinging around his neck heard her, he gave no sign.

The topside lift wrangler waited for them as the chairs glided toward the turnaround, radio raised to his ear, face tense and determined. Gusts flapped at his jeans and windbreaker; Lyn drew Ryan's coat closer as that same wind buffeted her. Ryan hadn't been exaggerating; high summer had turned sharply to fall.

Abruptly, the chairs slowed in pace, giving Ryan a luxury of time to flip the safety bar up and disembark. The girl clung tightly as he half carried her away from the chair's path, one arm wrapped around her waist.

Lyn fumbled with the unfamiliar bar as she, too, reached the summit, ducking away and to the side as the lift wrangler's radio drizzled static in response to his short comment. The chairs sped up again, and Lyn glanced down the long swooping lines of the cables in surprise; she'd expected them to call an all-stop until things were sorted out. But it didn't take her sharp vision long to pick out the cluster of occupied chairs heading their way in double time—E.M.T.s, officials.

She didn't plan to be here.

Ryan apparently felt the same; he'd transferred the teenager to the lift operator and now headed for the narrow trail leading uphill.

"Hey," the lift wrangler said, tangled up in the girl, "you can't go… They'll want to talk to you—"

Ryan spun briefly around to face him. "Go *where?*" he asked, wry enough to make the kid laugh.

Lyn took note. Not a lie, but misleading? *Oh, yeah.* Because she and Ryan had an entire extinct volcano over which to range—eighteen thousand acres of fragile, extreme Kachina Peaks Wilderness area above the more accessible trails.

On the other hand…

Don't overanalyze. Of course he'd misled the kid. Of course he'd do whatever low-key thing it took to keep them out of any official reports of the incident, just as she was prepared to do the same. And it didn't take as much as one might think. Already she could imagine the reaction to the description of Joe Ryan leaping to catch hold of that lift chair and pull the girl to safety. Skepticism, if not outright disbelief. Chalking it up to a natural inclination to exaggerate.

Such skepticism served the Sentinels well.

Ryan moved effortlessly up the tricky trail, maneuvering its short, zigzagging sections with ease. Lyn followed, custom-made boots finding purchase in spite of rolling cinders over rock-hard dirt.

She'd thought he'd just keep going—get them out of sight and head into the woods. But instead, when the trail widened out to a viewing area perched at the edge of a rock outcrop, he hesitated. He wandered to the fenced edge, looking not at the drop before him but out at the re-forming thunderheads of the waning afternoon. Lyn realized, then, with a startling snap of awareness—this was the very spot his dossier picture had been taken.

Yes, he knew this place.

He might even consider it his, in some ways.

He'd be wrong.

She wandered over to the token handrail. Ponderosas speared up at her from the plunging slope below; off to the side and farther down, ski resort personnel bustled around the teenager. Scattered groups of tourists appeared in the distant chairs on the lift. Good. With more people up here, their own absence would be less noticeable.

But while she tried to focus her thoughts on the power surges of the area, on the consequences of such surges, on her need to prove Joe Ryan a Sentinel gone dark, the gentle gusty wind snatched at her thoughts; the scent of sun-warmed pine beguiled her nose. The thin air slipped in and out of her lungs without leaving much impact, and her peripheral vision seemed ever so sparkly around the edges. Her fingers curled around the upper rail of the brown pipe fencing; she took a deep breath.

"Give it a few minutes," Ryan said, giving her a quick, sharp glance before he returned his attention to the panorama before them. "You'll adjust."

More so than the average tourist—an advantage of her robust shifter form, and one she'd gladly take. Plenty of travelers found the seven-thousand-foot altitude at the base challenging enough; Lyn hadn't even considered it until this moment. She took another deep breath, suddenly overwhelmed by the very alien nature of the landscape—from the volcanic rock formations around them to the distinct sections of forest and high desert prairie spread out below and the slash of the Grand Canyon far to the north-west…this place smelled different, it sounded differ-ent…it even *tasted* different, pressing in around her with clear, rarefied air and the unique trace of those creatures who dared to live at this cold, dry twelve thousand feet.

Perhaps that's why she nearly missed it. Another rumble of power, a mere bass hiss of presence, tasting of Ryan and of deep green wild…Lyn found herself closing her eyes, leaning into it as she might a pleasant breeze on a hot day.

Her eyes snapped open, riveting to him in accusa-tion—but the words she gathered to fling at him died on her lips. He stood braced against the rail, a frown drawing his brows, nostrils flared with the impact of that faint surge…or with effort, she wasn't sure. Even as she watched, eyes narrowed, he lifted his head—a little jerk of determination there—and turned to her.

And then she couldn't help it. Then the words burst out. "Don't tell me you didn't feel that. Don't tell me you didn't taste yourself in that surge!"

For an instant, he looked nothing more than non-plussed. And then his frustration snapped back at her. "No! It's *not*—I—" A quick step, another, and he'd closed the distance between them, by then under better control. "Tell me, Lyn Maines…did you recognize *your* voice the first time you heard yourself recorded?"

She blinked. "I…" Flashed back to that day, two children playing with an off-limits answering machine, her brother leading the way into trouble even then. The laughter at how they sounded, their insistence—*that really is you!*

She didn't get a chance to voice her answer; he turned away from her again, looking back out over the vista. It truly didn't matter—they both knew her answer. And so the question became…did he not know why his trace was tangled with the surges? Or had he simply not realized it would be detectible?

Voices muttered up from below as the next wave of tourists grew closer, the Snowbowl management and emergency personnel in discussion with the lift operator. "They'll be looking for us," Ryan said, but it came as an afterthought, an aside to whatever else ran through his mind.

Lyn said, "If the Core siphons the energy of this place…if they store it in their amulets, if they use it against us…if they use it against the rest of the world—"

He didn't turn on her, but she got the impression it was only through strength of will. "Then this ancient place will change forever," he said, his voice low. "Irrevocably. The people who revere it, who draw their spiritual strength from it…those nations would never recover. There's no telling what would happen to the delicate ecosystem up here."

"And you?" she said, words that slipped out before she could think better of them. She tightened his jacket around her, realized suddenly that it was *his,* and pretended that it didn't matter. "If *you* siphon energy?"

He laughed—a short, bitter sound. "They think I'm

that good, do they?" He gestured out over the slopes—
hard red-brown cinders cropping up in dramatic patches
between the pines, while above them the trees stunted
down and gave way to lichens and scrub. "Look at it!
Can't you feel it, lurking here, as big as the world?
What would I do with it all?"

She shrugged, determined to be unaffected by his
passion for this area. "Personal glory? A little something to make up for what you've lost?"

No laughter this time, but he grinned, and turned so
the gusts lifted the hair from his forehead as he looked
back at her. "Don't you think it's all just a little bit
bigger than I am?"

"Well," she said, taken aback at both the grin and the
matter-of-fact nature of the response, "I do. But people
who break rules usually think they're the exception."

He nodded. "Okay," he said, and turned to her,
leaning his hips against the top pipe rail with an insou-
ciance she could not have mustered, not with the fatal
nature of the drop behind him. He nodded again,
catching her eyes. The sharp shadows thrown by his
own features turned his dusky hazel gaze to something
darker. "Okay," he repeated. "That's good. You think
like that."

She must have registered her surprise. He grinned
again. "Thinking like that will find the truth. That's
fine by me. That's not the same as already having made
up your mind, and coming here with some old grudge
already in hand."

Lyn's jaw dropped; she groped for words. Her
temper filled the void. "How dare you even suggest—"

He cut her off with a snort of a laugh. "What have I
got to lose?"

And that stopped her temper cold, floundering; she

was unable to do anything but search his eyes. From below came filtered conversation—clear to any Sentinel, if not the average person. The lift wrangler said, "They've got to come down soon."

"We should go," Ryan said, dropping her gaze. He pushed away from the railing and then quite suddenly froze, and the hint of natural burnished color in his face paled away. His step faltered to the point that she reached for him—and that's when she felt it herself, another angry aftershock of power, whispering through her veins and briefly clouding her head. Only the merest of grumbles, but here, so close to the source...

An instant of panic skittered down her spine, fluttered in her chest. *So much power, and we're sitting right on top of it...*

What if she hadn't even thought of the worst of the possibilities? What if brevis regional had missed it, too? Because...what if whoever had disturbed the mountain hadn't done it *right?*

If the area had been unbalanced, destabilized...it could be on the verge of an eruption such as the world had never seen. Not magma, but pure power...

Take a breath. She did just that. *Get a grip.* Not quite as easily done. She took another breath, deeper... slower. She gathered her own energy, what little grasp she had of it. She was no Joe Ryan, to perceive and impose himself on the world's deepest powers, but she could damn well control her own. She pulled it into herself, found it tainted with her fears, and hunted the inner note that had always cleared away such things...a silent hum. It grounded her...centered her.

And when she opened her eyes, she found him there—*right there*—his hand reaching for the side of her face, his expression equal parts intensity and wonder. "How…?" he said. And, "I thought you were a *tracker*…."

"I am," she said, the calm lingering; she didn't so much as blink to find him so close, though she couldn't help but lift her chin slightly.

He shook his head. "Whatever. Damned fine job of…" He shook his head again. "It wasn't shielding, or even just centering. Nicely done."

She shrugged. "Are you all right? You looked—"

He waved off the rest of the question. "I had a bug earlier this week. I'm fine." But he glanced down slope and took her arm, escorting her back to the trail and moving a little too quickly for her comfort.

She shook his hand free. "Where now?" she asked, and she lowered her voice in deference to those who were looking for them. She and Ryan were vulnerable now—silhouetted against bare rock and sky until the trail rounded the next hump of ground.

He looked back at her, ready to offer a hand if she needed it. "Following my feet," he said. "You've seen for yourself…they pretty much lead me to trouble. Today, I'm counting on it."

Chapter 4

Alien and familiar at the same time, the alpine zone of the Peaks never failed to draw Joe's awe, here on the rarified trails across the towering Agassiz Peak summit to the saddles and dips between the other five Peaks. Arctic tundra, right here in the Arizona desert, with lichens and a threatened groundsel species and even a variety of buttercup; on the gentler slopes of swooping tundra meadows there were enough grasses, sedges and moss to keep his nose twitching—not to mention a shrew or two.

But he wasn't here for shrews today. He glanced at Lyn; she, too, looked out over the cold rugged landscape, her eyes bright and alert, her ears flicking in tiny, precise motions.

So very Lyn.

The wind ruffled her thick, rich fur, rippling down along the length of a truly amazing tail. What would fur like that feel like beneath a man's hands?

You'll never know, boy-o.

They'd followed the trail at first, passing out of Snowbowl turf into the Kachina Peaks Wilderness area, where they definitely didn't have the necessary permit. And so as soon as they found a grouping of rocks big enough to hide the jacket, Lyn had taken the ocelot, and Joe had turned his face to the sun and let the cougar come out.

From here, the power pushed at him with an inner rumble and a strong directional flow. Unlike warders with their discrete lines and precision knots, Joe saw broad tides and flows, overlays of movement over earth and sky. Tides and flows couldn't be tied into knots or moved with precision. Might as well try to herd a flash flood. Managing power on this scale took deep concentration, a sense of conviction behind clear vision of *what should be*…an utter belief in success.

Even if Joe still had that belief in himself, it seemed that brevis regional did not. And looking out over this natural magic of delicate ecosystem backed by a power so deep that every native nation within reach had considered it sacred, Joe felt the resentment of it. *I've done a good job here.*

Probably part of the problem. They probably had no idea of the subtle adjustments he made, the corrections to natural flows gone astray in the face of modern incursions. Even if they'd read his reluctantly submitted reports, they'd never truly comprehend.

He stopped, flicked a whisker, briefly flattened annoyed ears. He *had* sent that last report, hadn't he?

Damned paperwork.

The ocelot looked back at him, silent. Had she been more simpatico, they could have communicated clearly in thought. *Also not gonna happen, boy-o.* Joe padded past her, heading them down into the scoop of the meadow and toward the tree line on the far side— aiming through the Fremont Saddle to pick up the Weatherford Trail. "If they've been here," he'd told her before the change, "they probably came this way." Pretty much the only way, on foot.

They being the Core, of course. Those for whom he'd already intended to look today. Not because brevis had warned him, not because consul Dane had sent him any message or his adjutant Nick Carter had bothered with a heads-up, but because anywhere things went amiss as profoundly as the recent power surges, it was worth looking for Core influence.

The tree line rose up around them in an amazingly abrupt transition, stunted and gnarled spruce, firs and pines. Something of a rodent nature rustled low in the grass off to the side; Joe ignored the catlike impulse to play *toss the squeakie*. He threaded through the trees, heading for the trail in an efficient line—leaping onto rock outcrops as though they were mere steps, bounding over water-worn mini-gullies in the fragile soil.

When he struck the trail, he gave it over to Lyn. They'd had no discussion of it, but it made sense. He could track with his nose, his whiskers, his common sense, but the best trackers could sense any faint trace of used power, including the corrupt presence of Core amulets, and he was betting his little ocelot—

Right. Not yours. Not a tame ocelot. Don't forget it.

But he thought Lyn could do it.

She didn't hesitate to move out in front of him. She stepped onto the trail and trotted easily along. The unwary might have said she wasn't paying attention, but Joe saw the swivel of her ears, the alert, graceful posture of her neck…the slight kink of tension near the end of her tail.

Quickly enough, she stopped short, her ears trained forward—presenting him with a perfect view of the yellow spot on the back of each small, perfectly aligned ear. He came up beside her, watching her whiskers quiver. The quiver traveled through her whole body until she gave a quiet, disdainful little sneeze and shook it off with distaste.

Core. His pulse quickened. And if they were indeed on this trail…he knew where they were headed.

She opened her eyes and instantly stiffened to find him so close, so large; she was ten inches shorter than he and nearly a hundred and fifty pounds lighter. She hissed.

He immediately crouched, not in submission but remorse. Hadn't been thinking, nope. *Sorry,* he said, an apology she wouldn't or couldn't hear. But when she flicked her tail and stepped out to move on down the trail, he didn't follow. For that scent in this place…he knew where they were headed, and that meant he was no longer just out for a ramble in the high, free air beside a beautiful companion. Not now.

Now, he was predator.

Lyn scowled. It came out as whiskers tipped back, baleful green eyes glowering at him, ears slanted. A powerful look, used to good effect.

Ryan ignored it. He may have tried to say something to her. She had the uneasy sense of it, enough to make her skin twitch. She couldn't hear him; she didn't want to hear him.

Even if it meant watching him turn away to lope downhill with directed strides, slipping between the gnarled, sun-scented pines where the shadows turned long from the early-evening sun. She sneezed again—this time from pure vexation.

Trust him, then. She'd know soon enough if he was leading her into folly…and now that she'd been to this place, she could find her way back with or without him.

She didn't admit to herself that it was a relief to return to his smooth trace, the baritone feel and the textured depth of it. Something she could sink her mental fingers into, but not a sensation that would ever turn boring. It didn't matter that he was already out of sight, or that her nose could track him as easily as her eyes. She slipped onto his trail without benefit of either, indulging in an all-out sprint, tail undulating behind her, until she caught sight of him flicking through stunted trees. He paused by a conglomeration of jumbled rocks and gnarled miniature trees to let her catch up.

His whiskers quirked in quick greeting. And she realized, startled, that she'd allowed the feel of him to capture her senses. She instantly closed her eyes to filter him out, pushing the *Joe Ryan* awareness back to a trickle and casting the area for other influences.

Nothing. Just the feel of this place itself, a deep rumbling hum with a touch of discord and the uncomfortable random prickle of physical static. They'd have to go back to the trail and start again; he'd merely led them astray.

But when she opened her eyes, she found him… gone. She gave a startled *mrp,* full of sudden suspicion, thoughts racing—had he led her into a trap? Abandoned her here, thinking she couldn't find her way back? Gone off to—

But by then she had opened herself to the feel of him again, and the baritone corduroy came flooding back with such intensity that she knew he was still close.

Claws scratched rock above her; she glanced up to find him comfortably ensconced on the outcrop, one massive paw outstretched, claws exposed to knead stone and a cat grin on his face.

She would have blushed, had she been in the human form—this, then, was the reason she could never work alone. Too vulnerable, when those moments of utter concentration blocked out all else.

The skin over her shoulder twitched—no doubt he'd said something to her. She scrambled lightly up those rocks to stand beside him; he withdrew his outstretched paw and tucked it beneath him, classic cat, eyes squeezing closed.

Good God, was that a *purr* she heard?

If so, it was brief and barely evident, but he remained settled. In his element. For the moment, not concerned about Lyn, or about what they might find here. Certainly not concerned about what she might expose of his activities here.

Another flash of uncertainty hit her. Either brevis had been wrong all along—*she'd* been wrong—or he'd simply led her so astray that he already had complete command of the situation.

She'd prove him wrong. And damn fast.

She settled herself on their perch and went deep again; she wouldn't let it be said that she'd stinted the search. She filtered him out—harder this time, with his contentment now coloring his trace—and she hunted. The land gave her a trickle of something fresh and bright and near, and at the same time nudged her with the distant unrest of a developing storm cell. And there, at the edges…

Something bitter. Something corrupt. The faint traces of power ripped from its living vessel and stored away, as decayed as any corpse but still entrapped. *Amulets.*

Her eyes popped open. She found Ryan watching her with such interest in those predator's dusky hazel eyes that she felt a quick, ephemeral thrill of fear—it ran down her spine and just like that, puffed out the considerable length of her tail.

He blinked, drew back. Looked, if it was possible, embarrassed. He sat, turning away to look out over the land. For the first time she realized that on the other side of their approach, the rocks tumbled away in a V shape. They sat at the apex, and directly below them, from within the steep cleft of stone and moss, a seep of water eased out to fill the most modest of pools near the base of the structure.

Suddenly she was so very thirsty. And she thought, from the sly flick of his ear and the way he didn't quite look at her, that he might be laughing again—that she'd been so caught up in the hunt she hadn't yet realized that he'd brought them to water.

The birds alone should have alerted her, flitting so actively from twisted evergreen branch to lichen-covered rock, or the light scent of the tiny white flowers so thickly scattered along the gentle slope below. She gave another inward blush, another acknowledgment of how very focused she became when on the trail of something. *They should have sent me with a partner.*

But they hadn't wanted Ryan to feel threatened enough to act rashly. They'd wanted him just as he was—aware of Lyn but underestimating her. If that meant she needed to pay a little more attention…

Well, then, she'd do it. She'd had her warning.

And now she scrambled to catch up, because Ryan

had moved ahead, descending careful step by step on the nearly vertical clifflet. Here, Lyn found herself at an advantage, light and swift; she reached the spring before him, lapping neatly from its fresh, cold water, then moving aside so Ryan could join her—noisier, not quite so tidy.

Men.

That the thought held humor surprised her, and she was still somewhat bemused as she padded out beside him, heading toward another, much lower rock formation. Except this time he gave her a little sideways glance, and it was but an instant later that the first wafting stench of it hit her.

She stopped short. Her eyes widened; she sneezed. Corruption filled her nose, her sinuses, her inner self. It brushed against her soul with Brillo-pad harshness; she slammed her defenses shut. Another sneeze and she dropped to rub her paws over her face, and that's how the change caught her; she came to the human curled up over her knees with her hands over her face.

Dammit. Another weakness, and one of her worst. She hadn't intended to change, but when the trace came on that strong…it didn't matter whether she was human or ocelot, she found herself jarred into whatever she wasn't.

But Joe changed right beside her, already crouching down to put a hand on her shoulder. "Are you all right?"

She sneezed, one more mortifying time, her face still buried in her hands. "I'm fine," she said, her words muffled even to her own ears. Even now, the trace was strong—but she'd adjust. She'd push it back until she could filter out the details, just as she had pushed back the feel of Joe Ryan.

Except now, with the corruption so strong around

them, she gave in to sudden impulse—she let his trace wash over her, as textured and deep as she remembered. She took it into herself, absorbing it like a decadent balm, and then took a breath, clearing her thoughts, finding her own inner note of centered calm…pulled that centered space around her as if it were a cloak.

Ryan made a strangled noise. His hand clenched down on her shoulder—until he snatched it back to himself, sucking in a quick breath. Lyn looked up from her centered, peaceful place to discover him staring at her, darkened eyes wide and alarmed and something she couldn't read, his withdrawn hand clenched and…

Yes. Trembling.

Chapter 5

Joe took another deep breath. What the hell had she done? That centering thing of hers, but something else, too—something that had grabbed him and folded him in and damn well caressed him from the inside out, touching nerves he hadn't even known he'd had.

And she clearly didn't have a clue.

At least, not to judge from those big, brown eyes aimed his way, puzzled and a little concerned—but more suspicious than not. So Joe took one last deep breath and counted himself glad for clothes, and he turned himself brusque and matter-of-fact. He tightened all those feelings down into his clenched fist and allowed himself that small crutch while the rest of him went on. "We can't stay this way long," he said, certain the cold wind already bit into her as it did into him. He stood, held out a hand and pulled her to her feet.

She tucked a strand of wavy hair behind her ear and gestured at the area. "How did you know?"

He shrugged. "I guessed." He pointed back at the little spring. "Believe it or not, that one's not on any maps—none of the trails go anywhere near it. I call it the top of the world. It's a place where…" He hesitated, narrowed his eyes slightly—and decided maybe not. Not when she'd already decided he had a thing for power. So instead he asked, "What's it like? The traces? What do they feel like?"

She looked taken aback, as she well might. It was a personal question, in its way. Probably too personal, and probably she wouldn't answer, but—

"It depends," she said, wrapping her arms around herself—cold at that. Her eyes still watered slightly from her sneezing and she hadn't quite recaptured all her hair; a wavy tendril from her temple fluttered in the breeze. Reluctantly, she added, "They come as smells, mainly, but also as…inner sensations. The sneezing…the amulets are particularly pungent, in all ways. Corrupt. Like sticking your nose into a liquefying corpse."

He recoiled. "Tell me *I* don't do that to you," he said, the words out of his mouth before he thought them through.

She reacted much the same. "God, no," she said. "You're—" and then she caught herself. "No, not at all. Don't worry about it."

All right. Yeah. He changed directions again, back to where he'd been. "What I feel," he said, "is too big to fit inside me. Like being inside a slow wind that goes right through your skin. Sometimes it gets gusty and fussy, but unless someone's messing with it—" *like lately* "—it's pretty steady. Feels different, depending on the source. It's…"

And there he ran out of words, for how could he explain the thrill of riding power, of having it fill him and pass on through, leaving the taste of wherever it had come from and where it had been along the way? Like jumping off a high cliff and soaring on thermals and bounding downhill and flinging himself wide open to all the possibilities of what might be, all at the same time—

Mistake, boy-o. She'd seen something in his expression…something, perhaps, of the words he hadn't said. Her eyes narrowed. And so, totally lame, he pointed to the rock formation over the spring. "It's a natural channel…easy to monitor the area from here."

"Right there," she said flatly, and then repeated words that somehow now seemed childish. "At the top of the world."

He suddenly felt exposed, scraped raw right down into a silly, insignificant core. Hardest thing he'd done in a long time, meeting her gaze just then. But he did it, and he said, "Yes." And he gritted his teeth together a moment or two, clenching jaw muscles he hadn't had occasion to use in such a fashion since the days of pain and loss—his sister, his partner, his *life*—and then managed to add more casually, "Once you caught trace on the Weatherford Trail, I figured our Core friends had headed this way. They just didn't know the straightest route to get here. They probably circled in on it…had some kind of detection device."

"Fabron Gausto," she murmured, and shivered, rubbing her upper arms. Maybe the cold, maybe the thought of the Core's local sept prince.

And then he realized she wasn't just referring to the influence of the local Core when she named the man. She meant *Fabron Gausto*.

She meant *here*.

Right then she looked at him, and said, "He's been here, all right," a pronouncement filled with both satisfaction and trepidation.

"Hold on," he said, and his temper suddenly felt hot within him, a rare thing for a man who'd become so resigned to so very much. "You *expected* to find him? You *knew* that son of a bitch Core prince would be *here?* And no one's told me? Warned me? Done so much as dropped sly damned knowing *hints?*"

Her hands stilled on her arms; she looked back at him, nonplussed. "Of course we—" she started, and stopped to frown. "Didn't you—?" And then gave a giant shiver and hugged herself anew.

The cold wind cut just as sharply through Joe's shirt, tugging at his hair, gusting away the last remnants of the startling sensations she'd roused. He badly needed to take the cougar, and even more badly, she needed to take back the ocelot. To bask in the sharp intensity of the high altitude sun, buffered from the wind by thick coats.

But not until she explained why brevis regional, the Southwest office to which he reported, on which he depended for updates on the millennia-long clash between the Atrum Core and the Sentinels, had failed to mention their intel on Gausto's location.

For although the simmering conflict between the Core and the Sentinels rarely exploded even on the most local of levels, Fabron Gausto had recently changed all that. A regional septs drozhar going against his own Continental septs prince, his own advisors, and the wisdom of every generation since the two organizations were both founded from the same family—by two brothers with the same Gaul mother, but fathers from two different nations—Gausto had broken rules that hadn't been challenged for hundreds of years.

Early enough, the Druidic-born brother and the Roman-born brother had realized that whatever their clashes, their survival lay in their clandestine nature. Never mind that the Roman-born brother, finding himself completely without the inborn ability to manipulate earthly powers—including his Druidic brother's amazing faculty for taking the form of a wild boar—turned early to darker, cruder options, justifying his actions as necessary to police any unsavory act his brother might commit. And never mind that the Druidic brother quickly set about refining his abilities, and set upon his descendants the obligation to continue his work. *Vigilia,* the Sentinels had been called back then— and, wisely keeping the strong, prepotent nature of their lineage to themselves, they thrived and grew and expanded…they spread across the continents, learning, growing…becoming sentinels of the earth.

The Atrum Core had taken their name from the Vigilia…*Dark to the Core*, they'd been called, and then *Dark Core* for short. It wasn't supposed to be a compliment. No one ever expected them to take the name for their own. And while the Core ran itself on stolen power, half monarchy and half dictatorship, broken down into regional septs, the Sentinels had a more developed structure—more democratic.

Or so they liked to say. And so Joe had used to believe.

He'd given her too much time. She said, "You were told. Just as you were specifically asked to deliver your most recent report—the one that's so late—and never did. That looked really good for you, by the way."

"I—what?" Now it was his turn to stand and stare, until the next gust of wind hit him and he turned his back to it; he didn't miss the way she angled around to use him as a wind break. Too cold, too high, too remote, with rain building up again in a little western thunderhead that might or might not dump on the mountain before it dissipated into evening darkness. No, humans didn't belong up here. "Hell, it's late…it's always late. What's the big deal?"

Dean used to rag him about that…his casual disrespect for paperwork. "You're gonna get nailed, boy-o," he'd said, more than once dropping forms on Joe's desk or leaving sticky notes on his monitor. And with Dean around, the paperwork had, somehow, always gotten done on time.

Not so much since Dean's death—nor since Joe had been both officially cleared of and unofficially convicted of causing it.

Lyn Maines snorted; it turned into half a sneeze, left her eyes watering as she said, "The big deal is that Nick requested it—he needed it to assess this situation. When he didn't get it, all we could do was guess what's been happening up here." She narrowed her eyes at him. "Maybe you've gone dark…maybe not. But letting down brevis because you just don't care enough to do your job—?"

Joe recoiled as if she'd hit him. Hell, she *had* hit him. He'd *never* not cared, he'd *never* given this job—this *life*—less than everything he had. Being a little slow with the reports was one thing…ignoring a direct request for information, something else entirely. Lives depended on fulfilling such requests. "I *never*—" he said.

But suddenly it had the same old familiar feel to it. *Not me. I didn't do it. There's been a mistake.* And so he turned from her, quite abruptly taking the cougar—

a quick, hard transition that found him already
bounding back up to the top of the spring upon completion—and this time, if she'd had anything left to
say, he was the one who wasn't listening.

Lyn thought she'd never get warm again.

She took another sip of coffee from the simple machine in Joe Ryan's barely detached casita—nothing like
the home-ground beans from his own kitchen, just your
basic Mr. Coffee and grounds from a can. Still, she was
grateful for it, even with the bitter aftertaste going down.

Rather like her entire day. Definite bitter aftertaste
there.

She hadn't expected to end up here, in this little
studio structure so common to Southwest homes—
open kitchenette, full bath and a daybed. He'd offered
it to her when they'd emerged from the Snowbowl
woods at his car, and she couldn't decide if he was
trying to prove he had nothing to hide or if he just
didn't care. His words told her nothing; his eyes held
dark secrets and a bruised soul.

Someone else might think it a sign of his innocence,
that hurt. She found it less than convincing. The most
dangerous were those whose hearts went dark because
they felt justified...felt the world owed them something.

But when she curled up on the daybed in the cool
night air beside the open window—when she wrapped
herself in an old quilt that smelled faintly of Joe Ryan's
natural scent and vibrated even more faintly with his
trace—she couldn't help but regret her convictions.

Up on that mountain, they had run together. They
had worked together. They had created a partnership
where, for isolated moments, it hadn't mattered who

she was or why she was here, or who he was and what he'd done. Even after he'd turned away from her, he hadn't gone far—only to the top of the spring, where he'd basked, eyes half-closed, immersing himself.

There, while she felt nothing more than the distressing tingle of amulets, Joe Ryan sat at the top of the world and sifted vast natural flows of power.

Even thinking about it, here in the casita with only a single dim light to disturb the night, she shivered slightly—and she couldn't blame it on the cold this time. He not only felt those waves, not only rode them…he could, in subtle ways, manage them. Manipulate them.

The good a man like that might have done the Sentinels…might have done the world…

And the harm he might yet do, with those soul-bruised eyes hiding the secrets of his inner world.

Lyn shivered again.

She threw aside the quilt, dumped the coffee down the sink and stalked to her tidy little backpack purse to grab her cell phone.

Brevis regional, she knew, would be waiting.

More specifically, Nick Carter—adjutant to the brevis regional counsel—would be waiting. Not that the brevis consul—a man named Dane Berger who'd become just a little too reclusive these past several years—was ever inclined to make day-to-day phone calls and communications, but sometimes Lyn got the impression—

No. Pondering her suspicions that Nick Carter now silently ran Southwest brevis regional was *not* the thing to do right now. He had an uncanny knack for plucking unspoken thoughts from her—and everyone else's—head.

So for a long moment, while the cell phone warmed

in her hand, Lyn thought of what she'd learned on the mountain that day. The confirmed presence of Fabron Gausto—no doubt completely bypassing the will of his septs prince. And he still had his sept posse, loyal in spite of his spectacular failure in Tucson. Didn't have any choice at this point, Lyn imagined—no other Core sept would take them in.

She'd found more there, while Joe Ryan sat on the top of the world and absorbed the power flows. She'd found the disgusting trace of discharged amulets— powerful amulets, and a number of them. And Ryan, once they'd gone human again, had allowed that there was a ripple in the power flowing through that area, but couldn't suggest its cause or meaning.

Unlike Ryan, she reported as expected. And that meant flipping the cell phone open and hitting the autodial that went straight to Nick Carter's direct line.

"Carter," he said, with noises in the background that made her believe he was at home—baying and carrying on, most boisterous.

"Is blood being shed?" she asked, amused, before stopping to think.

"Lyn," he said, after a pause in which he'd obviously sorted out her voice. "Hounds and their toys…" Then his voice changed, hitting a businesslike note. "You're in place?"

"I'm in his guest cabin."

"He invited you?" Surprise there, enough to make Lyn wonder. "Does he know—?"

"That I'm not exactly his advocate? He picked up on that right away." A flush of regret took her by surprise. Even full of suspicions and deep-seated determination to clear out the dark Sentinels, she'd seen a hint of something other than jaded resignation on Ryan's face.

Something that might have even been hurt, quickly covered.

So he's wounded to be under suspicion again. Doesn't mean he's innocent.

"Lyn," Nick said, and she could hear the hesitation in his voice and envision it in his pale green eyes. He was a wild one, that Nick Carter, a wolf wrapped in civility and manners, hoarfrost hair neatly trimmed, a lean, coiled power in his movements. Lyn suspected that his constrained manner was the only way he kept himself from startling people with his quickness, with the glimpse of the untamed showing through.

She'd never had a problem with keeping the ocelot tucked away—keeping that aspect of herself well behaved, covered with a tidy veneer of what society expected. She didn't lean on her Sentinel nature, as did some; she didn't need to. She was tenacious; she clung to lessons learned young. And she damned well knew what that hesitation of Nick's meant. "You knew who I was when you sent me here," she said. "I'll get the job done, Nick."

"I'm not concerned about your dedication," he said dryly. He must have gone through a door; the noise of the dogs abruptly diminished. "Nor your ability. So don't even go there."

"What then? I've hardly had a chance to get started."

"Your focus," he said bluntly. "We need answers—whether or not they fit your personal mission."

"You're the one who thought he'd gone dark in the first place!" she blurted out, too surprised to be circumspect.

"And I still do. But even so, I need someone who can look for what's actually there, and not for what you *want* to be there."

For a long breath, she couldn't say anything. She

walked up to the casita's large window, looking through the darkness at the house beside her, and the drop of the mountain beyond that. No blinding nighttime lighting for this property—nothing to interfere with the rich scatter of stars overhead. Only the most muted of lights from the second-floor loft area to indicate Ryan was still in there at all.

If he was. She didn't think for a moment that her presence would stop him from ranging out. She should be keeping track of him, not losing herself in this conversation, familiar dismay lumping in the pit of her stomach. "You went digging," she said. "That part of my background is supposed to be off the record."

"Your brother—"

"Has nothing to do with this!" Except— "No, I take it back. He opened my eyes. He taught me important lessons. And do you really want this phone call to be about me? Because I don't."

"Do you have news already?"

"Don't sound so surprised." Her turn to be dry. "We went to the top of the world today, as it happens." And she summarized their ascent and discovery of the trace. "But it could have been a throwaway." A gift to make her think he was cooperating. "If so, he lost nothing of real value by revealing that spot... I couldn't track them from there. Something about what they'd done with the amulets obliterated all but those first traces."

But even as Nick absorbed her words, she realized the things she'd left out—the way Ryan had reacted to her flawed shielding technique, the way he'd reacted to the power surges...how in some odd way, they seemed to hurt and not help him. Things she'd usually report and wasn't quite certain why she hadn't.

Because I'm not sure yet. Not sure what she was

seeing, or if she'd really even seen those things at all. She needed more time....

But Nick, knowing none of it, was still thinking of the words she *had* said. "So the Core is there. Then it's not likely Ryan is doing this on his own. Too much co-incidence, for them to show up along with the power surges, even with Ryan's trace clinging to them."

"He was surprised about that, by the way," she observed. "It struck me as completely genuine. Which doesn't mean he isn't involved—only that he didn't know his trace would show up, and didn't recognize it when it did." But that wasn't the only thing that had sur-prised him this day, and she had to add, "He said he hadn't heard from brevis regional regarding the Core's suspected presence here."

"Not quite the same as claiming he didn't know they were there." His voice was dark and certain.

She wouldn't, she realized, want this man on *her* trail. "He also says he never got a message asking him to expedite that late report."

They both sat on a beat of silence, and then she said, "I think you need to follow up on it, Nick."

Surprise, there. "You believe him?"

"I think," she said carefully, "that we should be ready to counter that claim if it isn't true."

He made a noise she couldn't quite interpret. "You know," he said, startling her with the same words she'd only just thought about him, "I wouldn't want you on *my* trail." But she heard the grin in his voice, and he added, "I'll look into it. And you—be careful. I can have a full team out there within two hours, day or night—it's not your job to confront the Core, or even to corner Ryan. Just get us close enough so we can get the drop on them."

Right. That had been the point all along—coming in

with a team too soon would tip off the Core, and spook Ryan into dropping whatever he was up to.

Supposing he still could. Lyn couldn't help but wonder if he even had control any longer—if he'd *choose* to continue with a process that was affecting him as this one obviously did.

On the other hand, maybe he'd been telling the truth. Maybe he had gotten a bug, and it was messing with his Sentinel skills. It happened.

"Anything else going on?" Nick asked her, interrupting what she suddenly realized had become a long silence.

"No," she said. "Sorry. Just thinking through it all. Same team, do you think?"

"You make the progression sound like a foregone conclusion." His voice still held amusement. "Some of the same people, if it comes to that. I doubt I can tear Dolan away from Encontrados and Megan…she might be a natural with those wards, but she's not ready for the field."

Lyn wouldn't expect it; it hadn't been long enough since Dolan, the Southwest's rogue Sentinel, had found Megan, bringing her back to the Sentinel fold after so many erroneous years of neglect. "And Dolan?" she asked. "Did he ever come in?"

"You mean did you talk him out of his grudges long enough to see that we need him?" Nick let out a breath. "He came in. If I had to guess, I'd say he's thinking about it. Not for too long, I hope. I need Sentinels I can count on."

Lyn heard what those words really meant. *I need Sentinels who will stand with me when things get rough around here.*

"I'll be there," she reminded him. For as much as she

hunted those gone dark, she could well recognize a man leading the way for those who didn't.

"I know," he said. "But we'll need…"

"More," she finished for him, and couldn't help a fleeting acknowledgment that Ryan's strength, his solidity—his depth, even—could have made him valuable to Nick. *Could have.*

"And Lyn," Nick said, his voice hitting a warning note, "keep in mind that there's a third possibility when it comes to the things Ryan said he never heard from us. Because he could be telling the truth, and still be dark. There's more than one tangle in play here."

"Got it covered," she told him. "Untangling trails is what I do."

Chapter 6

Joe prowled in from the early morning sunshine on the roof, stretching hugely. He flicked his ears, resigning himself to the end of solitude.

Not that he'd found much solace in the night. Not with the echoes of the faintly twisted power from the top of the world still churning through his body…not with everything he'd learned the day before still tumbling through his mind. For it was clear now—while he'd been thick and slow with that cold, his territory had been invaded.

And the people who should have had his back now blamed him. This woman—the tightly wound tracker with precision in her movement and precision in her features—she blamed him, too. Had come to find proof, but made up her mind before she even got here.

The feel of what she'd done to him—unwittingly, unknowingly—out there on the mountain…it, too, had followed him through the night, tingling along awakened nerves to leave him restless and wakeful. Even the solace of the roof had not lured him into better-late-than-never sleep.

But it meant he was awake when Lyn Maines left the casita for an early-morning walk around the house, stretching her legs and yawning, her hair tumbled loose around her face and her neat travel outfit from the day before replaced by crop cargo pants and some sort of shirred top that had made him want to lean closer for a better look.

He hadn't done it. He knew better than to provide any movement for her eye to latch on to. Only after she returned to the casita did he pad down from the roof, hopping lightly to the second-story porch and through the warded sliding-glass door...from there, straight to unclothed human form and then straight to the shower, the casual habits of a man who lived alone in a wild spot of land.

When he finally emerged onto the front porch, jeans and a loose-weave pullover blotting up the leftover dampness, he found her sitting on the porch bench seat, her hair now drawn back into a tidy clip. She looked up at him with a wary expectation, and he said, "Breakfast?"

And that was how she ended up cooking in his kitchen. Not because he couldn't—he'd already started the coffee and gathered bacon, eggs and appropriate pans—but because she seemed so uncomfortable just sitting there that he asked if she'd rather. And that left him free to deal with the paws batting at the lower cabinets, where the little black shorthair waited.

"Because I haven't fed you in a week, maybe two," he murmured, hitting the pantry up for cat kibble. They were indoor cats, other than the escape artist of a brown tabby; special wards contained them when he left the upstairs door open a crack so the cougar could return. But this little black shorthair still managed to find trouble. This morning, rather than eating, she fussed and shook her front paw with a frantic need.

Lyn looked up from the bacon as she repositioned it in the pan. "Is she okay?"

As if this little scene was truly a domestically cozy moment, with two companionable people sharing a good-morning breakfast, the paper turned to the comics section and the scent of frying cholesterol in the air. *Right.*

He scooped the little cat up and murmured sweet nothings in her ear until she purred and barely noticed as he deftly rolled a particularly nasty goat's head sticker out from between the pads. "She's fine," he said, rubbing lightly at that spot just between her eyes. "It must have come in on my shoe."

"I *hate* those things," Lyn said, vehemently enough to take him by surprise—to amuse him. She'd actually let something of herself peek out that time. And though she withdrew almost immediately, her eyes lingered on his fingers as they stroked the sleek black head and crumpled back delicate shell-pink ears to make the black cat purr.

"As it happens," Joe said, a murmur to fool the cat into thinking he was talking to her, and indeed she purred more loudly in response, "I actually like my bacon a little burned."

Lyn's eyes widened; her nostrils flared slightly, taking in the same sharp odor he'd already noticed. Her lips formed a silent curse, and she whirled to tend to the fry pan.

Joe smiled at the cat, bringing that purring creature up so they could briefly butt faces. Distractable, Lyn was—focused in, and therefore not aware of the larger world. He'd already seen some of that up on the mountain, and could well understand why she didn't work without a partner.

It did surprise him that brevis would have sent her without one. They trusted him to some extent, then—albeit probably only to maintain his supposed cover. And whatever they thought of him, he wouldn't let her down. Not this dark-eyed ocelot with her fierce drive to clean up the Sentinels, not even if she didn't realize they were on the same side.

Damned if he was going to let the Core get away with messing with this mountain.

The cat made an abrupt decision to be done with purring and face-butting, possibly inspired by the clatter of eggs being dished out. Lyn moved assertively in the unfamiliar kitchen, looking right at home as she finished up the meal.

"Juice?" he asked her, heading for the refrigerator to do at least that much.

She glanced at him, flicking the gas burner off. "Milk?" she said, a hopeful note in her voice.

"Sure, plenty of it." He poured her a serving, set it on the marble counter with a decided clink of glass on stone, and went back for his favorite mix of tropical juices.

As his hand closed around the carton, it hit.

Not a bad one, just sudden—his hand spasmed around flimsy cardboard…for an instant he lost awareness, swamped in the harsh atonal power, a slow, thick ooze filling his lungs so his vision grayed and prickles of pain and weakness raked him from inside.

Lyn pushed in beside him, prying the carton from his hand, muttering a curse. But by then Joe had control—or at least partial control—pushing away the power so he could fumble for shields.

But Lyn had no hesitation, and no fumbling. She reached for that same centered place she'd created up at Snowbowl—he felt it build around them, gliding into place like a balm. And then his head snapped up and he sucked in his breath, because she'd gone that one step further—done that which breezed through him from within, caressing those very nerves that had been scraped with pain only a moment earlier. The contrast shocked him, wobbling his knees, and he snatched at the edge of the sink for support. In her smudge-lined eyes he saw reflected shock; she stiffened, jerking slightly. And then she narrowed her eyes, and the connection slammed closed.

He lost his knees entirely, falling back against the cabinets beneath the sink, breath grunting from his body and mixed up with an inarticulate, involuntary noise of protest.

That, too, startled her—she looked as though she wanted to skitter away, putting distance between them. But she stood straight and still, and after a moment she let out a long sigh of breath.

"Well, damn," Joe grumbled, trying to ignore the incredible emptiness she'd left behind. There was no graceful way up from here, jammed back against the cabinets with his bare feet propped too close and his knees askew at chin level. "No offense, but whatever you're doing…I think it needs practice."

"I could say the same for you," she responded tersely—but she stepped forward to brace herself and extend a hand. A small hand, but he didn't make the mistake of supposing it lacked strength. She was, after all, Sentinel.

He took the hand and he took the strength she loaned him, and soon enough he was back on his feet, looking down at her again. He said, "Shielding…not my best thing."

"No," she agreed.

That stung a little. "Hey—it's my job to keep track of what's going on around here. You think I can do that if I fling up shields at every opportunity? When I was in Nevada, Dean—" He stopped. He didn't want to talk about Dean Seacrest with her. He didn't even want to bring it up. Not knowing she thought him guilty of Dean's death.

Well, hell, maybe he was. But not in the way they thought. So he cleared his throat and said, "I was in better practice then." Back when he hadn't been isolated, when he'd had more cause to shield, and more tightly defined duties. Now it was all his, a lightly populated area considered so stable that one Sentinel could handle it.

At least, one Sentinel of Joe's skills. Because, let's face it, there weren't many. And he had plenty of reason to rue it these days, when it seemed brevis consul and his posse had decided they couldn't quite trust what a man of such skills could—or would—do. Even when they didn't know it all.

But Lyn's brows had quirked up. "That makes sense," she said. "Although you should put in some practice."

He couldn't help but hope as he settled back against the edge of the sink. "So now you believe me?" That he'd have reason to shield, that he was as much a victim of what was happening here as anyone.

She gave him the driest of expressions; the hope died.

"I'm riding a line," she told him, blunt as she had been when she first approached him in the woods below. "For all I know, you started this thing and now it's out of hand—or the Core went their own way and left you hanging."

"Whoa." He couldn't help it; he shook off the words—physically, literally. "That's a hell of a way to go through life. Thinking like that." He thought about it; still didn't like it. "I'll stick with my way, thanks. But you're right about the practice. I'll get to work on that." As if they'd been discussing the weather, he turned back to his partially crunched carton of juice and unscrewed the little plastic cap on the side. "Hope you like your eggs cold. I think that's how we're going to get them."

"Eggs cold, bacon burned. Just as it should be." She said it with such deadpan perfection that he jerked around to look at her and caught the barest glimpse of a smile tweaking the corner of her mouth as she turned away to take the plates to the small round table in the tree-dappled sunlight of the breakfast nook.

His answering grin came in spite of himself. Because whether he liked it or not, whether she knew it or not, his heart was right out there for her to see, as it had always been.

It was just a matter of how hard she crunched it before she was through.

Chapter 7

They'd eaten breakfast in what amounted to silence, until Joe put his plate on the tile floor and grabbed the now-cool fry pan from the stove to put beside it, making the rolling baritone purr that brought the cats running from four different corners of the house.

Lyn added her plate to the offerings and said, deadpan, "Tell me you put them in the dishwasher afterward."

He only raised his eyebrows at her, very much *wouldn't you like to know*. But as he swiped a hand down the tortie's silky back, he stood and put himself into a more businesslike mode. "I'd like to go to the museum today."

He'd taken her by surprise. "Why the museum?"

He pondered the best answer. *Because you so clearly don't really have a clue* just didn't seem like the way to go. He said, "When we talked yesterday, it was pretty clear that brevis is approaching the situation from a streamlined point of view. I think you need the bigger picture."

She made a little *ffft* of sound that suited the ocelot perfectly. "Streamlined. That's diplomatic. You mean narrow-minded."

"A little too focused," he admitted, though that was as far as he'd go.

She seemed to sense that; she let it drop. And she said, "Tracking is tracking…I don't really need any picture at all. But in this case…"

"You need to interpret what you find," Joe said. "It's not just about the end of the trail this time."

"No," she agreed. "It's not." She narrowed her eyes. "Let's go, then."

And so he found himself on the road, his legs bent to fit the front seat of the Ford Focus hatchback rental in which Lyn looked perfectly at home—even if she had no idea where she was going as she drove them down off the lower sweep of the mountain and toward Fort Valley Road, which, when they hit it, would take them either into town or out to the Grand Canyon. "Head south," he told her. "Toward town."

She found a gap in the traffic and neatly inserted the Focus across traffic, a swift left-hand turn, and she was barely getting them up to speed when he said, "Okay, there—on the right. See it?"

"That's a museum?" Her disbelief showed clear as she pulled into the small parking lot and chose a spot that looked directly at the rustic stone structure tucked in among the pines.

He grinned. "Yup. It's got research projects, displays, collections…it's even got a campus. But this is the building we care about today. The exhibits." And after that, he said little; he let the museum and the exhibits speak for themselves. Twelve thousand years of history, all but the last few hundred years accomplished without the benefit of eminent domain—from the disappearing Anasazi populations to the distinct nations remaining in the Four Corners area: Navajo, Hopi, Paiute, and Havasupai…never mind the rest of Arizona. Busy place, this territory had been.

A sudden series of trembly little power fluctuation aftershocks rattled his teeth as she stopped before an image of the Peaks; he threw up the shields he'd had waiting, and missed what she said as ragged power scraped through that protection. He braced himself against it, reinforcing the shields, stopping to think through what should have been automatic.

Yeah, not a good time to be down on the basics.

"Got it?" she asked him, and this time she was looking at him, those smudge-edged brown eyes seeing far too much.

Bad enough to have fallen into such bad habits, here where he rode power as naturally as he breathed. Worse to be repeatedly caught out at it. He nodded at the displays as if it hadn't happened at all. "You see what I mean? About this place? We're not the only ones keeping an eye on this mountain. We're probably not the only ones who know it's sick. It's arrogant to think we are."

"We're probably the only ones who know exactly *why* it's sick," she said, with some asperity. "The Core is our responsibility, and you know it. They wouldn't even exist if it weren't for us."

"That's one way to look at it." He moved aside to the next exhibit, a timeline laid over images of ancient high desert starting with the Hohokam in 300 B.C. and tracing through a millennium and more of complex

Anasazi and Pueblo societies, with a period of Sinagua farming near the Peaks and even the eruption of Sunset Crater not far north of Flagstaff. Complex, complete, successful societies in a rugged and challenging desert terrain, with the Peaks an oasis of life and spiritual support. "I can't help but think it's more complicated than that."

She shook her head. "It's not. Don't make it that way."

He shot her an exasperated look, knowing she wouldn't understand. "I don't have to make it that way. It just *is*. Everything *is*, whether you want to believe it or not. The world is made of interlocking layers, not separate units. You think you can just excise the parts you don't like, without regard to the rest? Well, guess *what*—it doesn't work that way."

Lyn took a step back, obviously more startled than affronted. "Wow," she said. "Where'd that come from?"

He snorted. "Do you even have to ask? Or have you forgotten that you're here to take me down? If I want to see this mountain saved, I don't have any particular choice but to help you." He'd thought he'd been resigned…that he'd reconciled with the inevitable— knowing he'd do his best to keep the Peaks safe, but it likely wouldn't save him in the end.

Apparently he'd been wrong.

Something about the day before, about working with her at the top of the world…at the top of *his* world…

He'd liked that. He wanted more of it. More than he'd get if he let them take him down…again.

Her eyes widened; the light from the exhibit glanced against them, illuminating shades of brown and darker brown and specks of black. "If you're innocent—"

He snorted, making an effort to lower his voice here

in this quiet building with its respectful echoes of the past. "You forget. I already know better than that."

"Ryan—" she said, and gave up, just shook her head.

"You know," he said, "I used to see things that way, too. Simple. We are what we are—we do what we have to. Hell, I grew up groomed for it. Because what does any teenage boy think, right? That I could be one of the best. And I already had my partner, too—grew up with him, trained with him. Just as I'd always planned, in my perfect little world. And for a while, it even looked like maybe it was just that simple." He pinned her with a look, and she took another step back—not frightened or wary, just claiming that distance. "For a while," he repeated. And then Dean had been killed.

He didn't want to talk about Dean at all. Not to her. "What do you think?" he asked, abruptly enough that she'd know the subject had been changed.

And she did, but she clearly didn't follow. "About…?"

"Brevis," he said shortly. "What's happening there? It's not all nice and neat and simple, I can tell you that much. You know as well as I do that I didn't get those messages. Or is admitting that too close to admitting you might be wrong that I've gone dark?"

"I asked Nick to look into it."

"Nick." Joe looked away—looked back to the timeline without seeing it. Definite hard-ass, that one. Like Lyn, he'd made up his mind about Joe's guilt before they'd even met—truly believed that Joe would take out his lifelong friend and partner to pay off his half sister's marrow transplant bills. That he'd allied with one of Vegas's most influential crime lords to do it.

Because that's so very me. *So very something I would do.*

"He'll check it out," she insisted.

"Sure, so he can find some way to prove me wrong." He knew from the way her expression shut down that he'd guessed that one right. "Given the way things have been going down there, maybe I should just give national a call."

The notion clearly alarmed her. "National doesn't interfere with the brevis regions."

"Not with the day-to-day stuff," he agreed. "They sure as hell have an interest in whether things are running straight. And don't tell me they don't care about something as big as the Peaks."

"You're right, but—" She stopped, shook her head. "Not yet. It'd just blow things wide open down there, and no one's ready for that. It would ruin the consul…and possibly Nick."

"I'm supposed to care?" He leaned against the narrow wall space between display windows, and crossed his arms. "I'm going dark, remember?"

She bit her lip, clearly standing on the edge of words not quite said.

"Either you believe me and expect the right things from me," he said, "or you don't, and you can't."

Ryan's words stood in the silence for a good long time. Long enough for Lyn's ocelet's hearing to realize there was a group of excited schoolchildren in the building, no doubt lingering in the special therizinosaur exhibit. Long enough for him to shift away from the wall, raise a dark eyebrow at her and watch her with a question in eyes that currently sparked more green than hazel.

No. More like a dare.

I came up here for a reason, she told herself, looking for the conviction that had come so readily in that Tucson conference room. Even if conviction clashed, somehow, with Ryan's instant action to save the young woman at the Snowbowl Skylift, or with his gentle handling of cats he claimed weren't actually his, or even with the expression on his face as he watched the high desert from the Skylift overlook. Not to mention what she'd felt from him only this morning in the kitchen, the caress of texture and sensation when she'd so suddenly faced the impulse to fling herself completely open to him. And though she'd panicked, cutting him off so suddenly that she'd pretty much taken him down the rest of the way, in retrospect…

Some part of her still craved more.

And so she thought of all those things, and she looked at the dare in his eyes, and she hesitated.

But only until self-recrimination curdled in her throat. Because how many times had she wanted to believe better of her brother? How many times had she let hope push away truth?

He must have seen it in her, dammit. Too perceptive by far. That question in his eyes died out; his expression went flat. "Okay, then," he said. "Watch yourself, Lyn Maines."

Her eyes narrowed. "Was that a threat?"

He snorted. "Of course not. Me, I'll do just what I think is right. But you…best not set any expectations on what that might be. I'm not living up to your expectations, or Dane's, or Nick's. Just my own. And you've told me what you think of that, so…best watch yourself."

She frowned, crossed her arms over the snug shirring of her shirt, and supposed he was right at that. "This is the strangest conversation I've had in…*ever.*"

"Wish I could say I haven't been through it before," he told her flatly, and turned away, moving past the timeline to a protected display of Sinagua artifacts from Elden Pueblo—potsherds, bone tools, wood arrows, rock tools and a handful of items from other cultures indicative of Sinagua trade patterns.

But Lyn stopped there, and her nostrils flared at the sudden acrid bite of trace lingering in the air. He quickly dropped the resentment so clearly carried in his shoulders to flick a careful gaze around the room, and she said, "These Sinagua…"

"Si-nah-wah," he murmured in correction of her hard *G*, as if that were important now—except she realized that to him, it was. It was all part of respecting the mountain, and how did *that* fit in to labeling him the man who would steal from it?

She drew a breath, and the stench of amulet corruption focused her. "Is there anything particularly significant about their relationship to the Peaks? More than the other tribes?"

"They lived at the base of the mountain," he said promptly. "Elden Pueblo is partially open to the public, if you want to go there. There are trails that lead up into the Elden Summit—although Elden isn't actually one of the Peaks. The Havasupai lived on the northwestern slope for a time—that's this side of the mountain—so they were actually closer to the heart of the power, at least as we're concerned about it. But they were also in the Canyon area, and that's where their land is today."

Her gaze landed on the display built into the wall just beyond him—her eyebrows shot up, her mouth opened on words she no longer bothered to say. She nodded at the display, and found new words. "Or maybe that's all just too complicated, and it's about what's within reach." For the projectile points there were wired to the display right out where they could be touched for the *ooh* and *ahh* factor.

He made a noise in his throat, something surprised— a noise that might have come from a startled cougar, in truth. Before she realized his intent, he reached for those knapped-stone points, his fingers brushing carelessly over contaminated obsidian—but only for an instant. He snatched them back, a snarl in his throat. Astonishment took his features, and then pain, and by then she squinted against the flash of electric-blue lightning, pulsing and tangling around him. And even as she struggled to understand how the amulet-contaminated artifact had created this struggling, painful transformation, the blur of light and motion dumped him out on the floor, panting, dazed—and fully cougar. He sprawled out across linoleum, his claws digging in as if he might otherwise spin away.

She gave a quick glance toward the wide entry to this exhibit area, unable to help the panic icing her veins. "Good God, Ryan, take back the human! Right now!"

But the cougar only stared dumbly at her. A thin trickle of blood came from one nostril of his rough, black-edged nose; his ears were neither alert nor reactive—just slack—while the rest of him clung to the floor, awkward and ungainly.

Another glance at the doorway, a quick tip of her head—no footsteps running, no voices raised. She went down to her knees, right up close and personal, her hand hovering—indecisive, but only for a moment. She took his massive big cat head between her hands, all too aware of what those teeth could do to her if he was truly as confused as he seemed. Her fingers sank into short, thick fur; she forced herself to relax. "Ryan, *now*."

A drop of blood spatted on the floor. She forced

herself to take a breath, then another. "Ryan," she said, more quietly now, "you need to find yourself. Take back the human." Another deep breath. *"Joe,"* she said, and he blinked. His claws flexed, scraping tile. His tail twitched. His tongue, pink and raspy, tasted of his own blood at his nose.

"Yes," she said, stroking the side of his head, her fingers curving over the strong bone of his temple and down along his neck. "Come on, Ryan. Take back the human—" *before anyone freaking sees us,* but she didn't say that part out loud. Didn't push, just looked into those familiar eyes and tried to connect, to draw him out. "Come on," she muttered, more to herself than him, because if he didn't respond soon she would have to try the centering move, really truly bring him in, and she didn't know at *all* how that would work out—

His gaze sharpened; his body tensed. It was all the warning she got, and then the light of change flickered all around her—smooth and fast this time, so she quite suddenly found herself holding the man, her hand in his hair, his eyes wide and hell, yes, frightened, and the blood still running from his nose. Just that fast, he broke contact, rolling to his feet with the smooth power she'd come to take for granted in him, turning away to duck his head and wipe roughly at his upper lip.

Lyn rose to her feet more slowly, brushing at her pants—straightening just in time to turn toward approaching footsteps—the museum docent who looked in on them with restrained disapproval and said, "There's no photography allowed within the museum."

Camera flash. He'd thought he'd seen camera flash. And Lyn had no intention of disabusing him of that notion. "I'm sorry," she said. "We didn't pay enough attention. It won't happen again." And she looked at Ryan's back, the incongruous tremble of his broad shoulders, the blood drops on the floor and the deep scoring across the linoleum.

It had better not.

Chapter 8

She'd given him space. Time spent perusing exhibits she didn't quite see, except to realize, again, how seriously he took the many-faceted nature of the mountain.

For someone who had only been here a couple of years, he'd certainly become invested.

Then again, what else did he have? His sister had died, she knew that much from the file—his half sister, who'd been his only remaining family. His partner had died. He'd sold his business when he'd been reassigned, pulled from the area in which he'd grown up. He'd been a person of interest to the Henderson police in Dean Seacrest's death, gone cold case for lack of evidence…a situation very much echoed within the Sentinels. And now here he was. What else did he have, indeed?

Did you get in too deep, Ryan? Want too much?

By the time she'd worked through those thoughts,

he'd composed himself, turning back to her with nothing more than a faint gleam of blood at the base of one nostril, the lines of his face subtly harsher than normal…as though he still held himself together by dint of will alone. He said, "I know what you think of me. But do you really think I'd do *that* to myself?"

She shook her head. "Not on purpose."

His jaw hardened…and he simply turned away, heading for the main atrium of the small museum— and the exit.

"Check it out, then," he said. "I don't think it's anything but a practice piece—they tried to draw on the Elden connection—but you won't want to take my word on it. I'll wait outside."

"Wait," she said, caught by surprise at his abrupt departure. "That's it? That's all there is to see—?"

He barely hesitated, glancing over his shoulder. "There's plenty more to look at. I'm just not sure you'll actually see it. Either way, you know where it is."

Okay then. She wasn't in the mood to argue…and frankly, they needed to get out of this place. But she said, "I'll be a few minutes," because she wanted a better feel of that artifact—something she hadn't dared do while he was in the room, in case it stirred currents of power that he couldn't handle.

She moved in on it cautiously, her nose wrinkling, her eyes tearing as the stench of the trace became more intense. Amulets, for certain. Something of Fabron Gausto—not surprising. But the traces led nowhere; they felt like an experiment failed, or not yet completed. They posed no danger—except to a Sentinel named Joe Ryan. She'd recognize it if she came upon it again.

Still, she hesitated; her hand hovered above the

knapped obsidian. For certain she'd be e-mailing Nick at the soonest opportunity, asking for a consult with one of the brevis amulet experts. *Note to self: Make sure we have one on the team.*

In the end, she withdrew her hand without touching the projectile. Satisfying her curiosity wasn't worth the risk…and she didn't have the expertise to glean anything meaningful from the touch in the first place. So she curled her fingers back into her hand, did a once-over of herself to make sure she hadn't become too disheveled during her encounter with the cougar, and strode for the exit in his footsteps.

She found him chatting with the short, sturdy woman cashier who'd taken their money. Her copper skin tone, round face and strongly bow-shaped lips were features fast becoming familiar to Lyn, here in northern Arizona so close to the reservations. But what she noticed most was the woman's quiet ease with Ryan. There he stood, pretty much recovered from his encounter with the tainted projectile, once more radiating that understated but definite confidence that came with strength and power, and this woman accepted it and let it flow around her.

The realization startled Lyn…made her face the fact that she, too, could have handled Ryan's presence in this way, instead of taking it into herself…instead of reacting to him.

Couldn't she have?

The woman was saying, "Your cold sounds better. You shouldn't have been here last week…you weren't listening to yourself very well."

"I'm a guy," Ryan said, and grinned. "We're not supposed to have listening skills, are we?"

The woman responded with a mischievous grin.

"Not that I've noticed. But I'm glad you're feeling better. Will you be at the ride later?"

"The Save the Peaks ride coming in from Gray Mountain? I'll be around. Not sure you'll see me, though."

"Right. The mysterious Joe Ryan." She nodded with overt faux solemnity that didn't last, then leaned down behind her admissions stanchion to come up with a tissue. "By the way, Mr. Mysterious, you've got a nose-bleed thing going on there." She nodded at him rather than gesturing, a quick point with her chin.

He made a casual face, as if the circumstances behind that nosebleed hadn't torn at him from the inside out. Just an embarrassed-guy face, *aw shoot and shucky darn*. But he took the tissue and obediently dabbed it to his nose, and it was then that Lyn realized he'd noticed her approach long before, that he'd slightly angled his body to include her, should she ever decide to move into the conversation.

"This your lady friend, then?" The attendant fixed him with a disapproving look. "There's no way you can take someone through here so fast, not without making her eyes spin around in her head."

"Other obligations," Ryan said cheerfully, as if he and Lyn hadn't just been talking about guilt and fate and consequences. "I just wanted to make sure she saw enough of it to want to come back."

The woman nodded. "That's a good plan, then. It meets with my approval."

Ryan placed his hand over his heart as if he was faint with relief. "See you next time, then," he said, and led the way back out into the heat of the parking lot.

Overhead, the clouds had built into low-hanging rumblers, reminding her again of their altitude. A gusty breeze kicked someone's litter across the parking lot, all the more incongruous for its place amongst scattered pine needles and cones. She stopped to eye him. "Other obligations?"

He shrugged. "None. Just an exit line."

Her mind went straight to the practical. "Actually, I need to fill the rental with gas. And do you have Internet access at your house? Cable or wireless?"

"Cable," he said. "Plenty of room on the router for you to plug in. And if you turn toward town when we leave, five minutes down the road there's a gas station."

"Great," she said, knowing her voice didn't sound it. Too unsettled by it all…unable to just put it behind her, as Ryan seemed to have done.

Then again, he had more practice.

The gas station also sold snow cones. Good chipped ice, just the right amount of flavor. Lyn parked the car off to the side after it was gassed up, taking advantage of a niche of shade beside the convenience store. Out in the sun the heat had beat fiercely on them, but here in the shade, flavored ice sliding down her throat, the day somehow seemed like luxury. Across from her, one arm hanging lazily off the roof of the car, Ryan looked utterly at home. A twitch of his shoulder there, a faint tilt of his head here…she realized, suddenly, that his cougar ears would be swiveling, his whiskers tipping and flexing. That he was, even in this quiet moment, following the patterns of power in this place.

Had it been only yesterday that she'd ridden a wave of disrupted power at the top of the Skyride with the sudden flash of fear that it might well be too late to fix the deeply disrupted mountain? That the Peaks would erupt again, this time with much more than mere magma?

If it wasn't too late, it soon would be. Nick hadn't said it; Ryan hadn't said it. But she'd heard the concern in Nick's voice…seen the look on Ryan's face. Watched his concentration now.

"If they're here," she said of those who'd made the trace at the top of the world, "where are they staying? A hotel? A B & B? A tourist trap? Or do they have someone in place here, a private residence?"

"You're welcome to search my place," he murmured, eyes half-lidded.

She bit her lip on a flare of annoyance. "Look," she said, and she took herself around to the other side of the car, looking up into the strong lines of his face—noticing for the first time that he set his jaw just the slightest bit crooked when he hit this level of concentration, "even if you *are* in on this, you have to see it's gotten out of control. It's like you said…you wouldn't do this to yourself. I don't think you would do it to this mountain, either. So—"

He stopped her short by the reaching for her without looking, his hand cupping the side of her face. It startled her into silence, and then into gathering protest, but something about his eyes—gone from half-lidded to truly narrowed—and about the stiffened nature of his shoulders, the sudden hitch in his breathing as though someone had hit him but not terribly hard…

"What?" she asked, afraid she already knew the answer. If he was riding the power…if he'd found something else…

His hand tightened against her cheek. His head lifted, cocked slightly, face tense—a cougar blind to outer sight, listening to inner sight. Foreboding prickled along her spine, flattened her mouth.

His eyes snapped open—still not seeing. He growled,

a noise she felt more than heard. She didn't wait for it—
she flung her shields up. He recoiled from that but only
slightly, his attention still entirely elsewhere—until
quite suddenly he was back, sharply focused on the gas
station, the convenience store, the intersection.

A second roll of power came through. Lights within
the store sparked and went dark; a woman cried out in
surprise as her car engine, instead of starting, exploded
into smoke and sparks and grinding failure. The gas
pumps seized; a motorcycle cruised to a dead-engine stop.

And there at the intersection, an oblivious woman,
baby in her arms, elementary school daughter at her
side, stepped out into the crosswalk—even as the cross-
traffic light sputtered, flickered through its phases, and
settled on green.

Green both ways.

A third wave, and bracing himself wasn't enough;
she saw his knees start to go. "Shield yourself, dammit!"
She wanted to shout it, but managed to keep her voice
low—and still he didn't do it. And then she saw what
he'd anticipated, the cross-traffic car heading straight for
the family—the girl skipping with her small hand
twined around her mother's belt loop, the mother
laughing at something she'd said, adjusting the baby's
blanket.

Ryan made a hiss of sound—it might have been his
breath through his teeth as that third wave rolled on
past, it might have been warning. Lyn gasped in surprise
at the new shift of power washing over her—gasped in
the realization that it came not from the mountain, but
from right beside her. Targeted, precise…it growled
into the intersection, smooth and dangerous as it flowed
around Lyn's shields. Lights flickered and died, drivers

hesitated…and the single car at the focus of that push quite abruptly…died. No engine, no power…

Lyn wondered if the driver would ever realize he hadn't coasted to a stop, but rocked in place with the force of the additional interference.

And then she realized what he'd done.

What he'd *been able* to do.

What no one at brevis had even guessed had been within his reach.

And she saw what it took out of him. He flicked a wry look at her, wrung out and leaning against the car for real, somehow keeping his feet, with that fourth wave of disgruntled mountain power sweeping down to—

He's got no shields.

He'd deliberately left himself open to deal with the repercussions of that wild power—and there was no way he'd pull shields together now. Not after that.

So she did what she really didn't want to do. She reached for the calm she'd created around herself; she drew in a deep breath and as she exhaled, she expanded her awareness—carefully in this charged atmosphere, gently…enveloping him. Drawing him in.

And, oh yeah…here it comes….

The overwhelming sense of Ryan. The textures and layers and intensity, washing through her and into places she'd never intended but had known wouldn't evade this connection. Not under these circumstances and not, she was coming to realize, with this man. The swell of sensation—the pounding of her heart, the way her inner awareness felt too large for her body—felt unexpectedly sweet, and brought an equally unexpected longing.

He straightened, no longer distracted, looking only

at her. Dusky hazel eyes widened; something within her contracted in response, far too intimate. She gave a faint gasp of surprise and suddenly he was right *there,* expression gone feral—as though she was his to take, and the moment loomed inevitable.

Her response came so quickly, so freely, she felt like two different people—one of whom welcomed him and the other of whom stood frozen as he pulled her against him, her feet barely touching the ground now, their faces so very close, their mouths so very close…

"Ryan," she managed—nothing more than a choked whisper, a struggle against the forces swirling around and through them. A tiny cry in the wild.

His eyes widened even farther, ever so briefly—and then he closed them, giving his head a hard little shake, taking a sharp, deep breath and holding it an instant before he let it go. His hands slowly released her arms, easing her down from her toes. He turned away— elbows against the car, the heels of his hands rubbing his eyes—obviously still trying to find control.

"It's okay," she said, her voice low. Trying to con- vince herself. "It's the shields. I can't drop them, not yet. I wish there was another way—" Shielding some- one else…it wasn't anything for which she'd been trained. And though she'd done it now and then, it had never had these results.

"I'm sorry," she said, even as she fought the impulse to step closer to him again, to change the thrum of interlocking powers into the thrum of interlocking flesh.

What am I even thinking?

He lifted his hands just enough to throw her a side- ways glance; his voice came ragged. "It is what it is."

"I—what?" He'd said that as if those feelings were

real. Not created by circumstances, but *real*. She took a step back, alarmed beyond all reasonable measure at the thought.

"Relax," he said dryly. "I can deal with it." He pushed off the car, looking weary—looking *wary,* as though her reaction had dealt him a blow harder than anything the mountain had thrown at him.

Regret assailed her. Her alarmed expression, the reactive body language…it must have felt like a slap in the face.

Because you really did want him. Right here, right now. And the thought that anything so strong, so overwhelming, could be anything but induced…

Not with this man. Not with a Sentinel gone dark.

A Sentinel who just left himself wide open in order to save four people.

But that didn't mean he hadn't gotten himself into this. That he hadn't overestimated himself and underestimated the Core…or just plain been betrayed by them. Because troubled men could otherwise mean well…could even be admirable.

And a troubled man could damn well drag her down into the dark with him, if she let him.

Chapter 9

Joe settled into the passenger seat of the little car, which had not nearly enough leg room. His head tipped back against the headrest, eyes closed. No one in the gas station corner had even noticed the too-close-for-comfort exchange; they'd been completely engaged with the action at the intersection and the sputtering, flailing electrical systems all around them. Murmurs of *electrical failure* and *was there an earthquake* and *terrorism!* bespoke their inability to recognize the power surge. And so Joe had climbed into the car and Lyn eased in beside him and started the little Focus, pulling smoothly but swiftly out of the gas station and back onto Fort Valley Road. Back toward home.

Yeah, you can handle this, boy-o. The increasing waves of power; their increasing effect on him. The suspicion that today wasn't the first time he'd have to choose between protecting himself and managing that power…or that Lyn might not be quite as prompt to share her shields again.

They still hummed around him…hummed through him. Like subsonics, too low to hear but still effective, keeping the hair on his arms just a little bit raised, and the hair at the back of his neck a little more so, and other parts of him just way too—

Down, boy-o, he told himself. And yet the feel of it all was strangely comfortable, too.

"Things were out of control," Lyn said, as if they'd been having a conversation. She was flushed beneath those smudgy eyes. "People don't understand, but if we get more surges like *that*…" She shook her head. "I've got to get to the bottom of this. I need that Internet access…I have some checking to do."

"On me," he said. When she didn't answer, he said, "Wouldn't it make more sense to ferret out the Core? If they're here, they're still doing whatever they came to do. They need to be stopped." He shrugged, flipping the car's dash vent so it blew directly on his face. "If you don't happen to nail me in the process, you can always come for me afterward."

"No," she said, and the word had a panicky edge to it. Her hands tightened on the steering wheel; her gaze remained resolutely on the road. After a moment, she said, "You're my backup. I need to know just how far to trust you *when* I'm going after them."

He grinned, shook his head. Not that it didn't sting… it always stung. Downright hurt, even. But at least she didn't favor him with the sideways glances and words gone unspoken. Nope, she'd just come right out with it. "All right," he said, as if they weren't actually talking about him. "You need Internet access. Not a big deal.

There's a room downstairs where you can work, if you can convince the cats you need the chair. And—?"

"And we need to figure out where Gausto is staying."

"There's not much out this way," Joe observed. Such practical talk, thankfully, subdued his reactions to the shielding. To *her.*

"The other side of town?"

He pondered it. "Direct access to Elden Pueblo… I'm surprised they didn't try to pull that artifact stunt there." But that thought stopped him, and he half turned in the small space, looking at her. "You know, there's nothing to say they didn't."

She nodded, all business. "Then we'll check it out. As well as the hotels. I'll need to generate a list."

"Tourism is serious business in this town," Joe pointed out. "I think the yellow pages will give you what you need."

"Me?" she said, casting him a quick look as she slowed for the turn that would lead to his isolated back road. "Am I in this alone, then?"

He snorted. "I'd really appreciate it if you would decide if I'm part of this team or just your target. Because you're heading for that point where you can't have it both ways…and you're doing it at a pretty high rate of speed."

She grimaced, a mere watermark of an expression on a face otherwise engrossed with following the un-familiar and winding road. After a moment, she said, "I know." And then she said, "I stuffed my map in the glove box so you could sit there. Is this our turn?" And then, when he laughed out loud, she scowled. "It's not funny. Just because I can follow any trace on foot doesn't mean I instantly memorize a driven route. Two entirely different skills."

"Uh-huh."

"Get over it," she muttered, but she sounded embarrassed. "Is this it or not?"

"This is it." He braced himself against the door as she whipped around the corner just a little bit faster than necessary, and laughed again.

But not very loud, not once she snatched a moment to glare at him, true frustration showing through in the set of her mouth. Ah, that's the way it was, then. It bothered her, this slight imperfection. He held his hands up in surrender, but didn't have the chance to respond, not with the house coming up on the right—his neighbor, distant though she was from him, and the yellow scarf tied around her mailbox. "Stop here," he said, straightening in the seat, his hand already reaching for the door handle.

"What—?"

He turned for a quick glare, his voice dropping into a register he rarely used—had never used in her presence. *"Stop the car."*

Baffled, she did as he asked—there, in the middle of the road. And though he opened his mouth to explain—*the driveway*—in the end he simply flipped the lock and unfolded himself from the car, figuring she'd figure it out faster than he could explain it. He took the gravel driveway at a jog, bounding up the three porch steps in one effort and foregoing the doorbell for a sharp series of raps on the door itself.

Unseen behind the door but evident enough, the severely self-important bundle of hair that called itself a dog rushed up to the door on the inside, barking fiercely; by then Lyn had pulled up into the driveway's turnaround area. Joe knocked again. "Mrs. Rosado?" he called above the dog's barking. "It's Joe. Are you all right?"

Lyn emerged from the car and trotted over, moving like the ocelot—not as rangy as his cougar, but graceful and self-contained. "What's going on?"

"The scarf," he said. "It's a signal we— Here she is."

In fact, it took another minute before the door swung open to reveal Mrs. Rosado, the dog now ensconced comfortably in the crook of her arm and a warm smile on her lined face. "Joe, I'm so glad to see you." She glanced at Lyn in surprise; Lyn made no attempt to hide her bafflement. No doubt there had been no mention of Mrs. Rosado in his file. "And you have a friend!"

"Imagine that," Joe said, but his dryness did not mask his affection for the woman. "You all right?"

Her expression fell, as though he'd reminded her of troubles. "My phone is out. Is yours? Two days now. I had hoped if it was more than just me, they might fix it on their own…."

"You've been two days without a phone?" He let sternness enter his voice. "Mrs. Rosado, you *know* I'd be happy to add you to my cell phone plan. You could have an emergency phone."

"Oh," she said, and didn't meet his gaze. "Gadgets. My Leandro always managed the gadgets." Her voice softened on her deceased husband's name, and Joe flicked a glance at Lyn—and saw, then, that she abruptly understood, and that her expression softened in response.

"I'll call the phone company," he said, relieved it hadn't been more serious. Normally he made an effort to check on her daily, even if just to ease past the house in twilight, leaving cougar tracks behind—but this past week had gotten away from him. "I'm sorry I haven't been by. It's been an odd week."

"Summer colds can be so difficult," she agreed, her

words soft on the edges, still influenced by the language into which she'd been born. Even aging—and she'd told him once she was in her mid-sixties, but he wasn't sure she wasn't guessing—her features retained their distinct Hispanic stamp, strong bones in a square face, her hair still more black than gray. She wore a pair of conservative slacks and a brightly flowered shirt with a button-down collar. "And before that, there were those business associates of yours."

That stopped him short. "Those what?"

"Those men, more than a week ago?" She held up one finger, shifted the dog in her grip and turned away to the small table just inside the door. After a moment of shuffling noises, she turned back and triumphantly displayed a business card.

It took all of Joe's self-restraint to take it so casually, holding it by the very edges…and giving it to Lyn the same way. "Take a look," he said. He'd already seen enough to know that they'd matched his old business cards perfectly, albeit with different personal names imprinted. *Make It Happen.*

They'd done that, all right—he and Dean had. Ten years of making it happen, once they'd decided that bunking together on the field stipend just wasn't enough—from naive young men thinking small in a new business to seasoned men who thought big. Big enough that one of them was eventually killed for a client.

At first Joe hadn't been surprised that brevis had no apparent awareness of the work being done by Make It Happen. After all, it wasn't Sentinel business. But later…when consul never seemed to get it, when no one at regional ever seemed to *get* it—that the business had grown, that it was more than just facilitating unusual requests and last wishes and oddball events—

He blamed them now.

He caught Lyn looking at him, hand extended… waiting patiently, those big eyes watching him far too closely. She accepted the card by the edges and she eased down her shields and she quite suddenly sneezed. She turned to Mrs. Rosado. "Do you mind if we take this?"

"It's for Joe anyway. They were hoping to catch up with him."

Joe doubted that. They'd probably given that card away only to convince this savvy old woman to talk to them. "What did they say?"

He'd tried to keep his voice interested, without bite…but to judge by her expression, he hadn't quite succeeded. "They wanted to be sure they were on the right road." Mrs. Rosado's fingers tangled in the mop-dog's hair while it chanced a sly lift of its lip at Joe, giving a tiny soprano growl so low that only a Sentinel would have heard it at all. Some dogs could deal with him, some couldn't; the mop had never adjusted. "It was all right to send them to your place, wasn't it?"

The house couldn't be seen from here…but Joe was the only one out at the end of this road, where the asphalt crumbled into a short span of dirt and gravel and the loop of his driveway.

"They had the card," she said, a little anxiously now.

Joe shook himself out of his thoughts. "It's fine," he said. "It's too bad we missed each other, that's all."

"They said they wanted to surprise you," she told him, watching his reaction; concern deepened the wrinkles between her brows. "That didn't sound like something you would like. So I told them I wouldn't hide their visit from you, but that I probably wouldn't see you for a while." And that, no doubt, had likely saved her life.

"Thank you," he said, and gave her a smile so her concern might fade. "I'm sure we'll catch up with one another. Soon, even."

"But you know…" Lyn glanced at him, proceeding cautiously, respecting his relationship with his neighbor, he realized, "…probably best to avoid them if you see them again. If you can. They're…" she glanced at the card, bit her lip "…pranksters."

Joe snorted. "That's a good way to put it," he said, and meant it. Mrs. Rosado was now warned—but not unduly alarmed. Not made to feel vulnerable. "Is there anything else I can do for you? Is it just the phone? You made it out for groceries this week, didn't you?"

She *tsked* at him. "I'm not a helpless old lady," she told him. "I drove in to Basha's. They had chicken pieces on sale, you know. And polenta, too. But I *am* having this leak under my sink—"

Joe grinned. She always slipped such requests into the middle of otherwise innocuous conversation, as if it was the only way she could bring herself to ask a favor at all. He'd long ago learned to ask about the weather, or her small raised garden, or her recent errands, if he wanted to pry out the things she needed. "Well, let's have a look at that."

Lyn made a startled noise, no doubt ready to get back on her trails. And though her urgency was far from misplaced, he nonetheless glanced at her, his message clear enough. The few minutes they'd take here would mean the world to Mrs. Rosado, even if he didn't get the leak fixed, simply because she wouldn't feel quite so alone.

And Joe knew what it was like to feel alone.

Chapter 10

Lyn still tasted iced tea at the back of her throat as she navigated the rental car into Joe Ryan's driveway…and she still tasted surprise at the back of her mind.

"You don't know him very well yet, do you, dear?" Mrs. Rosado had said, stroking her Shih Tzu's ears as she settled back in the old overstuffed chair bearing a Mrs. Rosado–sized imprint. She glanced into the kitchen, a bright and airy place with plenty of light to showcase Ryan's sprawl—his legs looking longer than she'd realized as they stuck out from under the sink in those worn jeans and, as he braced himself to apply torque on a pipe, his butt looking quite suddenly stupendous.

As well it should, given how often he ran these mountains in his Sentinel form. *Stole from them,* she reminded herself, and then, uneasy at such thoughts while her shields still stretched between them, she let them dissipate—and ignored the way those sprawling legs momentarily stiffened at the loss of the connection. He returned to work without comment.

Lyn cleared her throat as the little dog jumped down from the chair to come sniffing around her feet, and returned her own thoughts to Mrs. Rosado's surprising comment. "What makes you say so?"

Mrs. Rosado had only smiled. "Because you were surprised he would delay to check my sink. Don't worry, child, it's a very small leak. It could have waited, if you must know. But then he would have worried that I was letting things go undone."

He would? she almost said. But she clamped her lips closed and bent down—cautiously—to let the dog sniff her fingers. She'd already seen its reaction to Ryan.

"Don't worry," Mrs. Rosado told her, breaking a butter cookie in half on the little plate beside her tall tumbler. "It's only Joe who makes him growl that way."

Right. Which only meant the dog had never encountered another Sentinel. But even as the short-legged little thing swept its nose across her fingers and followed with a small pink tongue, its crooked tail swept over its back in a wag.

"You see?" Mrs. Rosado said. "It's a boy thing between the two of them, I do believe. And you, my dear, have the most unusual eyes."

"I— Thank you. Have you known Ry—*Joe*—long?" Smooth. Very smooth. But she hadn't expected to find herself faux-interrogating a genteel neighbor.

"Since he moved in," the older woman said promptly, her dark eyes bright beneath wrinkled lids. "He came over and introduced himself on that very day. My Leandro was still here then, and of course he warned Joe that I was taken. Such a gentleman, that Joe—he pretended great disappointment, you know. And he still brought me things—special fruits from the natural foods store, those hard candies I like—but he always asked Leandro if he might give them to me. He's a special one."

From beneath the sink, Ryan's leg twitched. But those who took the change were used to concealing acute senses and reflexes and strength, so Ryan reacted with nothing more than that twitch while Lyn felt a clamp of alarm as she looked into Mrs. Rosado's protective, affectionate expression as she spoke of Ryan's *special* nature and wondered just how much she knew.

It had turned out there was no need to ask. The older woman had leaned forward slightly and lowered her voice. "There aren't many like him," she said. "Who care the way he does. He feels things deeply, child. You keep that in mind. And he's been hurt. I wouldn't want you to add to that." And she settled back, leaving Lyn speechless.

They'd talked of other things for the remaining twenty minutes or so it had taken Ryan to finish up, from the little dog's place in Mrs. Rosado's life to Ryan's former business, about which Mrs. Rosado knew much more than Lyn's file had indicated.

And thus she sat here in the car with the taste of surprise in her thoughts, because she'd thought Make It Happen had only ever done contracting work. Someone with money wanted a fancy kid's party with sparkly hooved, black ponies, clown cars and a birthday cake in the shape of a ninja turtle? Ryan's company put the pieces together. Someone else wanted the environmentally-greenest-possible house, with no idea where to start looking for contractors and resources? Ryan's company would sort it all out, from finding the location to riding the builders until the work was done. They were the ultimate contractors, whatever the need.

But she hadn't realized the rest of it. The pro bono work, the entire families connected with networks of helping volunteers, the constant cycle of donated goods and services for needy individuals—the services they'd secured when the volunteers weren't to hand. Legal and medical and practical.

Just the sort of help Ryan's sister could have used, had she come to him in time. Talk about irony.

"Hey," Ryan said. He'd exited the car and now bent to look in the open door. "You coming? The Internet? E-mail from brevis? Remember? Gotta check up on me, right?"

She scowled at the windshield, yanking the key from the ignition with a twist. "I'll get my things."

Suddenly she didn't want to check up on his finances, didn't *want* to find out that he was every bit as guilty as she'd always thought he was.

And boy, did that make her mad. Mad enough that she didn't try to hide it as she slammed the car door closed behind her and stalked to the casita to grab her laptop and padfolio and her favorite pen. When she returned it was to find him waiting, bemused, by the car. But as he led the way to the door, he turned back to her and raised an eyebrow. "Don't scare the cats."

Her firm stride faltered; she ran headlong into abashed chagrin. She never would have meant to…and she should have realized. But no. He was the one to think of it. The man she suspected of pillaging this mountain of its power, of leaving it open and vulnerable to the Core. Making sure the cats weren't spooked by anger they didn't deserve.

Yeah, and Bond villain Ernst Stavro Blofeld had his white Persian.

Didn't mean a thing.

But she moderated her steps and she pushed her annoyance to the background. Because, really, when it came right down to it, she wasn't mad at anything or anyone but herself.

Because boy, did she know better.

He showed her to a cluster of small rooms off the hallway behind the kitchen. She felt like the invader she was, pulling her laptop and padfolio closer to her chest as he pushed open a door at the end of the hall to reveal a room of stunning full-length windows, some of which were open to screens. Pines filtered light into green shadow; their sharp, dry scent filled the air. "I could hook you up in the great room," he said, already dropping by the desk to root around in a cluster of cables. "But I figured you'd prefer some privacy."

When he came up for air, he had an Ethernet cable in hand, and he offered it to her, moving on to clear one wing of a wraparound desk—stacks of papers, a phone book—and then to clear the chair of its resident cat. "All yours," he said. "Plus a phone if you need it." He turned away—she thought to leave, but after she set her things down and glanced back, she found him standing before the windows and she faltered, drawn by the sight. *This* was the look, she realized. Eyes half-closed, head slightly tipped, the light bringing out the short black tracings in his tawny hair, the crisp defined nature of it in contrast with the way the rest fell longer and sometimes lifted in the wind. And the way he stood—tall, upright, shoulders somehow both relaxed and expectant…as though a small thrum of tension ran through him. Expectation.

He spoke to her of potential. Of power listening.

And she thought back to what he'd done at the gas

station and she realized that was exactly it. Power listening. Not currently in use, but poised within reach. Closely within reach at that.

The very reason she had to *know* he was clean, that power. What he'd done with it. What he *could* do with it. Did brevis even suspect?

She would have turned on her laptop then had he not taken a sudden sharp breath and opened his eyes, very like a man just waking up. He turned just enough to catch her gaze, and there she stood, caught and not even trying to break away, breathing in that moment of contact as though she'd possibly even craved it.

He was the one to turn away, a quiet smile at the corner of his mouth as he looked back to the window. "Still restless out there."

"Really?" She hadn't felt a thing.

"Ripples." He glanced at her. "If you could feel them, then you would be doing this job, and not—" He gestured at the laptop.

Ah. Right. Checking up on him. "About the gas station…"

He returned her a steady look. "You already said it. Whatever's been triggered, it's volatile. More incidents like that, and people will notice…they'll start to ask questions. We'll be fighting more than the Core if that happens."

Just what we need. She returned to the laptop, all business as she flipped it open and turned it on, clearing a little extra space for the open padfolio and unearthing the phone book from beneath his papers. Awkward moment there, not sure if she should politely pretend not to see the contents of those papers, or if she should grab the moment to learn what she could of him.

"Just wrapping up loose ends from the sale of the

business," he said, and damned if he wasn't suddenly behind her. "The new owners come to me now and then…consulting, you might call it. Wondering how we used to handle similar situations." He reached past her, brushing against her as if she might not find that contact remarkable at all, and plucked out a sheet of paper. "Right. This one, for instance. They had a bad feeling about it. Wondered if I did, too."

"Did you?" She didn't glance at the paper. She didn't lean into his presence. She watched her laptop boot up.

"In fact, I advised them to decline the job."

Okay, that made her curious. She risked a glance not at the paper, but at him. "What was it? Surely people don't come to you asking for anything illegal."

He laughed, a quiet sound. "You wouldn't think so, would you? But they do. Sometimes it's income tax dodging stuff, sometimes it's, say, the sale of a property tangled up in divorce, with one party wanting to make sure the other doesn't get anything from it. But sometimes it just doesn't feel right. This guy…he wanted a bomb shelter."

She frowned, turning to prop herself against the desk. "What's wrong with that?"

He shrugged. "His presentation was a little eager. A little intense. My gut instinct says he wasn't going to use it for a bomb shelter."

She worked on that one, not quite getting it, and finally shook her head.

Gently, he added, "I suggested that they drop his name with the police and look into any unsolved disappearances from his previous locations."

She got it then. "You're kidding. You don't really think… Would he really come to a service for a bomb shelter if he meant to…?"

He flashed her a quick grin. "You'd be surprised. Arrogant, some of these guys. He had money, he was in a hurry, and he was trying to work it long-distance. Those three factors were common to a lot of our jobs."

"Except the pro bono work," she noted. She shook her head; her arms settled across her stomach in spite of herself, looking as confrontational as she felt. "Why didn't you mention—?"

The lingering hint of that grin disappeared as quickly as it had ever flashed her way. "Why didn't you find out for yourself? Why were you—*are* you—so willing to pass judgment when you know so little?"

"If it was important, it would be in the file," she said, and when her arms tightened across her stomach she knew it for defensiveness now.

"Then why ask me now?" He wasn't going to make it easy, that was clear enough. Wasn't just going to let it go.

Fighting the impulse to squirm, Lyn said, "Mrs. Rosado made me curious. It doesn't have anything to do with what's happening here."

"Or it might," he said. "It might have to do with who I am. But if you ever truly learned who I am, it might interfere with this vendetta thing you've got going."

"Hey!" she said sharply. "That's not fair."

He snorted. "Tell me about it." And then he cocked his head and looked at her, something sparking in his expression. "Tell you what. Prove me wrong on that, and I'll take it back. I'll accept whatever action you recommend."

"Prove you wrong," she repeated, and oh, yeah, she felt trapped now.

His smile was predatory. "Do the job right. Do the *whole* job. Check me out. Figure out who I am. And then see if I still fit into that guilty spot you've got picked out for me." He raised an eyebrow, shifting just a little bit closer. In the distant background, thunder rumbled. The first storm of the day, trying hard to work up into rain. "Or is that just a little too threatening to your vendetta?"

"It's not a vendetta," she snapped. "How could it be? I don't even know you."

"Exactly the point," he said, satisfaction flashing as sharp as teeth.

Walked right into that one.

Only because it was there to walk into.

Damn. She didn't want to be that person. The one who lost sight of the trees for the forest.

But his focus on her, so intent in these past moments, abruptly wavered. He took a step back; he faltered. He lost himself in some brief inward struggle, and still…if Lyn hadn't gone looking for it, she never would have felt that tiny susurrus of power, that infinitesimal taste of his trace in the air. When she turned her attention outward again, she found him watching, fully attentive again—but some of his color was gone, something of his presence muted. She said abruptly, "It shouldn't be affecting you like this. These power surges. Riding them is what you *do*. And that…that was nothing. Just like the one up on the top of the ski lift yesterday was barely more than nothing. They all taste like you, and they're damned well messing with you. Why haven't you said something? Why haven't you reported to brevis?"

He scrubbed one hand through his hair and brought it to rest at the back of his neck, kneading slightly. "Wouldn't you just find a way to turn it into evidence that I'm involved?"

She recoiled, stung. "That's not—" *Fair.* Right. They'd been through that. Issue, opposite sides of.

"Look," he said. "I had a cold. I may have mentioned it." He had, and they both knew it. "Not a big deal. But it slowed me down." He watched her, taking in her expression—and she was well aware of the twitch of her own frown, the narrowed eyes of her skepticism; she didn't try to hide them. "You don't get it, do you? I'm just now figuring this stuff out. I'm not ahead of the curve, doling out little tidbits of inside information. *Because I don't have any inside information.*" He dropped his hand from the back of his neck, looked at her in what she could only call disgusted resignation. "I'm not in on this. I didn't start it, and I don't have a clue what the Core hopes to gain here. Until you believe that, you're not going to find me of much help at all…because you're going to look at everything I do and say from the wrong perspective."

"Okay," she said. She turned, scooped up the yellow pages and the padfolio, and held them out to him. "You want to help? I'd like to have the names and numbers of the hotels written out, with enough space beneath each for notes."

"Okay?" he repeated, failing to reach for the phone book and pad.

She shrugged. "It's a good argument."

He squinted at her in patent skepticism. "Yeah?"

"I'm not convinced, but it's a good argument." She gestured with the phone book, which was getting heavy. "Now, are you going to help with this?"

Exasperated, he crossed his arms, very distinctly not taking the offered items. "And if I don't? Do I get demerits?" He looked at her straight on, gaze dark and direct. "I'm not going to play the game where everything I do is weighed and measured and judged. I have no doubt *you're* going to play that game, but…" He stopped, shook his head. "I'm not." And he walked away, past the heavy offered phone book, past Lyn… through the door. His final trailing comment came in the form of short, deep rolling *R*'s—a quick baritone purr, one he was so at home with that he clearly didn't think about using it now. A call to his cat.

The cat in question—the tortie girl, who had been again eyeing the chair with interest—gave her an assessing look, dismissed her and followed Ryan out of the room, exiting with her tail smartly in the air.

Lyn returned the phone book to the desk and shook out her hand. *Huh.* And that didn't seem to be quite enough, so she said it out loud. "Huh." And though she frowned and maybe she even gave the chair a little kick, deep inside she felt an admiration for what he'd just done.

And a little bit of shame for what she was putting him through.

Even if she had no intention of backing off. Not with the stakes this high.

The rich smell of brewing coffee filtered back to her— oh yeah, home-ground. Lyn had never been a coffee slave, but she had a sudden image of herself curled up in a chair in her own seldom-seen apartment in the very northern part of California, lap quilt pooled around her feet, night closing in around her. And then she blinked, and realized her mind's image hadn't really been her apartment after all, but the briefly glimpsed loft of this very house, and that she hadn't even really been alone as night closed around her. That—oh my God—she'd been wearing one of his shirts, half-buttoned at that.

She squeezed her eyes closed, covering her face with

her hands. "That is so wrong," she muttered. She smoothed down her shirtfront; she lifted her chin to expose her flushing neck to the slight breeze from the window, and she stared down the muddy brown tabby who came to sit in the half-open door and observe her as it might watch a bug.

The ringing doorbell was a mercy—especially as she had no trouble discerning the ensuing conversation. Two children, neither of whom carried any special trace, and Ryan, his voice soothing against their shrill and urgently blurted words. "…lost track," one was saying, and "…can't find him," said the other, and "…going to rain!"

Right on cue, thunder rumbled overhead.

"Come," said the voices, suddenly overlapping one another. "Joe, come help us, Joe, come find him, Joe, please!"

And the next thing she knew, Ryan was calling to the back of the house. "I'll be back in a while!"

She wanted to shout back for him to be careful—of the impending storm, of the potential power surges, of the Core in the area—but instead she closed her mouth and she returned to the desk, where she finally brought up her e-mail program and logged in. As it downloaded, she flipped the heavy phone book open to the hotel listings and began to write.

A cat sauntered into the room—the tortie again—pausing before the chair to eye it with a proprietary air.

"Sorry, cat," Lyn told it, barely glancing away from her notes. Did they even have names? And then she squeaked with surprise as the cat leaped into the chair anyway, landing in the small space behind her. It kneaded her lower back a few times and curled up in that tiny space, quite obviously determined to pretend she wasn't there. She informed it, "Two can play that game," and turned to her e-mail.

Nick's e-mail update was short and full of *not-yets*. Still checking on who'd been responsible for getting requests and information to Ryan, although that name should have been clear and simple to pin down. That it wasn't made Lyn think there might just be something to Ryan's allegations. "If you'd gotten the report in on time," she muttered, "there wouldn't have been any problem."

Unless someone made sure it got lost.

Wow, where had *that* thought come from? Almost as if some part of her actually believed him…believed that there was someone within the Sentinels working to make things look bad for him. Someone within *brevis*.

Right. Just because he'd touched something within her that hadn't ever made that connection before. Because he'd opened the way for feelings she'd never had before. *Get over it, self.*

Except it wasn't just that, was it?

It was the way he never bothered to hide what he was thinking, even when she wished he wasn't thinking it. It was the way he'd put his heart into these mountains. The way he kept constant watch on this place…and had expanded those responsibilities to include that stranger on the ski lift and his widowed neighbor and whoever those kids had been. They'd come to him; they'd expected help.

They'd gotten it.

It was the look on his face as he took in the high desert far below, listening for problems in the flow of power. *Dammit.*

Before she knew it, she'd pulled the folder from the padfolio pocket, smoothed its crimped edges and flipped it open to that photo. The one she didn't really need to look at. The one she'd first seen as a target, and now, in spite of herself, saw as the person behind the target.

"You are in way, way over your head," she whispered…and didn't know if she spoke to the photo or herself.

Ryan returned nearly two hours later, with the thunder rumbling constantly overhead and fat drops of rain hitting the office windows, steady and building fast. Lyn had gotten her permissions, navigated the Sentinel servers and connected with one of the brevis consultants to delve through Ryan's financial records— where she discovered he was, in fact, on the high end of financially comfortable. The business, now sold, had been doing very well at the time of his partner's death.

In fact, his credit record showed he'd been hunting a business equity loan as a down payment on his half sister's medical bills around the time of Dean Seacrest's death. What sense did it make, to kill the partner who made such a loan possible?

Because a better deal came along?

None of the mystery money remained…none of it had actually ever been deposited in his account. His partner had died; the medical bills had been paid. That money had been traced back to the Vegas crime consortium.

You'd think a criminal organization in Vegas would know how to hide their tracks.

Huh. You kind of would, wouldn't you?

And so she'd made notes, and she'd sent an e-mail to Nick summarizing the events since her arrival, and she'd said to him, "I need more time on Ryan."

Best to concentrate on finding the Core presence

here, and following the trail from that end. Especially since she wasn't quite ready to say out loud—not to Nick Carter, not to herself—that she had doubts about Ryan's involvement. That she thought…if he was involved at all, he'd tumbled into it stupidly, in some foolish *trying-to-do-the-right-thing* way that turned out to be totally the wrong thing.

She looked up to find he'd done it again—that in spite of his size, he stood in the office doorway without triggering her awareness. For all the young Sentinels practiced such tricks in their massively annoying teen-aged years—trying to be more ninja than thou—Ryan did it effortlessly. Lyn had come to suspect it was about more than just quality of movement and deliberate stealth…it was the way he fit in here. A man who could ride the mountain's power was pretty much just part of the place.

But now he very much had her attention. A bit bedraggled—half-wet with rain, and no more comfort-able in that state than any cat…and yet more than that. The fatigue shadowing his features, the set of his shoul-ders…the sense that when he leaned on the door frame, it truly was the only thing holding him up. But with all of that, he said, "I see you've made a friend."

"I'm not sure I'd call her that," Lyn said, peering over her shoulder to glimpse striking tortie fur. "More like she's tolerating my existence because she has no choice." She straightened, suddenly aware that she now had a vibrator at her back; the tortie had decided to celebrate Ryan's return. "Do you need something? You look…"

"Like something the cat dragged in?" he said.

"Like the cat who got dragged in," she corrected him. She saved her work and shut down the laptop, gathering her hotel notes, maps and planned routes and stuffing them into the padfolio pocket along with his file. "Come on. I want to try some of that coffee you had out earlier, anyway. Kona?"

"Smooth stuff," he said, but he didn't perk up noticeably. "It's got a nutty edge. Too much for me in the morning, but right now I'll take it."

She stopped gathering her things to look at him again. Still leaning there. And his color…decidedly off. "What was that all about?" she asked. "With the kids?"

"Ah, the Martins." He grinned—half a grin, anyway, and it looked as tired as the rest of him. His hair, darkened by the rain, highlighted his unruly state. "Latchkey kids, just past Mrs. Rosado. Their youngest has recently become an escape artist. Headed for the woods…the other two lost him."

"In this weather?" Lyn glanced outside, where the day had darkened under the storm and rain thumped steadily against the house and grounds, splatting up a misty ground cover of bounce droplets. She didn't need a thermometer to know the temperature had dropped a good twenty degrees, with the breeze blowing up goose bumps on her arms. A young child out in this could chill to hypothermia in no time.

"Hey, I found him." Ryan grinned again, a little more convincing this time. "Sent the other kids in the wrong direction, took the cougar…tracked him right down. Backtracked, took the human, and 'found' him again. Not the first time, as you might guess."

She frowned at him. "No offense, but it looks as though it took more out of you than that."

His grin faded; he glanced away. "You probably didn't feel it. We've had power ripples since I left. Whatever's in them…" He shook his head.

"*You're* in them," she said, and immediately regretted

it. He hadn't come to this doorway looking for trouble. "I'm sorry. But I think that's part of the problem."

"They're corrupt and angry," he said, and anger touched his own voice—but not aimed at her. He looked beyond her, out the window to the woods he worked so hard to nurture. "It's the lifeblood of this area, bleeding out of a giant wound somewhere. *That's* the problem."

"You didn't shield?" She kept her voice neutral… careful.

He rested the side of his head against the door frame. "Couldn't. Not and keep an eye on things, with Jakey out there. Looks like I'm like you…I need someone to watch my back when I work in an environment gone this sour."

For once, she didn't feel that surge of defensiveness at her inability to divide her attention between tracking and…well, anything else. Maybe it was the complete lack of judgment in his voice as he spoke…maybe it was the understanding in his eyes. "Is it bad?" she asked. "The surges? Are you—"

"I'm shielded now," he said, abruptly, as if he could tell she'd been about to reach out and check—and indeed, he gave his head a quick shake, lifting it from the door frame to fasten his gaze on her, that weariness mixed with an odd combination of wistfulness and warning. "Don't. I couldn't, if you—"

For a startling moment, she thought he was going to stride into the room, pull her up out of that chair and kiss her senseless. In the next moment she saw nothing but a tired Sentinel leaning at the door, and she blushed hotly at herself. She said, "I won't."

He took a deep breath, nodded at the contented cat behind her. "You acquired a supervisor. And did you find anything condemning?"

She couldn't help it. She said, "You have to ask?"

His expression shuttered; he looked away again, over her shoulder to his tremendous windows and the violence of the storm beating against the glass. Lightning flashed, right on cue; he didn't even flinch—nor at the almost instantaneous crash thunder that made Lyn stiffen in the chair and brought the cat's claws out against her back. As the thunder grumbled away and the rain picked up tempo, he raised his voice above the increasing din of it and said, "You'd think not. But I've learned the hard way—that's not the way it works."

And he left her there in the dim space of the office, with thunder ramping up to grumble in her ears and regret humming in her heart.

Chapter 11

The storm passed quickly enough—they always did in monsoon season. Joe retreated to his loft under the skylights and sprawled diagonally over the mattress and springs sitting directly on the floor—uncaring that he still wore damp clothes, that it was only midafternoon, that the storm would pass and the long desert evening would brighten the sky again, bringing back daytime from this faux twilight.

Completely uncaring. As the four cats joined him, taking up their accustomed spots on the bed, he twisted to the rhythm of the mountain, half-real dreams of power pushing him around, buffeting him…calling to him. But not the *real* mountain…instead, the distorted results of what came from trying to claim it. Not the kind of power that he wanted to absorb, or even to ride. He groaned in frustration and in remembered pain, debridement from the inside out. And eventually, hand fisted in covers and face stuffed into a disarrayed pillow, he actually relaxed toward sleep.

He should have felt better when he woke. He should have opened his eyes to invigoration and determination and *raring to go.*

He opened them to movement, there at the top of the stairs leading to this big private space of his, space that held bookshelves and the bed in the corner, enough open floor for stretching and yoga and even for the sprawl of a cougar. Laundry dumped in the corner, enough pillows on the bed to make it work from just about any direction, a single Ansel Adams print on the wall where the sun never hit it and the light rarely left it.

Disgruntled, the brown tabby grumbled away, slinking into some corner so dark even Sentinel eyes couldn't see. Joe blinked at the intrusion and put a hand over his eyes. A growl escaped.

"Not a morning person?" She leaned against the loft railing, no fear for the full-story drop below.

"Morning," he grunted, and flailed around for his alarm clock, hitting covers and pillows and scattering cats before he realized how skewed he was on the bed and gave up. "What time is it?" Nighttime, obviously, in spite of her dry allusion to his slow wakefulness.

"It's going on eleven," she said, and concern laced her voice. "How do you feel?"

"I'm fine," he said, licking at irritability. "I'm just tired."

She let that statement stand on its own, and after a moment added, "I thought we'd do some hotel drive-bys. I've mapped them all—we can hit half of them with a couple of passes. They sure do like their hotel clusters in this tourist town of yours."

He couldn't argue that. At either end of Route 66,

down by the Butler exit for I40…that would easily en-
compass half of the local options. Everything else
would be a tedious one-by-one process. "You think
you'll be able to detect Core presence from a drive-by?"

"I think there's a good chance."

"And if you find them?" *What do you think, boy-o?*
The Sentinel team would swoop in, corner them and
grill them about Joe's involvement.

But she said, "If we can track them to wherever
their base of activity is, we will. If we don't get anywhere with that, we'll bring in the whole team. They'll
be in on it before the end in any event. This is too big
for me."

He grunted. "Too big for any single one of us. Or two
of us, for that matter—even if you actually trusted me."

There she was, again saying nothing for a moment.
She fiddled with the flashlight, and finally stuck it in
the side pocket of the cropped cargo pants, the ones that
made her legs look long and her hips refined and her
ass tight. The whole effect just begged a man to use one
of those many pockets to pull her close, to run his hands
over the shape of her to define it for himself.

He sat up and scrubbed a hand through his hair,
pushing wayward strands from his face. "I'll be right
down. We can take my car."

"I didn't mean—" she started, and stopped as though
she didn't quite know how to finish, her voice full of
regret.

"It is what it is," he told her. He took a deep breath.
"Don't worry, I get it."

She pushed away from the railing. "I'm not really
sure you do," she said, and headed down the stairs. And
murmured, distinctly enough for his ears, "I'm not
really sure I do, either."

* * *

He didn't know what that was supposed to mean. He didn't know before he brushed his teeth and splashed cold water on his face, he didn't know as he patted his face dry and scowled at himself in the mirror, and he didn't know as he ambled down the stairs, pulling on a fresh shirt.

She waited in the kitchen, frowning at the Senseo brewer as if she couldn't quite bring herself to try it. She started slightly as she realized he was there, briefly transferred the frown to his unbuttoned shirt, and said, "It's not the coffeemaker that gets me. It's the pod things. Don't you keep any around that are premade?"

He let his disdainful expression answer that question. "You want decaf, or the full whammy?"

"Decaf," she said without hesitation. "I'm plenty awake on my own…and I want to be plenty asleep when the time comes." But she made no comment when he pulled down the Tarrazu French roast for himself. He wasn't surprised. He had, after all, seen his face in that mirror.

Power surges weren't supposed to do that…weren't supposed to drain him. Power surges should have been invigorating, there to be ridden, each one the perfect wave.

The Core had a lot to answer for.

It was a thought that stuck with him as he pulled on a hoodie jacket and offered Lyn one of the same. It stuck with him as they drove out onto Fort Valley Road and into town, picking up 89 to head for Butler, the back way around Flagstaff and the fastest route to the first cluster of hotels. And Lyn, who'd hunched herself inside his jacket and leaned against the door of his hybrid SUV as though to get as far away as possible, gave him a frown and asked, "What put that look on your face?"

He was tempted to respond that it was playing chauffeur for a woman who could touch him from the inside out one moment and who wanted to take him down the next. He wanted to say that she never should have come here, staring at him with her smoky eyes and being so damned true to herself that she'd already captured him and she hadn't noticed.

But he didn't think either of those things would go down very well, so he told her the truth. "Thinking about the Core. What they've done to this place." And then he braced himself for some reminder that he'd probably helped them.

It didn't come.

In fact, as they navigated past the always baffling Enterprise and Butler exchange of too many lanes in too many directions at once and he flipped onto a side road shortcut that clearly startled her, he pondered her silence and realized aloud, "You haven't found anything."

"Not yet," she said, crossing her arms only long enough to realize she was wrinkling her map. "But we're really not even there yet." Indeed, the road curved around the backsides of the hotel lineup.

Joe eased the car to a crawl in the nonexistent traffic, keeping an eye on the rearview mirror. "On me," he said. "You haven't found anything *on me*. None of the dirt you thought would be there. The big obvious Atrum Core fingerprints all over me."

She sighed. She looked away. "No," she said. "But I still have some queries out."

He couldn't quite understand what he heard in her voice. Reluctance to admit failure? To admit he might be clear? "I don't get it," he said, and he didn't bother to hide his confusion…or maybe that was even hurt. "You sound as though you *want* to find those finger-prints. I was right, wasn't I? You came here with your mind made up. You want dirt…and maybe it's not even about me. Who's it about, Lyn?"

"You're off base," she told him shortly.

He stopped the car. Oh, nominally he pulled it off the road first, but that really meant straddling a curb and part of a sidewalk. "Screw off base," he said. "This is my life. There's no way I'm going to hold myself up as a target so you can act out some inner need."

She turned them away from him, looking out the window into the darkness along the back of this group of hotels; she crossed her arms and probably had no idea she'd only drawn the jacket tight over those modest and perfect breasts. *Ah well, boy-o.* At least the car sat in darkness.

"You don't need to know anything about me," she said tightly. "Your job is to track down the power surges and to back me up. The end."

Two could play the anger game. "Says you." He snorted. "Last time, I played by those rules and I lost everything. Now I've got things to lose again. I'm finding new things that mean something to me." *You,* he meant. He looked at her, sitting in those shadows, obviously enough that she turned to him in surprise, caught in his gaze, suddenly vulnerable. He said, "And I don't intend to lose them without a fight."

She struggled; her open expression showed the impact of his words, of his gaze—and revealed far more than she'd probably intended. The anguish in those big smoky eyes when she squelched her response to him— the effort it took to turn away. She took a deep breath.

"I need to concentrate if I'm going to find them. I need... I can't—" She pushed herself against the door. "Just let me work!"

It came out as a cry of frustration. And not, he thought, at him.

At herself.

A complicated woman, Lyn Maines.

Joe sat back and let her work, watching over her. He stretched his senses to search the night for anyone who might cause trouble, for those well meaning who might interfere. He cracked the window to add his ears to his eyes, to let the rain-damp scents of the area trickle in. And if he also slid a glance over to study her profile in the darkness—lashes sweeping her cheeks as she closed them in that concentration she had, nose short and straight, her lips full and curved—then no one knew any better. Her hair still curled with the storm's humidity, free of its ponytail and—inadvertently, he was sure—left in a mildly mussed bed-head sort of state that made his fingers twitch.

But he not only kept his fingers to himself, he kept them where she couldn't see them twitch. *Just let me work,* she'd said. He could do that. He could do any number of things he'd rather not do.

Even if sitting here in the car with her—with her silence, her breathing, her scent—only made it quite clear to him just exactly what he'd prefer to be doing instead.

Give it up, boy-o. He could all but hear Dean's voice in his ear. *Just because we called ourselves Make It Happen doesn't mean we can take ourselves seriously. Some things are beyond what a man can do.*

So he sat. And probably not for nearly as long as it seemed before she let out a sigh and shook her head. "Not here."

"Next stop, then." He started the vehicle, pulling it out into the nonexistent traffic flow—but only for a block or so, until they reached the next alley between hotels. This time it took only a few moments before she shook her head.

"Hang on," he told her, and pulled through the alley, popping out a curving pathway later to turn back onto Butler, this time crossing beneath the thruway to hang a right at one of the fancier hotels of the area—his own personal target for the evening. Somewhere, the Core had to be handling what they'd stirred up—doing whatever they'd intended when they disrupted things in the first place. But it wouldn't be wherever they'd chosen to stay. Not with that kind of power. Not unless they were a whole lot dumber than Joe had ever suspected.

"They've got to be harnessing the power in amulets," he mused, at the same time Lyn's eyes sprang open; one hand clutched the door handle and the other landed on his arm.

"They're here!"

Pride flushed through him, surprising him. "Yeah? You found 'em?"

"Not precisely." She bit her lower lip. "They're shielding pretty well. They're here, but just *where…*?"

Her dissatisfaction let him finish her unspoken thought. "And you want to be able to tell the brevis team which room."

The look she shot him was a challenge. "Don't you?"

For once, it wasn't a challenge of his guilt or innocence. More as if testing to see if he'd be happy with a job half-done. *Not a chance.* "You want to drive a circuit? Or walk it?"

"Walk it." She spoke decisively. "The drive curves

too far from the hotel in spots—all that landscaping. And there's a virtual forest of trees around this place." She shook her head, looking at it all.

"You should see them at Christmas," Joe said, somehow forgetting for a moment that she wasn't likely to welcome such casual chatter. "People come into town just to see the light show."

But instead of cutting him off, she merely looked at him a long moment, her expression unreadable even to his excellent night vision…unless that was wistfulness he saw. But she spoke matter-of-factly. "I think we'll have a better chance if we walk. But Gausto knows me, and they'd be fools if they didn't know what you look like. I don't suppose you could put that hood up—"

Joe did just that, flipping the jacket's sweatshirt-like hood up over his head to regard her with a dead-pan expression.

"Oh," she said, understanding immediately—and not without a little smile. "Right. Too gangster."

"We'll manage." He twisted to rummage in the backseat, coming up with a battered straw cowboy hat, one he'd shaped to death at the front so the sides curled up as it dipped down over his forehead. "Bet I can find a cap back here…."

"I can handle it," she said hastily, and she dropped her head, scrubbing her hair with her fingers. *I'll do that,* Joe wanted to say but of course didn't; she flipped her head back up and finger-combed the front strands forward, and suddenly had a serious case of big hair.

"Whoa," he said. "That's…scary."

"Humidity is my friend," she said. "For the moment." And then she unzipped the borrowed jacket halfway, tugged her shirt off her shoulder and stretched the neckline down.

Joe got out of the SUV. Quickly. He jammed the hat on his head, looked off at distant headlights and took a deep breath. By then she was beside him, assessing the effect of the cowboy hat and nodding. "You'll do," she said. "Unless you wear it around town where they might have gotten photos."

"We're good," he said. "This one's for when I help neighbors with their fencing."

"And that comes up often?" she asked, taking another look at the battered thing.

He raised an eyebrow at her. "Neighbors do for one another."

She made a vague noise of agreement, something that still managed to convey her skepticism. And not, he understood suddenly, that neighbors should do for one another. But that she'd seen through him, and realized he'd not truly been able to leave his Make It Happen work behind him. She left it alone, though. "Let's go walk the hotel. If we're really lucky, once I get a strong hit, I'll be able to back-trace toward wherever they're doing their work. Because I think you're right—it won't be here."

Right. So just a matter of finding the source before it was too late.

"No pressure," he said, a little too cheerfully. He set the hat more firmly on his head. "Let's get started."

Chapter 12

They headed around the hotel perimeter together—a relaxed and easy walk, a couple headed out for a late-evening stroll. Absorbed in defining trace, she lifted her head, kept her eyes mostly closed. Joe placed a gentle hand at the small of her back, a subtle guidance as they followed the irregular path.

She didn't protest; she didn't seem to notice. And Joe, for once shielded, kept his senses fully engaged—fully Sentinel. The slightly blue-washed depth and detail of the night around them came through clearly: pine branches reaching from above; a late coyote prowling boldly along the mile trail behind the hotel, thinking itself unseen. The storm brought out the distinct scent of thick fallen pine needles and the loamier scent of dirt; the wet ground muted the sound of a vole scurrying around for insects, if not the owl who hunted it. All to be expected, those rich sights and scents and sounds, along with the cool night breeze on his face. High desert darkness after the best of storms, refreshing a dry land.

He walked Lyn around the back end of the long hotel, enjoying her scent as it mingled with the night. He let her choose the pace, easing along past hotel windows.

And then she froze. She took several faltering steps, her head tipped in a listening attitude, her body tensed—and then took a sudden startling handful of quick steps directly for a room door, hard on the trail. Rather than stop her and risk her startled response, he put himself into high gear, scooping an arm around her waist to bring her along in his wake and completely bypassing the door in question. And though a very distinct part of him reveled in his fingers curving around her tight waist, the greater part focused on hustling her away from that door before she blurted protest.

And indeed, her eyes flew open, confused and resentful. "Hey!"

"Hush," he said, not without understanding. He understood all too well—she'd been in deep, and had no idea why he'd pulled her off the track, or why he now propelled her along the sidewalk.

She resisted him; she said, "I was on to something!" and she didn't do it quietly, still lost in her tracking daze.

"Yes, hon," he muttered, "you surely were. But unless you want them on to *us,* we need to move along. We can regroup once we're—"

A door opened behind them; men's voices filtered out. Joe muttered, "Damn," and tightened his hold on Lyn's waist. He had no trouble, even in this pool of sidewalk darkness, seeing her eyes widen with warning as he pulled her in. He did it anyway, tugging her up against him, their knees interlacing.

"Don't you dare—" she said, even as he cupped the side of her face, looking down on her. Behind them, the voices raised, alert and territorial.

"Shh," he said quietly, bending so their faces were a whisper away, tipping his head to keep his suddenly annoying hat out of the way. She trembled; he felt it from the gentle hold at her neck to the firmer grip at the small of her back.

"Don't you—" she warned, though this time she whispered it.

What? React to her? *Too late for that, boy-o.* But he gave his head the slightest shake. "Trust," he said. "You don't want it? I won't do it. This is enough for appearances." Her breath warmed his chin. "Besides, do you really think if I did the cliché thing and kissed you, I'd have any chance of keeping track of that guy?"

That guy being the man standing in the open hotel doorway, just visible in the corner of Joe's vision, squinting suspiciously into the night. But unlike Joe and Lyn, he couldn't see with anything other than the hotel's lighting, spread out over sidewalk and parking lot but leaving great pools of darkness such as this one. They were nothing more than a couple cozying up in the dark, murmuring to one another.

Lyn's fingers, once clenching his jacket to push him away, now just gripped the material as if to steady herself.

"Just a couple of gropers," the man turned back to the room to say, tones he might well have expected to go unheard. He muttered, "Get a room," before the hotel door closed.

Joe eased his hold on Lyn.

But he didn't let go.

She looked up at him and where he expected recrimination, she gave him only a troubled gaze. "I was going for the hotel room, wasn't I?"

Oh, as if he could help it. He brushed his thumb against the side of her face—the softness of it, there along her wide cheekbone beneath that sooty eye. "You were."

She shuddered, but this time it was acknowledgment of what she'd almost done, of how close they'd come. Two unprepared Sentinels, blundering into a drozhar's nest. If they'd gone down, brevis would have been none the wiser—clueless as to the Core location, clueless as to why their team disappeared. "Thank you," she whispered.

So tempting, that lower lip and its hint of a quiver. Definitely a quiver that needed to be kissed away, and his body tensed with the need to do it. Somehow, he didn't; somehow he lifted his head just enough to kiss her forehead instead, and damned if he didn't think maybe she leaned into him just the slightest bit. "You're welcome," he said. "Now. What's next so we can get those bastards?"

Lyn held the phone perhaps a little too tightly, there in the little guesthouse with darkness closing around her—all the lights off, her night vision perfectly adjusted to the postmidnight moon and starlight. She relaxed her fingers and said, cleanly and distinctly, "It's premature to send in the team. If you spook Gausto's people to a fallback position, we'll have to track them down all over again."

Nick Carter shook his head. Oh, she might have been nearly the length of the big southwestern state away from him, but she could see it anyway, right along with that dark hoarfrost hair defying its expensive style and the serious nature of his pale green eyes. "I don't like it," he said. If she'd woken him with this late-night phone call, he showed no sign of it. "You've got no one for backup."

"I've got Ryan," she heard herself saying, with surprising sincerity.

"Maybe you two fooled them tonight, maybe you didn't," Nick said. "Either way, tracking them now is a far cry from hunting trace on the mountain. You're too vulnerable."

"I want another day." Firm but implacable. "I want to see if I can pick up fresh trace from their room tomorrow. Or I might start at Elden Pueblo."

"Elden Pueblo?"

"A hunch."

"Yours?" Nick asked dryly. "Or Ryan's?"

"I don't think it's misdirection." Lyn glanced through the single main window at the big house, as if she might find Ryan watching…listening. Or he might well have taken the cougar this night, wandering silently within earshot…patrolling the land in spite of drained resources.

Not so drained that he couldn't pull off that moment at the hotel.

Right. As if she wanted to think of *that,* with Nick Carter on the other end of the phone line. Not the feel of Ryan's hand spanning the small of her back, not the flooding warmth of her response.

No. Definitely not.

She cleared her throat. "This is his turf, Nick. He wouldn't be much of a Sentinel if he didn't have some sense of it."

After a short silence, he said, "No. He wouldn't."

She moved on. "We're going to need an amulet specialist. And whoever you send, make sure they're strong on shielding. This place is unstable as hell."

Nick said grimly, "You aren't kidding. No one here has seen anything like it. The words *powder keg* have been tossed around…and not lightly."

"I was right," she breathed, struck anew by the frisson of fear that had first shivered down her spine at the Skybowl overlook. "They've unbalanced things to the point where this place could blow."

"That's one way to put it." A gentle brush of sound gave away his movement; the faint clicking of dog nails on tile followed. "Has your mountain wrangler said anything about it?"

Lyn smiled to herself. *Mountain wrangler.* Ryan would like that, she thought, even though Nick's tone had been just a little too sardonic for complete sincerity. "I think he's too close to have realized. These power surges are taking a lot out of him."

She could hear Nick's frown in his brief silence. "That doesn't make sense."

It sure screws with motive if we want to pin this on him. But she didn't say it out loud; Nick could follow that train of. thought well enough. "It's probably because his trace is tied to the surges somehow. And I've already told you about his reaction to the museum artifact. Whatever's going on here, it's complicated."

"You'll track it out," Nick said. "That's one reason we were willing to send you."

"That and you knew I'd do my best to pin him down." She was surprised to hear a touch of bitterness in her words…maybe even self-blame.

As was Nick. "Lyn?"

She held her breath, then blurted the words out. "I'm just not sure it was fair to him." She looked again out the window, finding the dim light in Ryan's loft. "You know how I feel about Sentinels gone dark—about *anyone* gone dark. You know about my brother. I might be the best tracker you could have sent, but the best investigator? I'm practically jury and judge rolled into one, and you know it."

"Do I?" He let the question hang a moment. "You'll do the right thing, Lyn. That's part of the package. You demand no less from yourself than you do from others."

She made an indistinct grumbling noise, and—cowardly—skipped a direct response. "Listen, Ryan's already been affected by the surges, even if he's not admitting it. You'd better make sure the team has someone who can do extended shielding, because he can't do it while he's working. I covered his ass so far, but if I'm going to be tracking—"

"What do you mean, he can't—?" The words came in surprised demand.

"Oh, don't tell me it comes as a surprise. He and Dean had a teamwork thing—*Dean* covered his ass in the field. He has decent shields in general, but he can't do it while he's handling power, and right now that matters. And I can't do it if you want me on trace."

"Damn sure I'll want you on trace," Nick mused. "So Dean was his cover all this time."

"Just like I need backup when I trail," she said. "Think about it." She certainly had been. Moving from place to place, assignment to assignment…it meant she worked with many different partners. But now and then she found one she trusted so utterly, meshed with so well, she couldn't help but rue the change when she moved on.

She couldn't imagine killing such a partner. And one she'd grown up with? Trained with?

Ryan had cause, she reminded herself. At the time, he'd been trying to save his sister's life.

Don't go there right now. She cleared her throat. "What about the missing requests Ryan should have received?"

She wouldn't have heard the frustration if she hadn't been listening for it; wouldn't have heard the weary undertone. "Double-backs and stream breaks," he said, putting it into her own tracking jargon. "We can't find any record of notification to Ryan—or anyone else in northern Arizona—of our concerns about Core activity, although my directive to send them is in my own records. My request for expedition of Ryan's latest monthly report…" He hesitated, and Lyn again heard the grim frustration there. "It's on my system as sent. It's not on our main server."

She understood the implications immediately, and swore softly. "That means someone with tech skills *and* access."

"Or with enough skills to have gained the access."

"Or it's just system glitches," Lyn said. "Gremlins in the works."

"Brevis Southwest," Nick said with distinct grimness, "does not have gremlins."

No. Of course not.

She checked the window again…discovered Ryan's loft light still on. Either he'd found a hell of a good book or he was out checking the land when he ought to have been grabbing sleep.

She could say the same for herself. And as if perceiving her distraction, Nick said, "I'll keep you posted."

"I'd appreciate that," she said. "Because as it stands, I'm not certain I'm receiving all my communications, either. And, Nick…" She took a breath, then took the plunge. "I'd like a roster of Sentinels assigned to the Henderson/Vegas area at the time of Dean Seacrest's death. Because if Ryan *didn't* do it…well, it takes a lot to kill a field Sentinel, especially up close and dirty."

Sounding wary, Nick said, "We got alibis for the other local Sentinels for just that reason."

"Doesn't mean someone wasn't in on it." She hated to say it—*winced* to say it. "Especially one of the logistics people, who wouldn't have any physical advantage, but might have useful inside info."

Nick released a gust of breath—not quite a sigh, not quite acquiescence. "All right," he said. "I'll see what I can do. But don't get too distracted. After Gausto's failure in Sonoita, he's going to be more dangerous than ever…more desperate. He's already jeopardizing long-term Core plans with his presence there."

"Mmm," she said. "That whole business of letting him go, leaving him to face his septs prince…doesn't seem to have worked out so well for us."

"No choice," Nick said, and that weary tone was back. "The official peace between us is uneasy enough… If we were to kill a local prince—"

"*Another* local prince," Lyn noted, since Dolan Treviño had already killed Tiberon Gausto in the very incident that stamped him rogue. Justified, given the torture he'd been undergoing at the time. But it had destabilized an area already rocked by the indulgent, power-hungry Gausto brothers.

"Exactly the reason we had no leeway in Sonoita."

"And now?"

"I've made some calls." It was as much as he'd say, she knew. After all, the Core didn't want exposure any more than the Sentinels did.

She thanked him; she flipped the phone closed and

pondered it in the darkness, realizing anew that nothing she'd seen of Ryan, of his personal records, of his past, had convinced her he'd gone dark.

Nothing had yet convinced her of his innocence, either, but just because she'd arrived here so eager to sink her teeth into a dark Sentinel didn't mean he didn't deserve due process.

Especially if he hadn't gotten it in Vegas.

She sighed; she stretched and dropped the phone on the couch and scrubbed her hands through hair that was still scruffed-up big hair, catching her fingers on tangles.

Grumbling, twisted, distorting rolling power, torquing as it came, splinters of angry shrapnel full of Ryan's trace—

Her head snapped up; her fingers tore through a tangle unheeded. It didn't take Sentinel ears to hear the yowl of anguish through the open window—to know the cougar was nearby, unshielded, and hit hard by the power he was so used to riding.

The house. She sprinted away from the couch, threw the door open and ran to the house—totally stymied to find the door locked. "Ryan!" She pounded against that solid wood in futility, and kicked it for good measure as she spun around to put her back to it, hands splayed against its solidity, head tipped back to breathe in...

His trace.

Of course, his trace. It filled her senses, that deep, textured sensation, almost to the point where she couldn't discern where it waxed and waned.

But not quite. Because this was what she did. And so she pushed off the door and headed into the confusing backwash flows of power around the house and its wards, trotting through the swirling eddies with assur-

ance—until a groan took her ears and she emerged
from the trace, discovering herself at the back of the
house, puzzled and alone in the dark. Here, she and
Ryan had raced for shelter the day they'd met—barely
less than two days earlier. Here, they'd tumbled into the
shelter of the overhanging second-story deck, where
he'd offered up cat laughter at the exhilaration of it
all—and, she suddenly realized, planted that first seed
of doubt in her heart about his guilt.

And here, she'd seen the first signs of his difficulty
with the power surges.

But he was not here now.

Except somehow he was. She closed her eyes, raised
her head and listened. She reached for him, even as
another wave of power jerked through the night.

That's when she heard it. There, from above—from
the deck that had once sheltered them. The one that led
to the sliding doors of his bedroom, and to the reinforced section of roof where the cougar kept watch
over his domain. A tortured noise, not human or animal,
purely wrenched from one who was both.

The roof. He was on the roof. He'd been checking
the mountain, dammit, even if it meant leaving himself
open to this agony.

She couldn't get into the house—not the usual way.
Maybe as the ocelot, but… She stared up at the deck
and she narrowed her eyes and she thought of how he'd
reached that far-overhead chairlift at Skybowl, how impossible it had seemed and yet how easily he'd done it.
Reaching for the Sentinel within, that's what it took—
reaching without changing, finding that strength and
power. And it wasn't anything she'd done, not since she
was a teen in training. A tracker used other strengths;
a tracker was too valuable to put in dire positions.

And yet there was that deck, and there was that man in his pain, and damned if she didn't do it, reaching deep and tapping Sentinel strength—a crouch, a leap, and her fingers found purchase; she twisted in flight, lithe ocelot in human form soaring over the sturdy railing and crouching just long enough to get her bearings.

But she had to go higher still, easily finding the reinforced footpath the man had made for the cougar—scrambling, this time, to the juncture of two roof slopes where he'd covered a platform in shingling, blending it in.

There he lay, but no longer cougar. He rode the platform on hands and knees, cradling his head on his forearms. Starlight painted his back and torso, shadowed the strong, sculpted form of shoulders and biceps. He wore nothing more than shorts, ragged cut-offs that did more to emphasize the lines of his body than to hide them.

Lyn's heart pounded—to have made it up here, to have found him, to realize how serious his danger, disoriented here at the top of a potential three-story fall. Instinctively, she reached out to him with her shields, extending the protection that had been so successful in the past—and then, just in time, jerked them back. *Three stories up.* Not the time to stagger them both with the uncommon reverberation of that connection. So instead she closed those shields down tight, and she held out a hand. "Ryan," she said. "Time to get off this roof."

She might as well have been speaking in tongues. She crouched, beckoned—put some command in her voice. Tried again. "Let's go, Ryan. Time to head inside. Shake it *off*, now, and come inside."

Shake it off. He did just that, a shudder passing visibly from his shoulders down his spine, and then, after the longest of hesitations, he said, "Lyn?"

"You were up here as the cougar," she told him, keeping the calm in her voice. "We had a surge. It's messing with you, and now you've got to get down before there are aftershocks."

"Get down," he said, more than a little blankly. And then, "I'm on the *roof*? I lost control on the *roof*?"

"Yes. Now let's *go*. Can you? I don't want to touch you—"

"The shield reaction," he said, his voice much clearer, his head raising. "Go. I'll be right behind you."

"Are you—"

"*Go,*" he said. "I'll make it. But I don't want to come down on top of you."

And she could see why, as she waited by the half-open sliding-glass doors and he descended from the roof in confident, familiar moves, only to abruptly lose strength halfway down. He tumbled to the decking.

Still, she held back—didn't rush to help, or put a reassuring hand on the gleam of his bare shoulder. Not even though the strength of the urge to do so took her well by surprise. If only she'd listened to her instincts, the first time he turned the full force of those honest dusky-hazel eyes on her—instead of the hard voice that needed so badly to clear her own stains by hunting others. Maybe they wouldn't be here right now, pulling a vulnerable Sentinel off the roof.

Maybe that made her the dark one after all.

And *still,* she held herself back—not trusting herself, and knowing that this moment couldn't be about what they wanted. He seemed to know it, too; he pulled himself together, long legs not quite steady, shoulders flexing as he pushed up, making it just about as far as the railing. His shields flickered into place, stabilizing as he brushed himself off. He looked mildly surprised to encounter the shorts—they must have been for her sake after all. Just in case.

Some bold, wry little part of her wanted to tell him he needn't have bothered, but she tucked that comment away, along with one betting he'd gone commando under those worn old shorts. "You good?" she asked him, not bothering to hide her scrutiny. "That was a hell of a wallop."

"I can't believe—" He looked up on the roof, then away over the dark woods. "Damned embarrassing."

"We've got to track it." She kept her voice low—let the intensity of it speak for her. "Nick says…brevis thinks it could blow."

"*Blow?* What's that supposed to mean? The volcano's dormant, has been for—" He stopped, frowning at her as he realized what she really meant. "God, no. The balance is that tipped?"

She liked that he didn't question it, didn't protest that he'd have felt it. "Brevis thinks so. You're probably too close to see it—drowning in it more likely." Her anger came through, contempt for those who had done this thing. "Gausto just wants to get his greedy hands on whatever power he can have. He doesn't care about the consequences. We've *got* to stop them." She threaded her fingers through her hair, pushing it back from her face. "I don't suppose there's any way you can follow this back to the source? Then we can track them down from both the corrupted power and their trace."

"Not when we both need backup," he pointed out. But he lifted his head to give her a sharp look. "Am I missing something? Because it suddenly sounds to me as though we're a *we*. As though maybe we can just get down to business and bust the bad guys."

She blushed, wishing she was sure the darkness would hide it from his vision. "I wouldn't say that brevis is convinced."

As if he'd let her get away with that. "And you?" he asked, taking a step away from the rail, looking suddenly not unsteady at all.

Lyn held her ground. She felt short; she had to look up to meet his gaze, but she held her ground. "I don't know any longer," she said, and then admitted, "It's not feeling right."

Wasn't it just like him to break out into a big grin. No hidden dark corners to Joe Ryan.

And that was just the point.

She took a step toward him, caught herself—covered her face. Not to hide a blush, oh no. Not much point in that anymore. But at the confusion within, the startling nature of that single step and what it told her about herself.

"Hey," he said, surprising her again—with the gentleness behind that one word. The understanding. And his voice was close, and she looked up to find him *right there,* and not nearly enough distance between them.

Not *nearly* enough.

He looked down at her with eyes so deeply in shadow she couldn't quite believe she saw that gleam of intensity. "You know I'm going to kiss you, right?"

She couldn't help but bristle a little. "You going to ask first?"

A definite smile at the corners of his mouth there. "I'm thinking not. I'm thinking I'll face the consequences." But he didn't, not quite. He bent his head and he watched her, the smile lingering, the intent clear…

savoring the moment, she thought. Or giving her that chance to step away.

"Oh, *hell*," she said, and drew his head down. She pulled him in for a fierce kiss, one that took him by surprise at first, but soon enough that big hand spanned the small of her back, feeling as though it belonged and arcing her backward while she found that tawny hair, smoothed the black tracings. She breathed in the wild musky scent of him, cougar-on-the-roof; she let her ocelot come out to play with a nip and a butt of her cheek against his, but only long enough to gasp in breath before taking him on again.

His chest rumbled; his hand tightened against her back while the other cupped her nape, so very careful, so very possessive. He nipped and nibbled and played with her mouth, making her ache to feel his lips everywhere, anywhere—and she gasped a faint sound of dismay when he broke away, setting his chin at her forehead and gulping for air while she listened to the wild pounding in rhythm with the visible galloping beat at his throat. Her hands had drifted down his back to rest on the curve of his butt, giving her reason to know exactly how tensely he held himself.

Yeah, she was pretty sure he'd gone commando under those shorts.

"Consequences," he said, his breath still coming fast to stir her hair. "Oh, yeah, consequences are hell."

Consequences. "I can't be *kissing* you. I can't be— what was I even thinking—"

She stepped away. She felt cold and bereft, but she stepped away. Even if she'd crossed a line where she felt the circumstantial evidence against him didn't stand up against reality, she had to maintain that distance. For both their sakes. What kind of idiot didn't know better than to muddy that situation with—

With what she really wanted from him.

She took a deep breath. "I need to think."

"Always a mistake," he said, even as he let her go. If the expression *rueful* had been looking for a poster child, it had found it in Joe Ryan.

Lyn winced. "I'm sorry—"

"Oh, *hell* no," he interrupted, raising his head to a tilt of challenge. "Sorry is 'oops, I spilled your drink.' Or 'oh wow, I just dinged your bumper.' *Sorry* is *not* what just happened here."

She smiled. "You have a way with words now and then."

"I choose my moments," he said, attempting great dignity, there in the dark and clothed only in those shorts—and obvious regret. "But I mean it. You may not want to do that again—I do, by the way—but don't you dare go all *sorry* on me. The things it would do to my ego alone."

But he faltered, and he frowned, and he stared off into the vague night. Lyn scrambled to sort out her inner senses, hunting the trace that came with the corrupted power waves, the trace that reflected so much of the man standing right before her. "Shields?" she asked him, reaching to check for that, too, and relieved to find that he'd kept himself protected in spite of…

Well. Distraction.

Relief was short-lived. He looked at her, and something changed in his expression. Something hardened. "You want to know the root of it all? You want to end this—to end any question of my allegiance?"

"Ryan…" she said, and instilled a warning into her voice as the power trickled in, ramping up to a level even she could discern. "You can't mean to—not tonight. You're tired. We're *both* tired. And after what just happened—"

"I *am* tired," he agreed. "I'm tired of being under the microscope. I'm tired of being judged guilty by Sentinels when human law didn't have nearly enough to hold me, and now of having that false stain follow me to my new home. If I've made mistakes, I've paid hell for them. And I'm done with that."

Chapter 13

Alarm stiffened her spine; Lyn's hand's clenched into helpless fists at her sides. "No," she said—she *pleaded,* astonished to hear that note in her own voice. "No! I've got Nick questioning the communications you didn't receive, I've got investigators all coming up clean with your finances and your activities—I've seen nothing here myself—"

"Ah," he said, his voice gone deadly soft. "Except for my trace, tied directly to the corrupted power flows."

"But not to your advantage!" she blurted.

"Haven't you said that I simply got in over my head? Do you think others won't conclude the same?" He closed the distance between them again, with the sliding-glass doors of his bedroom at her back and the house curving around on either side. She had to close her eyes, to give in to a sudden deep snatch of breath, a subtle tremor…knowing he was right. His touch brushed over her disarrayed hair, lightly smoothing it. Once, twice. His voice low, he said, "I've had enough."

Gripped by sudden fear, she snatched his wrist before he could retreat. "No!"

And knew it was too late. Knew by the brush of his falling shields—knew by the slight lift and tilt of his head, the sudden vague focus of his eyes. For a moment, she couldn't help but ride the wonder of it—knowing that even now the power flowed through him and that he found and followed it upstream, and that if it had been any normal power surge, he would have done so with the fierce wild freedom of inner flight.

But this was no normal surge, and she saw it in his face first—a tension, a tightening of his jaw. The play of muscle there, and along his neck and shoulder. The twitch at the corner of his mouth, the sudden stiffening of his entire body. His breathing turned abruptly harsh, his nostrils flaring with inner effort. Sweat gathered at his temple in spite of the chill air, darkening tawny hair where it blended into black. "Ryan," she said, her low voice loud in the quiet night. "Ryan, that's enough now."

He jerked as though someone had punched him; his torso rippled with it. There went his eyes, rolling back in his head—there went his knees, slowly giving way so Lyn ended up down there beside him, still holding his wrist. "Ryan," she said, and fear infused the urgency in her voice, "I mean it. Come *back,* Ryan. Come back…" and she finished the thought with something of wonder in her voice "…*to me.*"

But he didn't. He spasmed, and suddenly she couldn't keep him upright any longer; he fell back against the deck railing, his body arcing, every muscle clenched as he tore free of her grip. A gritty noise forced

its way between his teeth—nothing human about it, that
noise.

"God, Joe," she murmured, frustration burning in her
eyes, "what have you done?"

He twisted, muscles rippling—electric-blue light
glinting where it shouldn't, ragged flickers of impending change, energy building without discharging. He
cried out, arching to avoid the agony of it and by then
Lyn had had *enough*.

Because she could stop this.

She could have stopped it before it started, had
she had the courage. Because she knew, now, if she
opened her shields to him again, if she drank of his
trace and immersed herself in that deep beguiling
texture, *conflict of interest* wouldn't matter and
common sense wouldn't matter and *this isn't a good
idea* wouldn't even register. So she'd selfishly waited,
and now here he was contorted, battling waves of
power that scoured through his body and still, when
she knelt astride him, clamping her hands on his
shoulders, he tried to push her away. He muttered
something that through the gasps sounded very much
like, "Almost—"

It must have left him vulnerable, for he instantly
cried out, his body tightening so acutely as to lift her
off the ground, the back of his head thumping against
wood… Blood trickled from his nose, from his mouth,
even from his ears.

Lyn closed her eyes against tears. She centered. She
found that small, quiet space within, and she breathed
it large. She expanded it, silently humming the note, the
feeling that created her place of safety and calm. And
then she finalized it—one last minuscule hesitation and
then the last plunge as she breathed in his trace, taking

that, too, into herself, and gasping at the incongruous pleasure of it.

Beneath her, he stilled. A residual tremor worked its way through his body.

Nothing else.

"Ryan?" she whispered. She bent over him, her body a wash of foreboding; her hand shook as she wiped the blood from beneath his nose, the corner of his mouth. There, her fingers hesitated; what started as a simple gesture of caring turned into a caress, tracing the lines of his face, brushing across the night's stubble of beard. Her lips joined her fingertips, barely touching his skin…honoring it. She hadn't intended it…she hadn't thought about it. But then, she realized distantly that she was no longer truly thinking at all, merely reacting to what was between them.

If she hadn't been too late. Because though his breathing eased from panting to merely harsh, though his tremors subsided, she saw no sign of awareness, no reaction to the shielding, which had previously brought him to instant attention.

"Ryan," she breathed. "Come back now." She took his head between her hands, let her lips graze his. Kissed him lightly, tasting his blood; she kissed that strong stubbled jaw, breathed on the tender spot just below his ear…nuzzled his neck.

His breath caught.

She smiled against his neck, gave it a leisurely lick, and pulled back just enough to see he'd opened his eyes. But not with true understanding behind them—dazed, he was, and uncertain, with some part of him still lost. His groan was heartfelt and spoke of both his pain and his response to her.

"Ryan," she said. "Come back. Come back to your

deck, outside your house. It's just the two of us here. We're shielded…we're safe. Can you feel it?" She lowered her mouth over his, barely touching, and whispered to his lips. "Can you feel *us?*"

Just like that, he came alive. He clamped his hands on her arms, too tightly for comfort; she allowed it. He met her whispered words, turned the contact into a hungry kiss—a wild kiss, hard and demanding and mindless. His hands left her arms, found her hips—effortlessly lifted her into position over his own, as if clothing was no barrier at all.

She tumbled away from him then, at the wildness in his eyes and the missing spark of that final connection—at the sudden realization that he wasn't quite back yet, that she'd created something so strong between them that it had brought him back without truly restoring him.

Maybe I was too late after all. Maybe there's nothing left but this—

"No, dammit," she breathed, eyes narrowing as he rose to one knee, a hand to his head. She reached for his trace again; she surrounded it. His groan echoed the ripple of sensation that fluttered through her body, so intense that she almost lost herself to it. "Whoa," she said, startling herself with the husky nature of her own voice. And Ryan tipped his head back, flipping the hair from his eyes to pin her with a gaze instantly mesmerizing and terrifying, and she knew then…

That was the line she would have to walk. The power she would have to ride. Bring him along without letting him tip over into mindless, brutal reaction. Bring him along until the Joe Ryan she knew could find the safety she'd made for him here.

She stood on shaky legs. She searched his expression for the honesty that had won her over, for the unabashed passion he had for his life here, his love of the mountain…even his reaction to her. It had been right there in his eyes from the start.

But not now.

Not yet.

She drew him up, directly into her embrace. But this time she controlled the intensity of it—she kissed him and backed off; she stood on her toes to nibble his skin and when his hands grew too tight at her back, on her waist, she drew back—manipulating the shields as well as their bodies, riding that power until she tingled and gasped and nearly forgot what she was about.

She managed to lead him through the sliding door and into his bedroom, and to push him down on the floor-bound mattress, and never was she so glad for her Sentinel strength, that which allowed her to do all those things with just the right amount of *must* and *beguile,* a balance all the way. Once she had him there she came down atop him and deftly pinned his arms at his sides— but she still had her mouth, and her hips, and the subtle manipulation of the shields, expanding and contracting, filling and receding, and if it left her gasping and trembling, it did the same to him; he surged up against her, a demanding presence.

"Ryan," she said again, flipping tendrils of hair away from her damp skin, watching his eyes. Kissing him, taking that mobile and well-formed mouth and watching his eyes. Moving against him, watching the unfettered desire in his face, the reactions that told her what took him and when to give him space and—

There. Was that a flicker of something, behind his eyes, as things grew hot and desperate and Lyn's control flickered, her body tightened? Oh, it had to be—*had* to be, because she suddenly didn't know if she could do this, if she had the strength to hold them both, two bodies straining for completion, for each *other,* growing fevered and driven and wrapped in Sentinel magics.

"Ryan." And she rammed the shields at him in a way she'd never used them before, hadn't even thought to use them before. Not so much an enfolding caress, not so much a fulfilling completion...more a hard push. "I know you're there! You've got to be th—"

And there it was in his eyes.

Joe Ryan, honest and passionate and right there— flooding back to mix and mingle with the sweat and the musk of their lovemaking, the tight cords of his neck, the straining lift to his hips. The completion of Joe Ryan, right here beneath her, so she instantly released his hands and laughed out loud with relief, happy even to see his flabbergasted expression. Before he could even ask, she said, "Do you want all your answers now? Or do you want to finish this thing we're doing?"

"We're—" he said, and took that instant to assess them. And then he, too, laughed. And a beautiful thing it was to see on his face, with blood still smeared at the corner of his mouth, still drying at his ears and a touch beneath his nose, with his hair still damp from sweat that had come of pain and not their pleasure. "Answers later," he said. *"Much* later."

He hadn't the faintest idea what was going on.

Okay. *A lie, boy-o.* Joe knew *exactly* what was going on. He knew he'd gone after the root of the power; he knew he now lay on his back, recently released from the deceptively strong grip of one Lyn Maines, she who now rode his hips with far too many clothes on. He knew his body ached and his head felt strangely wrung out, that dried blood crusted at his mouth and ears and nose and, man, he didn't even want to think about the damage he'd caused himself.

Then again, he didn't really care how they'd gotten from there to here. He just wanted to finish *here*. And he wanted to do it *now*. Her shielding wrapped around them so tightly, so snugly…he knew exactly how she'd brought him back, if not exactly where he'd been. And now it pulsed around them and there she sat, right where it mattered, her cheeks flushed and her eyes bright and her hair tousled and her shirred top wildly askew, showing him a neat little belly button in a tight tummy, ribs softened by just enough flesh, breasts snugly encased by soft, thin material and every feature showing, every aroused pucker and every *hold-me* curve.

He reached for her pants and she reached for his pants and hot damn, then there were no pants. But as much as he ached and strained for her as she came back astride him, he pulled her down to his chest instead. He pushed her shirt up so they came delicious skin to skin, proving that yes indeed, she had no bra. Oh, yeah, he needed to kiss her senseless. And though the plump nature of her lips and the faint brush burn on her cheeks told him they'd already done some of that, he needed to do it while he was…well, here.

She hardly seemed adverse. She even seemed prepared for something less controlled—but oh, he liked that sound she made in her throat when he gentled their contact, when he played with her mouth, when he teased her tongue. He ran his hands down her back, found the tight round and wonderfully naked curves of her bottom, cupped her to him. He absorbed her purr as his hands admired her breasts, not so very large but oh-so-perfect. And he grinned against her lips as she caressed everything she could reach, while her shields enclosed them, cocooned them…filled them.

All of which had him pretty smug about life in general, pretty much in control again, back in his head, back in his body, back in his bed with this woman he'd wanted since he'd laid eyes on her. Right up until the moment she managed to work those small hands between them and take hold of him, fingers oh-so-clever, eyes glinting oh-so-wicked.

So maybe he lost it then. Maybe he arched up and maybe he cried out and maybe he tipped his head back hard against the bed. Maybe not so cool, maybe not in any control whatsoever, but then again maybe she wasn't, either, for suddenly she was astride him and taking him in, that small body somehow just big enough, those slender legs gripping him tightly as she took him, hot and ready. She cried out, a surprised sound; she quivered. And he froze, panting, afraid to move one way or the other because there she was and there he was and she'd somehow clamped those shields down, stopping the ebb and flow of energy between them.

"Let it go, Lyn," he rasped, teeth gritted, every in-credible flicker of pleasure in his body tightening in streaks down his spine, down his buttocks, heading for hot damn the place it would do the most good. "Let it—"

Another noise of surprise, a cry of discovery—and she released her hold on the shields and the energy came flooding through and—

And maybe he lost his mind just then and maybe he didn't. Maybe they cried out together, helpless and entwined every which way a man and woman could be, spasming in the culmination of all that energy and all that touching and all that exchanged emotion.

Joe only knew for certain that he'd never felt anything quite like it.

No, he decided, coming back to his senses with Lyn draped limply over his body, her hair sweeping over his neck and those sweet breasts pressing into his chest, he also knew for certain that he wanted to do it again. As soon as possible.

Well. Perhaps with a few moments to recover.

"Where did you go?"

Lyn's voice startled Joe from his very pleasant doze. In a night so surreal, he made no assumptions; he opened his eyes—and found exactly what he thought he'd find. The middle of the night in his loft room, his bed comfortably beneath him, if at some odd angle, a comforter scrounged from the pile of covers to lay lightly over himself and the woman draped over his side. Three cats had magically appeared in some unknown recent moment, taking up their accustomed stations at various points on the bed.

Yup. That's how it should have been, all right. So it seemed only sensible for him to say, "I'm right here."

She drew a deep breath, let it out slowly in a way that probably wasn't *meant* to tickle his ribs. "When you followed the power," she said, her words deliberate, "where did you go?"

And here he'd been so content to have her tucked into his elbow, his hand lazily wandering the spare contours of her body, his mind drowsy. He shifted, putting himself up on his elbows, awakening an entire host of aches and pains in the process. *"Ow,"* he said. "What did you *do* to me? While I was where I went?"

"What you did to yourself is more like it." She rolled away from him, leaning her chin in her hand. "Wherever you went, I thought it was going to kill you before I could get you back. And then…you weren't really here at all…as if some part of you had been trapped behind." She shook her head. "There's something powerful going on. Something unusual. And it's all tied up in you."

"Regretting that trust you so recently offered up?" he asked ruefully.

She scowled at him—an imposing expression, with those dark-rimmed eyes of hers. "Noting things worth looking into."

"Ha," he said, and settled back to stare at the ceiling far above. "If we weren't here in my bed, you'd be making lists."

Her silence gave her away.

"OhmyGod," he said, all one long amused word. "You want to be making lists."

She drew slightly away from him. "Lists," she said, somewhat stiffly, "can be useful."

He pulled her back, waited for her to relax, and said, "I don't know where I went. At first, it was what I'd expect. Swimming upstream. Okay, it hurt some." Hurt like unimaginable hell is more like it. Swimming upstream into acid rain from the inside out. But… He frowned, hunting memory. "I swear, I was doing it. I was getting close. And it felt familiar, but—" He went deeper, looking for where he'd been, casting about for something on which to pin that sense of familiarity. There was the pain, and a gray haze, and…and…

…and…

He startled at her hand on his torso, shoving him—and not gently, either—and slapped his own over it, stilling her. "Hey, *hey*—what's that all about?"

"You were gone again," she informed him, her hand now pressing down across his ribs as if to reassure herself, her face grim. Whisker-burned and smoky eyes and love-sultry lips and grim, didn't quite all fit together somehow. "Promise me you won't try that again."

"I didn't know I was trying anything in the first place." Following memories? Right there in his head? *Deep trouble, boy-o.* But he gave her shoulders a squeeze. "No fears. I won't go back. There's no information for us there. Just that sense of…" He hesitated, and then asked—most carefully, "Is there any chance you missed something at the top of the world?"

Where her hand had shoved, it now stroked—following the contours of his ribs, following the shape of muscles kept hard by running the mountain as the cougar and climbing them as the man. She found the faint line of hair that gathered at his navel and headed south, and would have followed that, too, if he hadn't stopped her. He captured her hand and rolled on his side to face her. "Lyn. The top of the world?"

"I was sifting through what you might have meant," she admitted. "I give. Missed what?"

So it was her turn to be obtuse. "Trace. Working amulets left behind. Some sort of…I don't know, *anchor.*"

Understanding brought a scowl, and instant denial. "If you even knew how insulting that was—"

He made a rude noise, bringing her up short. "This is beyond ego, Lyn. It's sure as hell beyond mine. It's got my trace and yet I can't follow it? Yeah, *that's* what I wanted to learn tonight. But we've got to assume this thing could be outside our experience in other ways."

She scowled again, but it was a softer expression—and it wasn't aimed at him. "All right," she said. "But there wasn't anything active up there, just the signs that they'd been through."

"I don't get the impression you usually have a problem following fresh trace." For he remembered her lashing tail, her poorly hidden annoyance, there at the top of the world where she'd grudgingly trusted him to keep watch while she circled and quartered and nosed around.

Some of that annoyance resurfaced even as he watched, and worked its way around her expression, and finally turned into long exhalation. "Ego," she murmured, and sighed again. "Ouch."

"Tell me about it," he said ruefully, and kissed the top of her head.

"The brevis team should have an amulet specialist." She stretched, scraping the hair back from her face, and if she had any awareness of what the sight of her tight, half-clothed body did to him, she showed no signs of it—at least, not until she shot him a single sly glance from beneath slitted lids. He ran a hand down her torso—part admiration, part possession. He almost missed it when she said, "I'll ask about it when the team gets here—see if there might be some new technique we should watch for. But that area…it's just not convenient enough for them, Ryan. No matter how you come at it."

"Mmm," he said, as his hand acquired a mind of its own and slipped beneath the comforter to caress her bare ass.

"Surely not," she said.

"You started it," he told her, quite abruptly tugging her closer.

"I didn't think—"

"Ego," he warned her. "Delicate, delicate ego."

"Wouldn't want to damage *that*."

"Oh, *now* you've done it." He rolled over her, licked her belly from navel to sternum, and eyed her breasts in a most pleased and predatory manner. "Oh, yes," he murmured. "Now you've really done it."

And she laughed.

But not for long.

Chapter 14

Lyn thought he was still asleep—Joe was almost sure of it. She'd eased out of bed, made use of the loft's bathroom and hunted down her clothing—none of which had remained on her body by the end of the night. The shirt, he thought, was pretty much a goner anyway. She seemed to think so, too, by the look of dismay she gave it as she held it up to the bare light of dawn.

"T-shirt," he suggested, as the black cat settled by his head. "Middle dresser drawer. Not that the neighbors are close enough to see if you make a mad dash back to the casita, but I wouldn't want any of your important parts to take a chill."

She whirled, dropping the shirt, and momentarily crossed an arm over her chest—but then dropped that, too, straightening.

Still, it made for a sad little tight spot in his throat. Second thoughts, all right. "You okay?" he asked.

She stood there a long moment, then came to sit on the edge of the bed, casually displacing the old brown tabby. She half crossed her legs to accommodate the bed's low direct-to-floor setup, her back straight, her body looking somehow slighter than he remembered. Vulnerable. Her bare shoulder held a perfect curve, lean with muscle; her waist nipped in and flared out again well above the level of those low-riding cargo pants they'd both roughed up so badly the night before. A single breast peeked out from beyond her arm, held high by her straight back. Not a shy breast, oh no.

She said, "I'm okay." But she didn't sound it. She sounded puzzled, and maybe even a little fragile. "I'm just trying to sort out my work thoughts from…this." And she made a vague waving gesture.

"Hmm," he said. "And here I am, trying to sort out *this*—" and he repeated her vague waving gesture "—from the way you were so hot on my trail when you first arrived here. And not, I would like to point out, in any way the same fashion you were hot on my trail last night."

She laughed, faintly, as he'd hoped she would. But she didn't turn to look at him. Her shoulders lifted in a sigh and she said, "You really deserve to know," and he didn't think she was quite talking to him. But then she said quite clearly, "My brother."

He thought it best to give her some silence, so he said nothing, his fingers automatically reaching to scratch the little black cat behind her ears as she eased closer to bump his head. *Her brother.* So many places that could go. Her brother had been hurt by a dark Sentinel, perhaps even killed…her brother had tracked dark Sentinels, as well…her brother had—

"He was human. My half brother, just as with your

half sister." She bent to pick up the T-shirt and slipped it on. "My brother and I grew up together. We always knew I'd go off to a 'special boarding school,' but those early years…I'm not sure we could have been any closer. And really—" she turned to look at him, her expression puzzled, her face still bearing one distinct patch of whisker-burn "—I've never been able to figure out when it started. When just being him wasn't good enough, because of who I was. When he started playing with drugs. When he started cheating and lying and—"

"All the way back to the beginning all over again," Joe said, with a tremendous ache in his throat for her. "The Druid and the Roman. But you know, as far as we can tell…the Druid didn't do anything to get the Roman started, either."

"And yet here we are, feeling responsible for the Atrum Core," she said, dryly enough to give him an inner grin. One tough woman, hidden ticklish spots notwithstanding.

The black cat licked his ear and Joe absently flipped her over and closed his hand over her belly, so she turned on him in a big ball of *fierce,* biting without teeth and clawing with bare paws. "And so you feel responsible for your brother…" He let the words trail off because he didn't quite see how the pieces fit, not yet.

"Felt," she corrected him, the word precisely formed. "He's dead now. The details…don't really matter. An inevitable result of the cheating and lying and etcetera. Mostly the etcetera."

Joe frowned. Definitely not seeing how the pieces fit. The cat leaped up, dealt his hand a series of wicked death blows and sprinted away, tail cranked.

She acknowledged his puzzlement with a weary shake of her head. "You don't get it, do you?"

"Well…" He took her hand, still flat on his back and

thinking, from the way that effort trailed down his arm and ached at his shoulder, that perhaps he might just stay there. "I could offer up some understanding babble. But, er, no. I don't get it."

"All those years he said he'd straighten out and didn't…I watched him break my parents' hearts until they died, I financed his schooling, I found him jobs…I tried tough love. Finally I just let it happen—I limited our contact as much as I could. But even then…I never quit hoping. *Never.* You'd think anyone with half a brain would figure it out, but not me." She turned away from him, just enough for the pretense of privacy.

"Lyn…" So much packed into that one word—the need to sweep her up and hug away that hurt, the need to make it all right again. The need to kick her brother in a beauteous parabolic arc right over the Peaks.

"You still don't get it," she said, turning on him— and if her huge brown eyes glimmered with unshed tears, they also darkened with anger. Not at him, not this time—but he'd seen that particular anger before. "I know what it's like when someone you love goes dark. Now add the very real damage a Sentinel can do to this world. Never mind that every dark Sentinel gives the Core their justification for existence—"

He snorted, but held his peace, for she was right enough.

"—a dark Sentinel is every bit as dangerous to the world as brevis regional thought you were to the Peaks." She disentangled her hand from his, regarded it as if it belonged to a stranger, and said, "And I can stop it. I'm one of a very few of us who can stop it cold."

Joe got it then. He got it good. "Because you can track us. Which of us is doing what. Someone else might suspect, but you…you *know.*"

She closed those big eyes, lashes sweeping her cheeks, the smudge of natural color at the edges of her lids more stark than ever, and she nodded.

"Except with me." He tried to infuse humor into his voice, and didn't quite make it.

Her eyes opened into frustration. She said, "Yes, dammit. Because the trace in the power surges is already set in motion. It's not about you sneaking out in the middle of the night to go do something nefarious."

"I could try that, if you want," he offered. "But I think you'd probably be the target of my nefarious intentions, so it really wouldn't be very sly of me."

She laughed, thank goodness. She laughed and she twisted around to startle him with a resounding kiss on the lips, and then she was up again, light and graceful on a morning when he could barely think about moving at all. "So now you know," she said. "It wasn't personal. Except…it's always personal." She stretched hugely, and added, "Well, except when it's like Sonoita, which was actually a welcome change of pace. Brevis flew me in from Europe—Spain, actually. You'd have liked my partner—big guy, black as night, packed more muscles into one body than I've ever seen before. He took the lion."

Joe, still flat on his back, managed a convincing growl.

She grinned. "Uh-huh," she said. "Hit the shower, why don't you. That's what I'm going to do. I'm thinking we've got work to do today, and if you use up all your hot water, you might just loosen up some of those stiff muscles." And she moved out of reach, away from the bed and headed for the stairs.

He groaned. "You're all heart."

But he was beginning to realize it was true.

* * *

She should have stayed with him. Stayed and massaged out those sore muscles—some of which she'd contributed to, and some of which she'd simply watched helplessly as it happened.

But no. Her thoughts had tuned in to tracking even if her body hadn't. So she had every intention of scooting in and out of the tiny casita shower, pulling on something casual, and then taking the ocelot for a quick jaunt to Mrs. Rosado's place. *Joe sent me to see if you needed anything.* It would go over well enough, if it wasn't too early in Mrs. Rosado's day. And, of course, if the woman did need something, then Lyn would see to it.

She had the feeling she'd be back before Joe managed to stagger out of his own shower. And if not…he'd do the polite thing, waiting for her to come to breakfast and plan their day.

Not that there was much planning to do. *Head back to the hotel. Hunt trace.* Because they had to figure out where the fallback was—where Gausto was hiding his activity. Lyn was willing to bet it wasn't within Flagstaff at all, but was somewhere remote—within the national forest, or at a rented warehouse at the edge of town. Might be time to cruise that back side of town again.

By the time she'd worked her way through those thoughts, she was swiping a token towel across her body, smoothing lotion into her skin and pulling a big wide-toothed comb through her hair. A pair of loose linen cropped pants, a chocolate-brown shirt with a baby-doll neckline and crisscrossed swatches across the torso, and she opened the door into the freshness of dawn in the shadow of the mountain. The sky above shone a hard, bright blue from the sunlight heating up the east side of Flagstaff, but Lyn shivered in still-chilly air.

No matter. She, too, could rejoice in taking her other form, in the ocelot. She stretched hugely in the doorway, defying the cold, and as her head tipped back, she closed her eyes for a quick check of local trace—hunting signs that anyone else might have been sniffing around the area, whether unknown Sentinel or amulet-tainted Core.

Not that she expected to find anyone. But the day she neglected to check...

With the area cleared, she quietly closed the door behind her, reached deep within and turned the ocelot loose. Her mind flickered brief blue lightning; her hands splayed, fingers reaching, stretching—

—claws kneading, landing in the dirt to stir up dust and pine needles and *oh! Lizard!* There at the edge off her vision, startled by her transformation into skittering away from beneath the doorsill and she *leaped* and flipped it into the air and let it land and scoot away and pounced and played and rolled around the creature in a completely unnecessary gymnastic, thereby letting it escape.

Whoops. With a *mrrrp* of embarrassment, she sat and gave the inside of her front leg a quick lick. Sometimes the whimsical ocelot nature took her that way, when no one was looking and the moment was hers to have. She pulled a pine needle from between her toes and glared into the woods on general principle—one never knew when the trees might be tempted to laugh—then shook the foot out and bounded into the forest.

The terrain grew unexpectedly rugged between the two properties, giving the ocelot more of a chance to stretch her muscles—a giant bound between two massive rocks, a scramble up a steep slope she could have found a way around if she'd really wanted—and then she came across the track that Ryan must use when patrolling this area and fell onto it.

She needn't have wondered if Mrs. Rosado was an early riser. As she padded closer to the property, glimpsing the house through the trees by virtue of its unnaturally straight lines and hard corners, a mighty alarm shrilled through the woods—the ferocious yapping of one small but alert lap-warmer. She instantly froze into stalking mode—and just as quickly shook herself out of it. *Not nice to eat the little old lady's lapdog, Maines.*

Even if she had no trouble leaping lightly over the back corner of the tall fence into a huge yard full of trees and natural features, with plenty of cover between her and the back of the house. The mop of hair stared at her, mortified, clearly feeling the thin line between being predator and prey. She trilled a noise at him, reaching for the human—and as she stood, it turned to laughter. "Poor little guy," she said. "That wasn't really fair, was it?"

His tail, cranked over his back and buried in hair, gave a hesitant twitch of a wag. She crouched, opening her arms. "You want a ride?"

His legs might not show, but they were sturdy enough. They propelled him straight for her, all his dilemmas solved with that friendly invitation, and she scooped him up to play a game of little-pink-tongue-everywhere as she walked toward the house.

Neither she nor Mrs. Rosado really expected to see one another when the older woman opened the back door to call the dog, her hand going to her chest as she found Lyn rounding the tree nearest to the house. "Oh!"

they said, pretty much at the same time. And then Mrs. Rosado looked anxiously around the backyard, her eyes following the fence line. "The fence isn't down, is it? Or surely after all this time I didn't leave the gate open and let my little Tigre out—"

"No, no," Lyn assured her. "I was on a morning walk and I couldn't resist him—I came in to say hello. I hope you don't mind too much." She offered up an embarrassed smile, caught out—because the ocelot, still in impulsive mode, had brought her in here…she hadn't thought ahead about encountering Mrs. Rosado from within the yard itself. "I'd wanted to stop by and make sure your sink was behaving, but I was afraid you might not be up yet, so I peeked around back and there he was…."

"Well," Mrs. Rosado said, as if she wasn't quite sure what to make of the whole thing, "he can be terribly hard to resist." She hesitated, concern and confusion quirking her brow. "Are you not cold, my dear? And… your feet?"

Because of course Lyn hadn't put on a jacket. And her feet… She looked down, wiggled bare toes against the ground. Just a little chilly at that, come to think of it. Well, damn. She'd been so stuck to her trail, so aware she planned to take the ocelot…she'd forgotten that little detail. She didn't try to hide her embarrassment— she let it work for her. "I'm visiting from Tucson," she said. *Among other places.* "I guess it still takes me by surprise, how cold it gets here at night. I didn't realize it until I was well on my way. You could say it's been a brisk walk."

It didn't account for the fact that no one from Tucson would consider gallivanting around in bare feet anyway, given the prickly, spiny nature of everything that grew in the mid-desert, not to mention the scorpions, rattlesnakes, coral snakes… But Mrs. Rosado was too polite to voice that thought. She said, "You might like to come inside? I'm not ready for visitors yet, but I can find you a sweater, maybe some sandals…"

The last thing she wanted was clothing that wouldn't transform with her, but getting a few moments to chat…worth the inconvenience. "Maybe I should," she said, letting her embarrassment linger. Embarrassment was easier than her guilt at misleading this nice woman, anyway.

Mrs. Rosado stood aside, holding the door open, and Lyn found herself in the back end of the kitchen, her toes even colder on the tile than they'd been against the ground. She set the dog down and hugged herself for warmth, nodding at the sink as Mrs. Rosado pulled a mug from the cabinet and poured a second cup of coffee. "The sink's doing okay, then?"

"That Joe, he does things right," Mrs. Rosado said, and smiled. "He's feeling better now? He didn't look himself the other day."

"You don't think?" Lyn tried to keep her voice neutral. This was someone who knew Ryan, had known him for years. Had a perspective Lyn didn't. She accepted the mug Mrs. Rosado extended to her, wrapping her hands around its warmth.

Mrs. Rosado made a *tsk* sound and broke off a bit of toast from the plate by the sink, absently flicking it down to the dog. "Even a strong man like that shouldn't ignore a summer cold. He's been pretending it was no big thing, but…" and she closed her eyes, her lips moving as she counted days "…he needs to see a doctor, that's what I think. Let someone else take care of *him* for a change." And she opened her eyes to give Lyn a meaningful look.

Lyn took a sip of coffee just to fill her mouth with something, and then had to fight to hide her reaction to the strong, bitter taste.

Mrs. Rosado laughed. "That Joe!" she said. "He's got you spoiled on his fancy coffee already, doesn't he? And my Leandro…he liked his coffee just this way. Cheap coffee, extra scoop. I never did like it…at least, I never thought I did. But then he was gone, and I couldn't bring myself to make it any other way. That's what our men do to us."

Lyn nodded vaguely. *Our men.* Oh my God. No, no, no.

And to think she'd come here with some expectations of controlling this conversation. Or at least guiding it.

"So," Mrs. Rosado said, breaking off another piece of toast. "Are you heading to Elden Pueblo to watch the riders this afternoon?"

Lyn must have looked as blank as she felt. Yes, this conversation was completely out of her control.

"He must have mentioned it." Mrs. Rosado frowned. "He always watches the riders come in from the Gray Mountain ride."

"Gray Mountain…" Who had mentioned Gray Mountain? Someone…just the day before…

Had it really been only that long? Had she really been here such a short time?

Joe Ryan had no need to steal power from the Peaks. He clearly had all the power he needed, to have turned her life so around, so quickly.

"The Save the Peaks protest ride," Mrs. Rosado said, responding to Lyn's confusion. "From that…*desagradable* plan to make snow with wastewater. For several years, the tribes have held this ride. Joe is always there."

"He mentioned it—I forgot it was today. Maybe we could still make it."

"If you don't have anything else planned," Mrs. Rosado said, a little too offhanded as she swiped some imaginary crumb from her light bathrobe. She sipped her coffee, gave Lyn a long, thoughtful look and apparently decided to say her lurking thoughts. "You haven't known Joe long, I don't think."

Mutely, Lyn shook her head—not liking the touch of possessive censure in the older woman's voice, but forcing herself to listen. She'd come here for information, after all.

"When he arrived here, he was an empty man. I don't know the details of what happened in Nevada— maybe he has told those things to you. I only know that he came here with nothing." She seemed to realize how that sounded, waved her hand in quick negation. "Not as with the house, the clothes, the things. *In his heart.* A tall, strong, handsome man who no longer knew how to breathe deeply of life."

"Why, Mrs. Rosado," Lyn said, around a sudden tight crimp in her throat, "you have a poet's soul."

"I'm Latin," Mrs. Rosado said, quite matter-of-factly. "Of course I do. And so does your young man. Whatever happened in Nevada emptied it for a while, but this mountain filled it again—he showed us who he was, soon enough, with his little excuses for coming around to see if things were all right, his little errands and the way he made us all aware of one another here on this mountainside." She crossed her arms over the pale lavender robe and regarded Lyn a moment. "And now, are you going to ask why I bring these things up?"

Lyn coughed. She made a conscious effort to loosen her hold on the mug. Ceramics weren't meant for

Sentinel strength. "Actually, I was taking it as a warning of sorts. *Be good to him.*" Assuming a lot, that.

Mrs. Rosado gave the matter a moment of thought, wrinkled eyes narrowing, and then apparently decided to let that one go. "It's because of what else is happening here these past weeks. Before you came."

Lyn set the coffee aside. The ocelot—buried deeply within—slanted her ears back, twitched her tail. Some Sentinels dismissed the instincts of mundane humanity, but Lyn wasn't one of them. Not when she was facing a woman as strong as this deceptively small, quiet widow. "Tell me," she said.

"Ah," Mrs. Rosado said. "You already know. You can see, too." She wasn't an elderly woman in a faded lavender summer robe just then, her permed curls flattened on one side of her head and askew on the other and her glasses perched on parchment skin. She was someone in whom Lyn trusted…in whom she was quite nearly willing to confide.

But if not quite enough, then she was someone to be heard. "Tell me," Lyn said again.

Mrs. Rosado nodded, just once. "Watch his face, when he thinks you aren't. There is something hurting him—something distracting him. He should be a man with much laughter in his eyes—with sons he swings around by their ankles just to make them shriek with glee."

Lyn hadn't even thought of it, but suddenly she could see it. Good God. There was that scary feeling again. She squinched her eyes closed. *No no no.*

"You'll see it," Mrs. Rosado persisted. "Watch for it. And then ask him. I've tried, but he gives me his stupid-man look and pretends he doesn't understand. Maybe you can get through."

"I've seen it," Lyn said, pulling herself back to the conversation with a confession she hadn't quite intended to make. She covered it quickly enough. "I've seen the stupid-man look, too. Trust me. I won't give up that easily."

And that much was the utter truth. Lyn Maines, once on a track, didn't give up at all.

The only problem was, somewhere along the way she'd stopped thinking of Ryan as tracking work. Somewhere along the way she'd stopped thinking of him as any kind of work.

Oh, no, no, no...

Chapter 15

Joe found her crouched by the side of the house, wrapped in an unlikely pink sweater, oversized flip-flop sandals on her feet with a jewel-encrusted butterfly on the thong between her toes.

Also unlikely.

"You raided Mrs. Rosado's closet?" he asked, bemused, not realizing until too late that she was deep in tracking and had no idea he'd even approached.

She squeaked, an undignified sound that—in some equally unlikely way—suited the pink sweater and the jeweled flip-flops. She also startled backward, which didn't work out as well; she fell, arms splayed out, legs askew. She lost a sandal. And she glared.

"Sorry," he said, and bit his lip, and briefly looked heavenward for strength in the straight-face department. It was hard to feel entirely guilty, given that he'd emerged from his shower to find her gone, gone, gone, and that she'd stayed gone through the morning chores—feed the cats, purr at the cats, water plants and of course the litter box basics. She'd stayed gone through the first cup of coffee, through his morning e-mail—finally, a formal communication from brevis, touching base on the missing report and the missing request for same—and now he'd found her out here with clear evidence that she'd gone visiting.

While Mrs. Rosado wouldn't have guessed why a grown woman would show up in the chilly post-dawn hours without a jacket or shoes, Joe pretty much knew what had really happened. "Your coffee got cold," he told her.

Guilt suffused her features. This, he thought, was an improvement. Two days ago, she simply wouldn't have cared. "I thought you would take longer."

He offered a hand; she took it. He pulled her up with enough force that she bounded to her feet with some surprise, bounced slightly on the balls of those feet— one in a sandal, one not—and finally steadied. "I couldn't figure out a way to turn her down without looking like a crazy woman," she said, smoothing down the front of the sweater. "Maybe we can drop them off later today."

"Sure," he said easily, hoping himself sly as he inhaled the freshness of her scent, allowing himself the luxury of remembering—*feeling*—her body against his. *Later for that.* "But first things first. What's up with my mulch?"

Just like that, her work face slid back into place. Serious, contained…not giving much of herself away. "I got to thinking, as I was talking to Mrs. Rosado… those men she mentioned. That business card. We never really followed up on that. At first, I assumed they'd been scouting you, that they had no intention of making contact. But that was sloppy. I should have *checked*."

"Lyn…" He couldn't help his own frown. "That was weeks ago."

She shot him a mildly annoyed glance. "And?"

His turn for surprise. "You can follow trace that old?"

She crossed her arms, cocked her head and looked up at him with that slanted glance. "Did you think that trace at the top of the world was recent?"

Um…yes?

Probably not the right answer, boy-o.

So he didn't say anything at all.

Not that she didn't notice. She raised an eyebrow at him, her arms crossed over the sweater, her composure regained—the single sandal not withstanding.

"Okay," he said. "What did you find?"

Composure fled. "Nothing yet," she admitted. "I was just realizing that I need to go ditch this sweater." His lack of comprehension must have shown; she gave him a wry grin. "Mrs. Rosado is quite the strong personality. She may not be a Sentinel or carry amulets, but she manages to leave her own kind of trace. Hold on, will you? I'll be right back." She put an unthinking hand on his arm to steady herself while she hunted down the errant sandal and threaded her toes into it; he grinned quietly to himself at the feel of her small hand. *Oh, yeah, memories.*

"*Men,*" she said. "Is that all you can think about?"

"All I *can* think about?" He gave that some serious thought. "Hell, no. But it's what I *want* to think about."

She gave him a cross look, as expected. But he wasn't so sure he didn't see the faintest bit of panic behind that expression. Whoops, that wasn't good. *Back off, boy-o.* Deep within, she apparently did realize she'd given some part of herself to him, something she couldn't just take back. And, oh yeah, it had scared her.

But not so much that she didn't do the also expected thing and step out past him, strides as long as those legs could make them, sandals flipping loudly against her feet—headed for the casita, if he guessed right, and if he was guessing right, she'd be right back. Because Lyn Maines wasn't the giving-up sort, and she obviously hadn't finished here.

So he waited. He rocked back on his heels, let his gaze wander uphill and let his thoughts follow. He couldn't see the top of the world from here—he couldn't see the Peaks at all, beyond the curve of the rising land and the pines climbing through the thick ring of white-trunked aspens. But even if he hadn't followed the previous night's power surge to ground, he knew it had come from above.

These were his mountains, his turf. He could damned well find the Core here.

Especially now that I know to look. No thanks to brevis for that. Even if Carter had sent him a heads-up gone astray, he might well have followed through instead of making a black mark. *Doesn't answer e-mail. Must be going dark.* Yeah, right.

Except…okay, maybe Joe had gotten a little jaded. Maybe he'd gotten a little less than communicative. Maybe he'd fallen into the habit of taking care of things here and letting brevis deal with his silence.

Dammit.

He'd expected to hear her coming, but she'd ditched the sandals and come out barefoot, her feet and arms both bare in the fast-warming day. He hadn't realized she had that snug shirt on beneath the incongruous pink sweater, its rich brown bringing out the warmth in her eyes; it both enticed and frustrated him, with the clever crisscross wrappings of the material—and that, he realized, was exactly what it was supposed to do.

Men, he thought, using Lyn's voice in his head. *So easily manipulated.* And grinned at himself.

She gave him a suspicious look, as if she might know what he was thinking and didn't want to know at the same time. "Ready?"

"Sure," he said, as amiable as he'd been way back at the beginning of this conversation. "What am I doing?"

"Making sure rocks don't fall out of the sky and land on my head," she told him dryly.

"Ah. Right. Backup. I'll stand around and look capable, then." He leaned straight-armed against the house, beyond casual. And yeah, he saw a little smile lurking at the corners of her mouth.

"I checked the porch already," she said, her expression sliding back into work face. "The obvious place. Nothing there. But here…" She glanced into the woods, her target the faint trail made by a certain cougar's regular trek past the house. Lyn gestured at it. "They already knew who you are—*what* you are—of course. So they knew what to look for." She offered him a pointed little smile. "Then again, so do I."

She crouched down again—and this time the faint play of flickering blue lightning gave him warning. And though Joe tried hard—*really* hard—to watch, to see that wondrous moment of the human taking the ocelot, his eyes gave way against the intensity of the ethereal light. Only a blink, but a blink at just the right moment and then there she was, petite and feline with the most amazingly long rudder of a tail, rich dark-rimmed rosettes chaining down her back against a gray desert cat background.

She twitched her tail, extended her claws briefly into the thin soil—finding the ground, he would have said—and then got right to work, closing her eyes and tipping her head much as the human would have done. But now her whiskers sprang out from her muzzle, quivering as she lowered her head to inspect every particle of soil, every pine needle, every old oak leaf. Another step and she repeated the process, the intensity of her concentration a wonder to see. Joe found himself crouching, watching her—watching every twitch of her ear, every nuance of her whiskers, every ruffle of her fur. She crossed into the gravel moat around the house—not quite mulch, it nonetheless kept moisture in and served as a base for the sparse natural landscaping—and she checked the other side. Without opening her eyes, she then turned around to come at it from the other direction.

He'd become consumed enough with watching her that he forgot they had a goal at all—until her eyes sprang open, her whiskers stiffened and her tail slightly puffed. "Whoa," he said. "You're kidding."

Out came her claws on one paw; as deftly as though they were fingers, she maneuvered individual pieces of landscaping gravel. When he crouched down to help, she *mrrled* at him and batted at his hand, and he quickly withdrew it. "By your command, princess," he told her, amused, and then laughed as she threatened him with a spread-open paw. But soon enough she'd found what she wanted, neatly uncovering a small, darkened bronze disk.

Joe's amusement vanished, flashing to anger. *They were here.* The Core had been here at his home, and they'd planted this thing in his path, and it had done who knows what—to him, to this mountain. Tied them together, somehow. And now it sat, dark and used and corrupt, offending everything it touched. He reached for it, unthinking, wanting it out of there—wanting it gone from his home.

The ocelot snarled a soprano warning, no less fierce for its register, and leaped at him—only twenty-five pounds of her, but all the force of her strong hind legs slamming directly into his chest, claws retracted, but those sharp feline teeth right in his face, her blue-green eyes glinting close and fierce. As he thumped onto his back, breath whooshing from his lungs, he jerked his head sharply aside—already warned by the flicker of changing light. Sure enough he lost what was left of his breath as her weight multiplied, human knees in his stomach and human hands against his shoulders.

Kindly, she let her knees slide to either side, straddling him to take the weight off his stomach. He grabbed at her wrists—not trying to remove them so much as trying to slow the action while he hunted air.

"What were you thinking?" Her voice snapped with anger.

He choked on his first attempt at words, tried again—looking at her, finding her eyes brown again and deeply furious…not to mention frightened. "Dead amulet," he said, going for shorthand. "Wanted it gone."

Her eyes narrowed; she leaned closer. "Who says it's dead?" And when that had registered—his grip relaxing on her wrists, his surprise obvious—she pulled her hands away from his shoulders, sat back and crossed her arms. She looked quite at home there, he thought, with his knees rising behind her to act as a brace should she want it. She said, "We're not making assumptions about *any* of the amulets the Core is using in this little conspiracy of theirs. They've done something… *changed* something." She gestured at the disturbed pile of gravel and its occupant. "I should have been able to detect that one the moment I set foot on this property, whether it was spent or new. And it *looks* spent, but that doesn't mean anything anymore. The one thing we know is that it was meant for you, and that means that *you* are the one person who needs to keep his hands— and paws—off it!"

Joe coughed, breathing more easily now that she'd shifted her weight back. He glanced toward the amulet and grimaced. "Point made," he told her. "It's all yours. Just get it out of there, huh?"

Her expression softened with understanding; she put a hand to his chest, fingers splayed…a gentle gesture. So was it his fault he responded to her, tensing beneath her, shifting ever so slightly? By the way her eyes widened, by the way her own body tensed—an entirely different kind of tension, at that—by the way she rapidly pushed off him and climbed to her feet, it would seem so.

"Ow," he muttered, and sat—and decided to stay there a moment and recover from the whole thing.

She said, "The Save the Peaks riders come in from Gray Mountain today. At Elden Pueblo. And the tainted artifact at the museum was from Elden Pueblo… Ryan?"

He shook his thoughts free from the mountain—or tried to. He couldn't stop his gaze from returning to it, or the slight shake of his head. "I need to find it," he said. "That's the root of it, up there somewhere."

She turned on him. "Don't even think of backtracking that power again—"

Joe snorted. "Hell, no. I'm going to go up there and find the Core."

"We tried that."

He found he could get to his feet. "For one afternoon. And we found signs of them. But we looked your way. I intend to look *my* way."

"And we can do that," she said, and for all her words tried to sound reasonable, her voice had grown tense. "But the riders come in this afternoon, and that could be an opportunity."

"Or a distraction from what we really need to do."

How swift her invisible ocelot fur was to ruffle, how quickly her ears went back. A reaction to more than just a simple disagreement…a reaction to something within her.

And then he remembered that moment of fear he'd seen, and he realized…a reaction to something *between them*. And he realized, too, he could quite likely ease things by shrugging, by getting his battered old Elden Pueblo handout, and by reaching out to locate the riders and time their arrival. They always came surrounded by their own spiritual strength, easy to find.

Except he needed to find the root of that power. It tugged at him, taunted him…a sandstorm from the inside out, ever reminding him of the danger the Core posed here. Who knew when they would trigger a cataclysm? *Powder keg,* brevis had said, and now it sang through Joe's veins, sizzling danger and urgency.

"Elden," he said carefully, "might be linked to all this somehow, but you haven't been there, so you wouldn't know… It's only a couple of hundred yards from Highway 89." Too public, too well traveled to be a keystone site for the Core. "It might help us put the pieces together, but it's there any time we want to check it out."

"The riders come in today." She was set to stubborn, all right, mired in her own private struggle. Last night…

Maybe it had meant something to her.

The thought cheered him. But it didn't change his mind. "Both then."

"Split up?" It seemed to shock her; she pulled into herself, walling herself up.

"I know you're used to working with someone," he said, not without understanding. But hell, if she was this conflicted about what had happened between them, maybe they were better off working separately. "But it's a public place. The riders will be coming in from the north after their overnight—it's a thirty-mile ride, more or less. They follow 89 down, but when they get close to the mountain they'll peel off into the foothills of Elden. Gorgeous country there, mainly wild. Anyway, they use the Elden Pueblo parking area as a pickup point. If you're at the dig, you'll be in the obvious position to watch them come in. No one'll even know you're sniffing for trace."

"But—"

"It's a safe place, Lyn. Or you can come with me, and we'll check out Elden tomorrow." He didn't mention that he'd get more ground covered without her. Not a smart move, not just then. "Maybe by then your Sentinel team will be here with their amulet enlightenment."

He saw her annoyance; he knew damned well exactly which expression the ocelot would have been wearing, and how far he would have kept himself from her claws. But if she'd ever mistaken his amiability to mean he'd give up when it mattered, or if she'd thought easygoing meant he didn't take a stand when there was a stand to take…

Then she'd misjudged him completely.

She looked as though she might just be thinking the

same. In fact, she looked at him quite closely, with a distinct scrutiny, one she made no attempt to disguise— and then she shook her head. "Something Mrs. Rosado said," she told him, in response to his obvious awareness. "But I'm not sure I see it."

Lyn's tail lashed up a storm.

It might not actually be there, in her human form. But she felt it nonetheless—the annoyance, the anger, and the very real physical sensation of the tail lashing back and forth, the ears flattened, the eyes narrowed...

Okay, that last one she was actually doing. Standing there with the Elden Pueblo archeological site at her back, not quite joining the scattering of people slightly downhill from her as they waited for the approaching riders, she'd let her eyes narrow into an ocelot's angry glare, and she'd let her very human arms cross beneath her breasts in that age-old defensive-aggressive stance.

No wonder no one had approached her with friendly words.

She turned around to face the Sinagua village ruins— a complex conglomeration of tumbledown walls that outlined living and storage areas, all surrounded by widely spaced Ponderosa pines and long grasses. Here, with as much privacy as she was going to get, she closed her eyes, taking a cleansing breath. Letting it go.

Or trying to.

She'd been surprised to find the lee side of the mountains so different in nature—more sparsely wooded, with scooped-out high desert plains between the rising asymmetries of volcanic cinder cones below the embracing slopes of Mount Elden. She'd come early enough to walk the several miles of Fat Man's Loop from the Elden Pueblo parking lot—running some of them as the ocelot to burn off emotion and then finding herself grateful for the frozen sports drink Ryan had tucked into her car before he'd left on his own trek that morning. Even the forested sides of Elden were more open, more sprawling, than the land north of the Peaks. Not that it didn't have its rugged features; she'd amused herself for some moments by crouching atop jutting vertical rocks while several hikers tried without success to gain control of their unleashed dogs, which leaped haplessly against the rock she'd scaled so easily. The hikers finally gave up and leashed the animals as they should have been in the first place. Ryan would have been both amused and pleased.

Ryan. What the hell was he thinking, splitting them up like this? He was the one who'd suggested Elden Pueblo in the first place; he was the one who liked to meet this ride.

She tried to decide if she'd feel better or worse if she had managed to find Core trace out here. Truth was, she'd found nothing…but for the first time in her life, she didn't trust it. Because this group…they'd covered their tracks more thoroughly than any sect she'd encountered.

She wanted to think it was because they'd done their homework after the Sonoita incident and realized who they'd have on their trail, but the timeline wasn't right. Assuming the visit by the two Core strangers was part of it, it had all been ready to go the moment Gausto called for it. It had certainly been in play before they realized a tracker of Lyn's status might be in the area, given how she was flown in at the last moment to go hunting the ancient *Liber Nex* manuscript and ended up tracking down a sect nest and the captive Megan Lawrence instead.

The whole thing was a backup plan to rule the world,

no doubt, since Gausto's plot to combine forbidden blood workings and the long-proscribed incantations in the *Liber Nex* had come to one great big fat failure. But Lyn had had backup there, backup who had stayed *with* her—

"Not fair," she reminded herself in a mutter, and took another deep, long breath. Ryan hadn't been assigned here as her backup; if anything, he had seniority. It was his turf; he was the one who knew how to read the nuances of the area.

Then why did he turn away from this incredibly obvious opportunity?

Oh, fickle ocelot. Only a day earlier, she'd put her faith in him. In more than just his integrity, but in his heart. Her deep, greedy need to be with a heart so true; her sudden conviction that she'd found one.

Maybe she'd just seen what she wanted to see, after all this time of needing.

Another deep breath, and she walked the perimeter of the largest building cluster, eyeing the foundational footprint of room upon room in the communal structure. From here, that tainted museum projectile point had come. And the Core had seen fit to use it—to place some clumsy node device on it, when everywhere else they'd used stealth. Because they hadn't had the stealth until after they'd gotten started? Because they'd been lazy? Because they hadn't thought it would matter, there in the museum?

Ryan might have some thoughts on it all. *If he were here.*

She had an image of him, then—padding along the crest of a ridge, high alpine lichens and delicate plants beneath big platter paws, lean cougar's head lifted to the chill breeze of the rarified air, eyes mere slits against the brightest of sunlight—and expression intense and serene at the same time. Doing what he was meant to do.

Here. You should be here.

Not that she'd found anything to justify her own insistence. This second stroll around the village revealed no more than the first. She might as well have gone with Ryan, might as well have waited for him to come along as the backup she so badly needed, even if her confidence in him had taken a sudden shaking.

She found she'd hidden her face in her hands, bitten her lip, made the kind of inarticulate noise of frustration one tried to avoid in public…wondering if it wasn't her confidence in herself that hadn't taken the shaking. The confidence in her ability to assess the man in the first place.

But no one saw her; no one heard. No one cared. Because a swell of excited chatter rose from those gathered slightly below her, arrayed just beyond a tiny parking lot now filled with pickups and horse trailers that were festooned with everything from professionally made Save the Peaks Coalition banners to homemade sheets and markers. The pickups held hay and huge five-gallon water containers; the trailers had tie straps already waiting for tired horses. But not, she knew, until the participants and their supporters ended the event with a Navajo prayer, just as it had begun. That, she'd thought, was the part that Ryan would have found irresistible, with its power drawn from the very area he shepherded, yet so separate from his own.

"There!" The exclamation was low but clear, and Lyn spun around to find everyone's attention focused northward. Her predator's eyes saw the movement quickly enough—just a flash of brown between the trees, and then the swish of a tail, and suddenly an entire horse came into view, a sturdy little buckskin. Soon enough half a dozen horses appeared, single file on the narrow trail—all seasoned trail horses on a loose rein, their riders bedecked in random traditional pieces: an old-timey shirt among the jeans, incredible heirloom turquoise pieces on both the men and the women, hand-crafted silver everywhere, and a few fancy dress western shirts in the mix. Western hats were a given—no one rode in this summer sun without them.

Lyn found herself content to watch in the shade, hunkered down without even realizing she'd taken that age-old watch-and-wait posture. A flurry of activity followed the arrival—family members greeting one another, offering cool drinks, checking the horses—but all in all, quickly assembling for a quiet in which one melodious voice rose, chanting. Lyn quite suddenly felt like the outsider she was, and couldn't help the urge to take a step back—just as the newspaper reporter and photographer below were now doing. But she quietly held her ground. Ryan no doubt would have felt very much at home here.

Another image, then, strong and clear: *the cougar, stopping in his hunt, his head turning unerringly north, his eyes wide and clear and knowing.*

And that's when she thought to look closer at the power flows—not a power wrangler, no, but if she went looking she could sometimes *see,* if not nearly with the depth and sensitivity as—

The cougar, now squeezing his eyes closed to feline smile, head tilted in that way that meant he was sifting power, tasting it...all the nuances, all the layers, the distance as nothing to such sensitivity and skill.

And then she could feel it, too, so much different

from the rolling bass power of the mountain, tinged with Ryan's trace; this came in gentle whispers, flowing across the contours of the land to mingle and mesh, drawing from a wellspring beneath the mountain itself. She felt her jaw drop; she felt the very stupefied look on her face as she realized how right Ryan had been, how he'd truly known—how narrow her focus had been, to think the Sentinels were the only ones who would realize there was a problem with the mountain, or that they would be the only ones affected by this particular aspect of that problem, should the Core steal and store enough energy to wreak its havoc unchecked.

In her mind's eye, the cougar crouched, immersing himself in sensations—experiencing without interfering. And Lyn, too, let it wash over her until she became aware of a scrutiny. Her eyelids sprang open, her gaze unerringly drawn to the man sitting on horseback beside the oldest man who led the prayer. Across that distance, they regarded one another; then the man nodded to her—just once, an acknowledgment.

Lyn, somewhat shaken, nodded back. Just once. And withdrew somewhat from her exploration of that power, embarrassed at her clumsiness.

The cougar snarled warning—

She reeled at the sudden onslaught of amulet-based corruption, springing to her feet and overwhelmed by the stench of Core workings in play. *Right this very moment* and what else could they want but to tap the power she'd just witnessed? Her scan of the parking lot, of the village site, showed her nothing—Gausto's people could be comfortably ensconced in one of those parked vehicles. The stench swirled around her, triggered by amulet but anchored right here at the old Sinagua village—remotely, too many layers for a simple severing. *The museum projectile point. They'd planned ahead.* Horrified, she turned back to the Navajos, saw she'd gotten the one man's attention—his frown told her that much, and his alert gaze held wary understanding.

She wasn't Ryan, to shift power around, to divert and block and manipulate it.

But she could shield.

She bit her lip, took an uncertain step forward, shields blooming to life around her even as amulet corruption mixed with the beauty the prayer had evoked—latching on to it with Velcro hooks, a swirling and oozing parasite. The chanting faltered; a young man stepped toward the elder with concern.

Lyn was no shielding specialist; she had no innate skill with it. Ryan's response to her shields...that had been a response to *her.*

But to stand here and do nothing?

Dammit, Ryan, you should have come with me!

And if she saw the cougar leaning into a new crouch, a predatory crouch, she quickly blocked it out, finding a renewed determination to stand solo. She centered herself, and she reached out—reaching to that shared spirituality, to take it within her protection. She let it fuel her, and instead of filling her as Ryan had, it filled her shields, pushing them outward...expanding them... expanding them....

She took another step forward, fists clenched, jaw clenched, determination narrowing her eyes—unheeding how it looked from the outside, that the reporter had noticed something amiss, that a communal murmur of concern had replaced the prayer—and she pushed the shield out until it was just barely big enough to surround the people below, if not the actual source of the spiritual power, then its conduit.

But the shield was brittle and it was thin; it wouldn't hold. She could feel the creeping grip of the amulet's hooked fringes scraping its edges, and her vision went gray around the edges and her knees started to wobble and she thought *I'm only a tracker*. She floundered in an instant's panic—and then she got a hint of Ryan's trace.

Not imagination. He'd really been there, watching her. Aware of the riders' arrival, aware of their prayer, aware of their power…aware of the attack from without.

And now he reached out with a deft touch and he flicked away the amulet's grasping claws. Just like that. He folded that darkness back in on itself and it popped out of existence with an extended shriek of ethereal sound that made Lyn cry out.

Something nudged her thoughts then, right through those thinned, brittle shields—but after an instant of panic, she knew. *Ryan.* He'd said something to her. Why he thought she'd hear him this time, she didn't know. She couldn't hear him and she didn't want to hear him. If he'd been *here,* he could have just spoken to her. *And why not?* she thought at him—but just right there, in the privacy of her own mind, as much a cry of dismay as a demand. *Why didn't you come today?* Had he tried to lure her away from this, knowing it would happen? Or tried to stay away, fearing it would expose him somehow?

Trust. Right. He'd just saved her, he'd just saved this entire group, and yet…trust him?

She couldn't find it in herself. Not when he'd thrown her so off her game; not when she'd thought she understood him, thought she could work with him, only to be so astonished he would split them up this easily. He knew she got too absorbed in tracking…knew she left herself open to trouble…

She wouldn't even contemplate the fact that it was easier this way. Easier not to trust, to return to her comfortable and isolated little world, the exacting tracker with impossible expectations, traveling to where she was needed and then…leaving. Alone.

God, was that self-mockery she heard in her own thoughts?

A rustle of sound alerted her; she stiffened and opened her eyes to discover that she was no longer alone.

High-level sect members had the same general stamp about them. A swarthy complexion, hard masculine features, black hair…all of which might have been attractive had they not been arranged around such a stylized look—slicked-back hair, plenty of silver jewelry, a definite touch of kohl around the eyes, hands neatly manicured and nails buffed to a high gloss.

Which didn't meant they couldn't cause a serious amount of damage, when so inclined. Especially when those hands were full of amulets. Only one of the men now approaching Lyn—spread out, already cutting off her escape through the parking lot, the village, or up into the woods—held amulets, but that was enough. Crudely stamped metal slung on cords, the amulets held stored workings, stored energy…there was no telling what any one of them did. Or what any one of them would do to *her.*

She backed a step—backing downhill, against all instinct. The ocelot wanted to take over, to take her far into the trees—far *up* a tree. But downhill was the only way left to her, toward the people she'd been trying to protect in the first place. Unless she wanted to change in front of them all, chancing that instant of vulnerability to Gausto's men as they closed in on her, chancing the blatant daylight change in front of a people who might just well believe her to be akin to an evil skinwalker—or, come to think of it, in front of that reporter and her photographer.

You see? she cried silently to Ryan. *You shouldn't have split us up*—

Never mind that she could have gone with him.

"That was inconvenient," said the man with all the amulets, and indeed, he looked annoyed as he stepped closer. "It would have been better for you if you'd stayed out of it."

"Hey, it wasn't *me* who messed with your creepy little amulet," Lyn said, taking another step back. Her heel landed on a rock, wobbling, and she hunted sounder footing while trying to look perfectly casual about the whole thing. "Don't you have some sort of amulet you can use to tell what's really going on?" she suggested. "*Something?* Because you're getting this one wrong."

The man shrugged. "Maybe. Maybe not. You're Sentinel. That's enough."

Lyn pulled her shields in close again, fortifying them—reshaping them. Hardening them. "Guys, we're out in the middle of a public place. Witnesses. A reporter, even. That's not good for either of us. Me, I vote we adjourn and take this up another time—"

The man with the amulets plucked one from his stash. "You're the only one they'll be looking at."

Did she even want to know what it did? It could force a change to the ocelot…it could short-circuit her brain to insanity. It could make her believe she was a chicken for all she knew—and the truth was, *no,* she didn't want to know at that. She didn't want anything to do with Gausto's stench or his amulets or his *Core.* She was a tracker, that's all. A small nimble ocelot who could follow a trail anywhere…

Ryan!

But Joe Ryan was miles and a mountaintop away.

Okay, now she'd stopped thinking rationally; now she was panicking. Now she'd given up what power she had, and she sure wasn't going to let them make the rules. Let the others see her change—let them wonder. That photographer would never be quick enough, and the riders would be busy enough hanging on to their horses, and—

Except she couldn't. Talk about going dark…talk about twisting the rules to suit herself…

Changing in front of witnesses wasn't done. Changing in front of reporters?

Not done.

Because protecting the secret of the Sentinel's existence was more important than protecting any given individual. And if anyone knew that, it was the tracker who hunted the dark.

Ryan! She took another step backward. Another. Gausto's man matched her, step for step, the one specific amulet now singled out and dangling from his grasp. Unhurried, certain of his prey. Smug, even. Nothing worse than smug on those Core-stamped features, and Lyn found herself gulping a breath on the heels of having forgotten to breathe at all, and then gulping again in surprise as she came up short against an obstacle where her memory told her none had existed.

It stamped a foot and breathed gently upon her hair, a surprised and curious sound.

Not a tree, then.

"Little sister," said a quiet voice, "are you in need?"

Gausto's man with his amulet had stopped advancing—looked, in fact, as surprised as Lyn felt. She dared to shift her gaze, tipping her head just enough to realize…it was not just this one horse and rider. It was *all* of them. Arrayed behind her as the landscape allowed, silent in support. And they looked not at her, but at the men threatening her.

Amulet Man had gall, she had to hand it to him. He said, "This isn't your concern."

Lyn couldn't see the rider's expression, but she well heard his dry amusement. "We have come to recognize those who would take from us. You tried to take. She helped to stop you. So it has become our concern."

Lyn was grateful enough to lean back into his horse—grateful, too, that the animal was so well seasoned that it simply accepted her in spite of her nature. Sentinels and horses…often didn't mix. She raised an eyebrow at Amulet Man and said, "You're the ones they're looking at now."

No disputing that. He didn't even try. Nor did he hide his displeasure, as he so casually pocketed the amulets. "We know you." He stepped closer, flashing his teeth in a sudden unfriendly smile. "We have the taste of you now. So we'll finish this later."

She managed to suppress her shiver until he turned his back on her. His movement served as a signal to the other sect members, who silently melted away—retreating to the parking lot in no great hurry. After a moment, two engines turned over, and one vehicle after another pulled neatly from the lot.

Lyn sagged slightly. She realized that she stood in the full sizzling sun, midday heat suddenly surging hard against her. The smell of hot horse, the creak of saddle leather, the palpable aura of support and kindness around her... She covered her face with both trembling hands, took a deep breath and straightened, turning to face the riders and their families. "Thank you," she said. "They meant me serious harm."

"As they meant *us* serious harm," the man said—a middle-aged man with a weathered face, the most amazing heirloom squash blossom necklace, and a turquoise bracelet with such weight and age to the piece that it spoke of significance. "We have been aware of their kind, mingling with those who would desecrate the mountain. This is the first time they have been so direct."

The oldest man, steadied at the elbow of a younger man Lyn could now see bore the stamp of the same features, said, "Doko'oo'slííd has been stirring, and these men are somehow behind it."

Careful, careful. She could no more expose the Core than she could expose the Sentinels. Thousands of years of existence had depended on such secrecy. She said, "That's what we believe."

"Ah," said the old man. "The one who isn't here today. The man. You came in his stead?"

"Something like that." She couldn't help her dry tone. And she couldn't help but wonder, again, why Ryan had insisted on the mountain today when he could go to the mountain anytime, and today—*now*—was the only time he could have met the riders here. When, if he'd been here, he could have stood beside her, a safeguard against that tight focus of hers. She wouldn't have been taken by surprise...there would have been no need to bring outsiders into the clash between Sentinel and Core.

She wouldn't have been alone, facing Gausto's men and their amulets with only the kindness of strangers to back her up.

The loneliness of it bit at the back of her throat. Cruel memory gave her images of the night before— of Ryan's face, of the arch of his tightly muscled body, the cry in his throat, the look in his eye as he reached for her again. That silly, you-got-me grin. Those moments when she thought she'd never feel alone again.

Right.

She looked back at the rider who'd backed her, at the old man who'd led the prayer, and felt the nuances of what had happened between the Core and her shields and Ryan's snarling rejection of the amulet's parasitic advances. *You came in his stead?* "Yes," she said, and nodded, this time a firmer answer. In his stead, or in spite of him, or perhaps regardless of him—because that was clearly the way it would be. "Something like that."

Chapter 16

A weary cougar sprawled out at the top of the world. Bone-tired, footsore…heartsore.

He hadn't expected her to respond to his silent query; she couldn't, as far as he could tell, truly perceive such private communication.

But he hadn't expected her to close him off so abruptly, either. Hadn't expected that clear, hurt zing of one betrayed. Still didn't understand it. He'd been watching, hadn't he? He'd known when the riders had reached their destination; he'd known when the prayer bound them together. And he'd felt the amulet's power—a slice of purulence across the bright day. Had Gausto's men thought he wouldn't? Had *Lyn* thought he wouldn't?

Maybe they'd thought he *couldn't.*

Maybe they'd *expected* his strange susceptibility to the power surges that now bore his trace.

Oh yes. Weary.

But that didn't mean he could simply stay here and soak up the sun. Or even soak up the power—quiet, natural waves of power this afternoon, as if the Core's distraction elsewhere had left the mountain alone. With miles beneath his worn paws and no particular success to claim as his, it was time to head downhill, take back the human and drive back home—to find Lyn.

She was confused within herself, he knew that much. Whereas he wasn't confused at all. He knew what he wanted. More than that—he knew damned *well* what he wanted.

He also knew better than to assume he would get it.

He'd certainly thought he'd have better success this afternoon. He'd crisscrossed the Peaks, his mind on precarious landing sites for a small chopper. Between Raspberry and Bear Paw springs…the best option for any pilot, but he'd found nothing. No disturbance, no scent, no sign. East of Flagstaff Spring, the same story. Surely they weren't coming in from Lockett Meadow, with its adjoining campground…way too public…

He sneezed, an annoyed cat noise, and rubbed his face against one big paw. In fact, he'd found exactly nothing. And that meant returning below with nothing to show for his time—for his insistence—but his sore feet and dusty nose.

Well, maybe he'd do something about the nose before he actually reached home. Water waiting in the car, the hem of his shirt…it would do.

And it did. He descended back down to the Snowbowl parking lot unseen, changed on the fly as few could and pulled his shirt off to use as a damp towel outside the car. He grinned at two bold college co-eds and their admiring applause, but didn't let it slow him down as he donned the damp shirt, starting the SUV even as he snapped the seat belt into place.

This would have been a whole lot easier if you'd been returning triumphant, boy-o.

He snarled softly. He'd been so certain the source of the disruption was up there…and dammit, he was *still* certain. But the way things had gone down today…

Might be a good time to pull out those good steaks from the freezer, fire up the grill and see about that chocolate fudge brownie ice cream he'd been saving for the right day. Hmm. Unless she was a pralines-and-cream kind of woman…

Well, he'd risk it.

Thing was, given a second chance…he'd make the same choice. And he had really hoped that Lynn would trust his instincts, his need to hunt the mountain for the root of the disturbance that had so deeply affected him.

Maybe it was easier to forget when she wasn't the one who'd gotten lost in that screaming gray pain. Maybe he'd expected too much, thinking that his experience and time in this place deserved a certain respect. But with his knowledge of the mountains, with her tracking ability…between the two of them, a second effort might have yielded more than his sore feet and formerly dusty nose. If he could, he'd still talk her back up there for the following day—but he had the feeling she'd want to haunt the hotel, to try tracking Gausto's men to their bolt-hole.

A whole *lot easier if you'd been returning triumphant…*

Well, he wasn't. He'd deal with it. He navigated the hairpin curves down Snowbowl Road, expertly riding the familiar swooping asphalt to the narrow turnoff that shortcutted briefly across the side of the mountain to his own remote section of the woods. A rumble from the mountain, so quiet all day, caught his attention. That's all it was, a rumble, but he turned his efforts to his shields—knowing better than to monitor the power on the go. Not *this* power. Not anymore.

Maybe it *was* time to turn this over to a brevis team. A collection of experts who could figure out what was going on here. Or, if they had their heads on straight, they'd work with him to do it. But he knew better than to count on—

Another ripple. He shored up his shields, reminded himself that he couldn't let his thoughts wander and keep them strong—others could, sure enough, but Joe and his shields… *Better be glad you've got me around, boy-o,* Dean would say to him, and flash up his rock-solid shields without a second thought.

Right. Because a man who could ride power *needed* them so often. "Ha," he said out loud. Not unless he and Dean had been on the hunt.

Almost home…and there was Mrs. Rosado's scarf, hanging off the mailbox. He pulled in the driveway, barely turning off the engine before he was out the door, out of the cool car air-conditioning and into the height of the day's heat, unrelieved by clouds. But he stopped in surprise when she opened the front door and came out to him, carrying a covered baking pan. "Coffee cake," she said. "An old family recipe. Lots of cinnamon, pecans… It'll go nicely with that coffee of yours."

He took it as she thrust it at him. "It smells wonderful," he said, baffled. "But what—?"

"It was an excuse," she said, giving him a once-over of much scrutiny. "I wanted to see you. And now that I have, I want to know what's going on. Have you seen a doctor? Are you well? What are you not telling me?"

"I—" he said, and then stopped himself, taking another look at her expression. Not one he was used to seeing…but one he knew better than to fight. "That obvious, huh?"

"To one who knows you." Freed of the coffee cake, she crossed her arms and waited, a short and determined person with many years of experience.

Joe shook his head. "Now I understand what Leandro meant. He said there were times when no wise man would defy you."

She looked startled, then pleased. And then she narrowed her eyes at him. "Nice try. Do I look distracted?"

Joe sighed. "It's…" he said, and then, "There's…" and finally, "It's hard to explain. I think that cold—"

She made an air-escaping *pfft* noise and waved her hand.

He met her eyes, so dark within wrinkled lids, and held her gaze a moment. "I'm trying to stop something from happening," he said. "It's not something I can talk about. But the circumstances…they're complicated. Difficult." He looked over toward his house, seeing it in his mind's eye, seeing Lyn there. Reminding himself that she'd come here to condemn him, feeling again his first glimpse of her, the impact of absorbing the essence of her…craving her.

Reminding himself that a glimpse of what it meant in return had scared her right back into herself. Away from him.

Quite suddenly, Mrs. Rosado put a hand on his chest—age-spotted, a knuckle or two swollen with arthritis, but the fine shape of the fingers still readily apparent even if they weren't quite steady. Her voice was steady enough, though. "This is what you need to listen to," she said. "Right here. And this is when you need to be strong enough to do it. If it was easy, my Leandro always said, then it doesn't mean as much to us when we get it. And then we don't fight hard enough to keep it."

"Leandro," Joe said, and grinned suddenly. "Wise man, that Leandro. Bet he knew a good coffee cake when he saw it, too."

"You can be sure of that." Mrs. Rosado quite suddenly stood on her toes and kissed his cheek, her skin papery-old against his, and then stepped away, back to brusque. "And you remember, Joe Ryan—you can't take care of the rest of us unless you take care of yourself."

Huh.

He touched his chest, right where her hand had rested. Huh. He gave her another grin, hefted the coffee cake in salute, and set it in the passenger seat of the SUV as he slid in behind the wheel. Almost home, then, and it could just be that a little afternoon coffee and cake would trump his plans for dinner. A little decadence in the cool space of the house, ceiling fans drying the sweat of the day…

The SUV parked beside Lyn's hatchback rental took him completely by surprise. He pulled in beside it and sat there a moment, listening to the engine tick. His shields had slipped; he shored them up—and then felt so blind that he immediately dropped them completely, letting his senses sweep over his home, over the surrounding land.

They'd hidden themselves well. He found Lyn—shielded or not, he would always find Lyn. And he found small eddies of activity—new wards, tiny riffs of power. Activity… *In his house?*

He'd gotten out of his hybrid before he even realized

it, the coffee cake forgotten, the door left ajar while he
stood there with his hands fisted, his temper rising. *In
his house.* Doing what, rifling through his computer in
search of evidence? Sniffing every corner in search of
Core trace? Frightening the cats?

Temper, boy-o. Maybe someone had to use the
bathroom. Maybe they were thirsty. Maybe Lyn had
invited them in, not realizing—as he had not quite
realized—how very strongly he would react to brevis
intruders.

They had judged him. They had judged him without
a trial after Dean's death, they had yanked him from
what was left of his life…they had left him here,
thinking him harmless in such a stable, deeply anchored
place as the Peaks. And now the Peaks had turned on
them, and they were looking for someone to blame and
they were *in his house.*

He left the car, ignoring the distant voice of inquiry
that might have been Lyn calling his name from around
the corner. He blew through the front door, solid wood
slamming back. And there they were. Someone in the
kitchen—indeed, getting a drink. A shadow of someone
in the hallway toward his office. Someone upstairs in
his loft, his damned *bedroom.*

He didn't mean for the change to loom, for the blue
charge to flicker in the edges of his vision or for the
snarl of the cougar to echo in his mind, surging to break
free. They froze, the three forms—one he could see, one
he could discern by shadow, and one he could hear
upstairs. For a long moment he said nothing, simply
because he couldn't—the words stuck in a throat that
couldn't decide whether to stay human. And then he
growled, "You are not welcome here."

The Sentinel upstairs eased to the half wall of the

loft, revealing herself—and, by her glance toward the hallway, revealing the nominal leader of this particular group. The man at the refrigerator turned just enough, opened his hands just enough, to make a no-harm-meant gesture.

Joe growled, deep in his throat. Completely and totally unconvinced.

From the hallway, the final individual emerged—a huge man, bearded, with a worn backpack hanging from one big hand and a laptop dwarfed by the other. He put the laptop on the center island of the kitchen, dropped the backpack beside it and turned to Joe—such casually slow movements, so offhandedly careful. He said, "Lyn thought we wouldn't want to waste any—"

"Not welcome," Joe repeated, his voice dropping another note or two, the fury so strong he could barely think past it. A brevis team in Flagstaff, he'd come to terms with. He'd prepared for. But not *here.* Not taking over his home.

"Okay, got that," the man said easily. "It's a misunderstanding, bro. We'll sort it out."

"Ruger," the woman said, a protesting note in that single word.

"Hey, it's his house." Ruger lifted his massive shoulders in a shrug. *Bear,* Joe realized dimly, taking a deep and deliberate breath. Three-on-one odds, he'd take… but a bear weighted those odds considerably.

They're on your side, boy-o.

Looking up at the woman, he didn't believe it. Looking at the man by the refrigerator, the one still standing in such an obvious, carefully neutral position, he didn't believe it. Of the man Ruger… *He's only doing what it takes to defuse the situation.* No, no trust there, either.

Ruger said, "I'm the healer. Shea is shields. Annorah

is wards and communications, and she's coming down-stairs now."

"But I'm in the middle of—"

"Now," Ruger said, ever so pleasantly.

Watching her descend the staircase—a curvy woman without the feel of full-field Sentinel but instead the look of stubborn bureaucrat with her mind made up— Joe's thoughts rattled, hollow in his own mind. This woman was here for him, as much as Lyn had been here for him at the start. And the man behind Ruger—a lightweight, that man, probably a coyote. His gaze went back to Ruger, locked there.

"The cats," he said, but stiffened—aware then of a certain questing power, a probe into his very nature. The most insidious form of invasion.

The woman. Communications, hell.

He didn't think twice, but gathered a quick surge of power, that which sifted constantly through him simply because of who he was. He hit her with it—hit her hard enough to knock her on her ass right in the middle of her so casual descent down the curving stairs. Didn't hurt her—didn't mean to hurt her.

But shocked her, yes—her eyes gone wide, her body stiffened, waiting for a follow-up blow. But Joe had no such intentions—and if he had, the shields that sprang up between them wouldn't have stopped it. Foundation power slammed shields just as hard as it did flesh, and she clearly knew it. So did the coyote Shea, to judge by the quick step he took, by the warning in his voice. "Ruger—"

But Ruger didn't move. He said calmly, "Annorah, that probe was a wee bit rash. One might even say *rude.*"

And Joe, as if he hadn't just effortlessly flung around the kind of power that Annorah had obviously never even seen and Shea knew well enough to regard with profound concern and even Ruger acknowledged with a lift of craggy brow, said again, "The cats. Where are the cats?"

Ruger tipped his head. "Haven't come across them."

Joe looked at Annorah. Straight at Annorah. Because the cats would have retreated to the bedroom, knowing that strangers never went upstairs. And flustered, she said, "Two of them were at the sliding doors—I put them ou—"

Out. But she stopped with a wince at Joe's expression.

"Then go find them," he said flatly. He looked at the coyote; he looked at Ruger. "Outside." He turned on his heel, leaving the door open behind him, and stalked out into the yard—token landscaping, token parking and surrounding forest—the cougar still flickering around his edges.

They came. The woman with her bruised ass and bruised dignity, the man without his water and Ruger with his backpack and his laptop, both of which he left on the porch bench. As the door closed behind him, he said, "Best find the kitties, Annorah." His genial voice didn't hide the nature of the order.

Joe rubbed his hands down his face, instantly easing down a notch now that they were all outside. "She'll only scare them deeper into the woods," he said. "I'll put out food when we're done here."

"Lyn can track them," Annorah said, hesitant.

He turned on them. "What the hell were you thinking? Did you think I would welcome you? Do you think I'm that stupid?" He caught Annorah's gaze—blond hair of the bed-head sort, big blue eyes, skin of amazing clarity; it showed her high emotion, staining her throat and cheeks. And she looked away. "Don't even tell me you've been assigned to field investigations before."

"I have," she snapped.

But Ruger laughed quietly, genuinely amused. "Give him that one, Annorah." To Joe, he said, "She works out of brevis with communications. Given what we're dealing with…the shielding, the power disruptions—we wanted a nexus here in the field."

"I'm not a radio," she said, but she looked away, and she sounded both sullen and embarrassed. "And there was something going on up there. Can't call it warding—almost like a power groove. But that's not my thing—it's just close enough so I can get a feel for it. We need a power wrangler out here."

Ruger laughed again. "We've got one, Annorah."

"She means one she can trust," Joe said darkly. "All you had to do was ask, Annorah. I do a lot of power riding off the roof out there. Damn straight there's a groove. I put it there."

Stubbornly, she shook her head. "It doesn't feel right."

"Ah," he said. "So you *are* an expert."

Ruger ignored them. "We've got an amulet master with us, as well. And backup for Lyn, a man she's worked with before."

Damn, that stung. It shouldn't have—Joe was never meant to be backup, had his own thing to do. But ow, yes, it did. But he said nothing, and Ruger added, "Lyn said you had Internet access in your office. Nick is waiting on instant message, wants an initial assessment. And he should have some of the information Lyn asked for."

"Yeah?" Joe said. "Like who diverted the communication that should have come my way? Or hey, how about the fact that no one's found any connection between me and the Core boys yet? Oh, wait—never mind. That's no problem. You'll just manufacture some if you really want it."

"Hey!" Annorah said, sounding truly stung. And she blurted, "No one thought you were connected to the Core, not at first. We thought—"

A look from Ruger stopped her, but not before Joe got it. He laughed short and hard. "Right, I know. You thought I was just off on my own thing. Power wrangler gone wild."

Ruger swapped that look to Joe. "How the hell many of us do you think can shove power around on a whim like you just did?"

Joe gave him a grim little grin. "It wasn't a whim."

But Shea looked grim in return, and Annorah simply looked away, unable to meet his gaze at all—and that's when he realized. He'd *scared* them. They hadn't expected that—not of him, maybe not of anyone. It surprised him; made him take a step back, a step down.

Because if they were truly concerned about what he could do, they weren't going to react rationally to anything he did do. They'd react….

Well, like Annorah.

The humor took him suddenly, dark as it was, and wrung another laugh out of him. When Ruger gave him an inquiring eye, he could only shake his head. "It's your own fault," he said. "You judged me. You put me here. Problem solved, you thought. Maybe you should have paid more attention in the first place." He shook his head again. "Tell you what I think—*get over it.* We've got a situation here, and it's not going to wait for you to deal. It's also not going to wait while you examine my house for molecules of evidence. You want to know what I think?" He didn't wait to see if they did or not. "Get a handle on this thing. Get a handle on the Core—round them up or chase them off or whatever current policy is. Then you can worry about whether or not it's all my fault."

Ruger dipped his head to scratch above one ear, casting Joe a rueful look from there. "Lyn said you were direct."

"Yeah," Joe said. "I am." A shallow ripple of power lapped at him—distraction and warning. A glance at the others told him that none of them had felt it; they were as deeply immersed in their current dilemma—namely, him—as ever. "Look," Joe said. "Lyn's got some ideas about what's next. So do I. Now that you're here, maybe we can split up—" He hated the words as they came from his mouth. They felt like defeat—like the first step of never being alone with Lyn again, of never having the moments for which he'd been heading home.

No. Denial kicked up, loud and strong. He'd do what it took to have those moments. During this crisis, after it…beyond. Certainty settled somewhere in his chest, solid and strong. Something within him relaxed; he took a deep breath.

Ruger nodded, moving ahead in his own thoughts. "It's possible," he said. "Lyn said you'd need someone to work with—I don't completely understand. Something about the tainted power."

"The problem is, my shields suck," Joe said, and saw the surprise at his blunt words reflected on all their faces. "Look, protecting myself from power isn't one of my concerns. I'm a screen, it's the wind. Get it? It just passes through. When I was working outside of Vegas and we ran into a…situation, Dean covered me. Out here, there's been nothing. It's not an active position, which is exactly why brevis put me here."

"Direct," Ruger said, straight-faced, "may have been an understatement."

Another series of power ripples riffed through Joe…his breath caught on the faint raking pain of it, stuttering his thoughts. But he caught himself, said, "The situation seems to call for it. Unless the words *powder keg* were carelessly used."

Annorah's stubborn bureaucrat expression returned. "They were not. I drafted the initial assessment for dissemination. Nick approved it."

Joe lifted his gaze to the mountain, well aware of the leading edge of more than a mere ripple, of power building to a wave. "I wouldn't dispute it. We've got to stop these surges…and then if we're lucky, we can restore balance enough so the mountain will take it from there."

Ruger crossed his arms over his barrel chest—a hard, big man made for T-shirts or flannel shirts and rugged jeans, and who knew better than to fight it. "So you want to split up, to send Lyn on the trail of the Core from one direction, while you hunt them from another."

"More or less. What I really want is to find their power anchor. They're not Sentinel. They can't just reach for it. They've got a hook somewhere, sunk into the source. How they've hidden it so well…that's another thing again." He settled his feet into a wider stance, swaying slightly with the building flow of power—not daring to back-trace it to see if it built further or if it simply ebbed away. It scraped at his nerves, already long raw. And the others still didn't feel it at all—Shea was lost in watching Ruger, waiting for some reaction; Annorah watched Joe himself, her eyes narrowing with some unknown suspicion.

Ruger nodded. "That can work," he said. "Shea and I can go out with you, maybe even Michael, our amulet expert. Lyn will have her backup. Maks takes the tiger, so he's muscle, too, when it comes to that. Annorah will stay here, work communications hub. Stay in touch with Nick via IM—"

"I don't think so," Joe said dryly. He tipped a thumb at the casita. "She can stay there. She wants to talk to Nick, she can give him a call. Or if she's that good at comms, she can do it that way."

"I'm that good," Annorah snapped. "But it's a stupid waste of energy when you can provide access right here in your—"

"In my *office*," Joe finished for her. "In my *house*. Where I don't trust you."

"Joe—" Ruger started, with all the makings of placation behind that single word.

"No." He said it with decisive finality, and not without rancor. "Of all of you, she's the one I trust least. She has fears about me, and no field experience to put them into context. She hasn't learned the difference between pushing and crossing lines. She scared the hell out of my cats and then she *put them outside.*" He glared at Ruger, spared a glance for Annorah's shocked and even somewhat hurt expression, and shook his head—too aware that his vision grayed at the edges from the tainted power they hadn't even noticed yet, but needing, if nothing else, to make this point. "She will *not be in my home* while I'm gone."

Ruger raised his hands, heading for placation—but his words weren't quite there. "About that," he said. "I think we need to talk."

Ah, he was going to pull rank. Or something. Joe ignored it. "Where's Lyn?" he asked. She was the one who understood about the power—who understood how he'd need to deal with it if it surged high. She would have felt it by now, he knew—she'd become sensitized in the past days, and more alert. "I need to talk to Lyn." He hunted her from where he stood—the sound of her, the sense of her. His internal focus narrowed, driven by a sleet of pain. *Shield from it, and miss the subtleties of what's happening...of what's* about *to happen*—

There she was. Distant. Concerned. Her voice raising in question. "Are they inside? I need to talk to Ryan...."

Ruger's bass obliterated those faint words without care. "You know as well as I do—we've got the authority to turn this place into a temporary ops base. Your situation is too damned precarious for you to give us crap about working here. If you're as eager to settle things here as you say, you'll— Whoa. Hey, man, you've got a nosebleed going there."

Lyn's voice, a little louder. "*You* figure out the amulet. There's power coming in, and I need to make sure—"

"Ryan," Ruger said. "*Joe*. You with us?"

"Don't trust him, Ruger—don't get too close." Annorah sounded distant, far beyond Joe's concern just then. Lyn was coming. She'd hold them back, buffer him while he sorted out this power wave. She'd—

His head lifted; his eyes half-closed, rolling back slightly. *Good God*. There it came, bearing down on them, a huge flash flood of power coming directly for this house—as if drawn by the Sentinels...or maybe just by Joe himself. They'd feel that one, all right—it would flatten them, flatten anyone with a connection to power. *Lyn*. It would blast her from the inside out...it could even kill her, as exquisitely sensitive to trace as she was.

"Ryan—" And if Ruger's voice held concern, it also held warning.

No time for that. The power tumbled down for them, a massive roiling and angry mess of damaging eruption, faster than any real flash flood could ever travel. Joe gathered himself, pulling power from within, and pulling it from all around them.

"Ruger!" Shea said sharply. He felt it, then—felt something, anyway.

Annorah, too. "He's pulling power, Ruger—! You saw what he can do!"

Ruger's voice rumbled closer. "Ryan! Don't!"

"Ryan!" Lyn's voice, clear and cutting over it all—the washed-out gray of his vision, the endless shards of pain, the immensity of effort to focus, to gather himself—to aim at that flash flood and split it asunder, wedging himself and his power into place against the rushing onslaught. Extending himself, feeling it roar around him, pressing against him. Locking his knees when they wobbled, clenching his fists, clenching his jaw, clenching his whole body—

Only when Lyn's voice turned to dismay did he falter. "Ryan, *no!* What are you *doing?*"

She didn't understand. It was coming too fast, still too distant. She wouldn't hold them back. She wouldn't buffer…wouldn't shield. Not from the very real physical confrontation now threatening the inner world he saved…not from the Sentinels who were supposed to be of his own.

"Ruger!" Annorah cried, panic in her voice. "If you don't, I will—!"

"Joe," Ruger said, a warning far from Joe's conscious thought. If he stood aside to face them, they would go down. The hell with them. *Lyn* would go down.

Lyn cried, "Ruger, please—"

It was all the warning he had. And he did the only thing he could. He jammed all his intention, all his ability, all his pain-ripped concentration, on driving *into* that flood, on splitting it farther and wider, on splitting it irrevocably…

"Ruger, *no*—God, Joe, stop scaring them! Just stop it! There's no reason for thi—" Her voice broke off, and when it came back it held a thin, sharp note. "Oh my God. Shields, people, *shields!*"

"I *told you*," Annorah snarled, dim in Joe's awareness, and metal worked against metal right before a sharp popping explosive sound and *sharp explosive pain and what have you done, little fool?*

"Annorah!" Ruger shouted, with the frustration of someone who knows he's too late. And then, with the sounds of a struggle, "No, Lyn—leave him. We don't know—"

"*I* know," Lyn said, panting, that struggle evident in her voice. "Let me go!"

And quite suddenly Joe couldn't quite concentrate any longer. He slipped away from his wedge of power; he watched it wash away in the flood, watched the flood reshape itself, reclaiming some of its former path. His numbed fingers groped over his chest…found the tranquilizer dart. His vision returned just in time to fade again. One knee quite suddenly went out from under him—the other followed. There he wavered for a moment, finding Lyn's desperate face, finding her arm secure in Ruger's grip in spite of the way she reached for him.

And then, as he flopped to his side in the pine needles and cinder gravel and packed dirt, his hands still twitching with his attempt to take back control and his inner sight completely blinded, she turned on Ruger. "He's not *shielded*—I told you—"

Ruger snapped, "Shea!" and Annorah suddenly cried out and Lyn repeated desperately, accusingly, *"I told you!"* And the world came crashing down and it landed on Joe Ryan.

Chapter 17

Lyn found herself huddled against Ruger's astonishing size. She'd come to trust him in Sonoita—seen him treat Dolan Treviño with compassion before anyone else understood the truth of what drove the man.

But he hadn't stopped this from happening. And now he and the rest of the team crouched together, finally understanding what had come down upon them if not how or why, everyone's shields at full and Shea's layered over all—while Lyn and Lyn alone reached out to cover Ryan. Teeth gritted, panting slightly with the effort, she still managed to demand of Ruger, *"Help him."*

Not that she blamed them for not seeing it coming. She almost hadn't seen it herself.

She should have. She should have known—should have been able to read Ryan's posture, his strained features gone sharp and a little bit hollow. She shouldn't have given so much weight to Annorah's fear, to Ruger's wariness. "Help him!" she repeated, crawling away from the protective huddle.

Ruger easily caught an arm around her waist. "Shea."

"It'll thin what's around us," Shea said.

"We're *all* holding shields," Lyn said. "Ryan has nothing!" Not strictly true. He had her. But against *this?* God, what if this was more than just a surge—

"Ruger," Annorah whispered, voicing that exact thought. "This isn't it, is it? This isn't—"

Ruger snorted—but gently, not disturbing anyone's concentration. "None of us has shields enough for this mountain if it really blows."

"Got him," Shea said after a moment; Lyn sagged with relief. And there they waited, listening to each other breathe—Ruger slow and deep, Annorah agitated, Shea barely discernible at all, so deep was his concentration. Lyn's breath hitching on emotion, her eyes fastened on the lone crumpled figure of a Sentinel tranked and left to face this tsunami of power on his own.

"He didn't deserve that," she said, her voice small, trembling with the tension of her body. She took a breath, steadying herself—and Annorah erupted, incredulous.

"Are you insane? You're the one who warned us! God, he just about went into a trance right in front of us, calling this down!"

Lyn took Ruger completely by surprise, a twist and a lunge, a swift grab at Annorah with an ocelot's speed—faster than the bear, faster than Annorah's human reflexes. Still on the ground, on her elbows with her fists wrapped up in the soft material of Annorah's simple boat-necked shirt, jerking the other woman in close. "You," she said, "are an idiot. *This is killing him.* Do you get it now? He couldn't call that power down on *us* without calling it down on *him*—and it hits him a whole hell of a lot harder than it would hit any one of us!"

Annorah, already pale, shrank back from her—and had nowhere to go, not with the four men crowding in around them, all crouched down low in an instinctive duck-and-gather-against-the-storm reaction. And now it raged outside them, outside all these layers of shields.

"It better be enough," Lyn said through her teeth. "You'd just better hope it's enough."

Ruger's hand landed on her shoulder, tightening in warning. But Maks shook his head. "Hell, Ruger, you think it's a small thing, one of us takes another down like this?"

The strain of the shielding showing in the muscles of his jaw and down his neck, Shea said, "Could be she was mistaken. That's not a chance we could take."

Lyn shoved Annorah away from her, exaggerating the release, her fingers splayed wide. "You think? Or did you happen to notice that things didn't get bad until you tranked him out?"

Disbelief wrote large across Annorah's face—and then she shut down, shaking her head. "I was too late, that's all. It could have been *worse.*"

But at Lyn's back, Ruger rumbled in what could have been interest—or could have been disbelief. "You're saying he was holding it back?"

"I'm saying he felt it coming long before you even imagined it." Lyn looked at Annorah as she said it. "I'm *saying* that he not only protected you, you have no idea what he went through to do it. This corrupted power is poison to him!"

Annorah only shook her head again. "And you *believe* him?"

Lyn growled deep in her throat, lost for words—her mind filled with the sight of Ryan sagged against the rental car after exposing himself to save the family at the gas station, at his dazed struggle after the contact with the museum artifact…to his lost expression out on the deck, when he'd gotten trapped away from himself.

Michael saved her the trouble. "Just offhand," he said, "I think she believes him."

Lyn finally found her words. "I'd rather work with him than you," she told the woman. "Anytime. He's pushed himself to the limit to cover my ass…repeatedly. But you'd take down one of your own rather than risk your own fears."

Something in that got through to the woman; she twisted away.

"Doesn't really matter now," Ruger said. When Lyn glared at him, he shook his head. "It *matters,* but…it's been done. There's no undoing it. When this fades—"

"Soon," said Shea, no longer looking so strained. "Now, if we want. It'd be unpleasant, but not unmanageable."

"A moment," Ruger said. "But even if he comes out of that trank a happy team player…Lyn, it's not going to happen. He's out of this one."

"What?" She let him turn her with the hand that had never left her shoulder. "*Why?* Ruger, he's the only one we've got who can manage this kind of power—"

"And maybe we need that, and maybe we don't. If we tackle this from the Core end of things, we've got enough team. But even if we didn't…do you really think we can trust him, after this? If you were him, would you trust *us?*"

Lyn closed her eyes—first to think about it, and then

in defeat. "No," she said. "If *I* was him, I'd tell you to fuck off. But you have to understand—" How to explain his dedication to this mountain? To its widely varied peoples? "He should be able to answer that question himself." *If he's able.*

Ruger gave an abbreviated shake of his head. "There's too much at stake."

She put a hand on his wrist where his hand still lingered on her shoulder. "Just *ask* him. He'll tell you, one way or the other."

"Oh, *right,*" Annorah snorted.

Ruger tipped his head at her. "That's it exactly. It's not a matter of whether he's trustworthy. Not anymore. It's a matter of whether enough of us trust him. Given more time, we'd work it out. But this is just a taste of what will happen if we don't stop Gausto's clueless stooges from tapping this mountain."

"But…" Lyn's voice fell to a whisper. She looked over Annorah's head to Shea, who nodded, and to Michael, who shrugged reluctant assent. To Maks, who couldn't meet her eyes. She didn't bother to look at Annorah at all. "That's not right. It's not fair."

"Not to Ryan." Ruger agreed more readily than she ever thought he would, tightening his hand on her shoulder in a manner that was meant to be comforting.

She shook it off, sat on hard dirt and grinding cinders and wrapped her arms around her knees. "I couldn't understand how someone so basically generous and honest could be so cynical about brevis. I guess now I do."

"Lyn," Ruger said, and his attempt to speak gently merely lowered his voice to a rumbly undertone. "We'll make sure it doesn't get out of control when it comes to debrief. But we have to work with what we've got…however we got here." He glanced at Annorah. "You won't be in the field again on this one, Annorah."

She took it like a slap, and Lyn should have felt some satisfaction at it—at the "But—" Annorah couldn't help but say.

Ruger stopped her. "What's in play is in play. You're a big piece of that."

She *should* have taken some satisfaction in it. But all she could do was look outside their safe little group to the rangy, limply twisted form of the man who could ride power…and who had been taken down in its path by his own.

And still Shea shook his head, and still Ruger kept a tight hand on her shoulder, as if he sensed that she would bolt out from under the shields at the first opportunity. Out of desperation, Lyn reached for Ryan with her inner voice. *Ryan.* Ryan.

Nothing. No response whatsoever. Not so much as the stray tickle at the back of her thoughts, just the dull sound of thoughts going nowhere. *Dammit.* After a lifetime of being perfectly comfortable alone in her own mind, she suddenly couldn't bear it? "Ryan!" she called, giving in to that futile urge. "Ryan, *please*—!" Please what? She didn't even know. She gathered herself…

"Lyn," Ruger murmured.

"No!" She turned on him, fierce and fed up. "Shea has shields out that far. I have shields out that far. If it's enough for him, it's more than enough for me."

Ruger exchanged a glance with Shea; Shea gave a little shrug. Ruger's grip eased and Lyn scrambled away, never quite making it to her feet.

"Ryan," she breathed, hands hovering for a moment,

not quite sure where to touch, how to touch. Gently, she turned him, bringing him back to rest across her knees—and gasped. Blood from his nose, blood from his mouth, blood from his ears… Oh, God, blood from the corners of his eyes, and he stiffened under her hands, his breath faltering with pain. And when he cracked his eyes open, the whites, too, were bloodred….

"Ruger!" Her horror put command in her voice, and damned if he didn't respond to it—albeit after the faintest of hesitations. He loped on over and knelt across from her, cursing softly. She glared. "I told you," she said. "I told you *all*."

"Quiet," he said, brusque if not unkind. "Let me look."

She'd seen this before—seen him work his own wonders, as he had with Dolan Treviño in the highlands of Sonoita. But this time, she didn't like his frown—didn't like the look on his face at all. "He's bleeding everywhere," Ruger said, and not quite matter-of-factly any longer. "What the hell was he doing, standing up in front of this?"

"Stopping it," she said bitterly. "Turning it. And if your precious communications expert had let him finish, it wouldn't have done this. He would have turned it away from us all."

He spared her a quick glance, one hand resting on Ryan's shoulder, one over the center of his chest. "You're assuming."

"No," she said, her voice tight but her hands ever gentle as she held him. "I'm believing. I'm trusting. I might be too late in that…but I'm doing it."

From the remaining huddle, Shea called, "It's passing—I'm dropping the extra shields. Hold your own and you'll be fine. I'll keep 'em on Ryan."

"Good," Ruger said, not looking away from whatever his inner sight showed him; his hand moved from Ryan's chest to his solar plexus. "Bring my bag, will you?"

"Ah," Shea said. "The noxious superbrew."

Ruger muttered, "It's going to take more than that."

It brought a chill to Lyn's spine, there in the heat of the summer day. She looked away long enough to find Annorah, to catch her eye and to command without apology. "Go inside and find a towel—dampen it."

Annorah did not argue. And Maks said, "I'm going to do a circuit. There could be fallout."

"I'll come with you." Michael showed no interest in returning to the amulet that had so intrigued him before the surge; Lyn caught his eye, stricken, checking to see if she read him right…that the surge would have obliterated what clues had been left to find. He gave her the slightest of shrugs—an apology—and headed out after the other man. Moments later the woods relinquished a brief flicker of flashing electric blue, barely visible against the daylight.

Annorah came out with a kitchen towel, warm and damp, and handed it over with impersonal distance. Ruger didn't appear to notice her—but he spoke nonetheless, startling her. "Annorah. Take my laptop. Hook it up to Ryan's router. Nick is waiting to hear from us. See what you can learn about brevis's take on this surge."

"All right." Annorah straightened, as composed as if she hadn't just faced the man she'd injured so badly.

"Annorah," Ruger added, catching her as she stepped away, waiting until she stopped, still without ever looking at her. "Don't touch anything else. Don't look at anything else. Don't snoop into anything else."

"All right," she said, more subdued at that.

"And leave that trank pistol here with me."

Annorah hesitated; she looked at Lyn and looked at Ryan and finally looked at Ruger again. Then she pulled the little pistol from the front pocket of her tunic and set it quietly on the ground. With another glance at Ryan— a more uncertain one this time—she hurried away.

Lyn glared after her—but only for a moment. Later for that. For now…there was Ryan. The blood ran down the side of his face, mingling with the dark tracings at his hairline; she wiped at it, and the corners of the mouth she had so recently kissed—*just last night*— and she realized she had also done this very thing just the night before, and she wondered how much one body could take, Sentinel or no.

And that's when Ruger shook his head. "There's too much," he said. "I don't have the resources…"

"No," Lyn said fiercely. "We do not take down our own and leave them in the path of danger and then *give up* on them!"

Ruger shifted from his inner vision to look at her— to *glare* at her, his eyes a remarkable gold-brown at this close distance. "No one's *giving up*. But—"

No buts. "Ryan," Lyn said, pressing the damp towel against his face. "Ryan, Ruger needs something to work with. He needs resources. *Power.* You can do that, can't you?"

"Lyn, he's nowhere near conscious. And he's better off for it. The most merciful thing—"

As if she was going to listen to that. Not when it could make the difference—and not when Ruger didn't *know*. Didn't *believe*. Didn't *trust*.

As Lyn finally did.

She leaned over him, leaned close—close enough so

their lips just barely touched. She reached out to him—
that sublime textured taste of him, the baritone hum faltering now, the sensual vibrations muted—and drew
him into herself. She filled every nook, every cranny,
reveled in what somehow was this time less arousing
and more completing, and let it reverberate back out to
him. Then she whispered to his lips, "Ryan. Ruger
needs energy to heal you."

So many things all at once, then—his eyes, half
opening to stare blindly in her direction, and then his
body stiffening, jerking against the agony of internal
damage everywhere, anywhere. The muscles on his
neck corded; his breath grunted out, turned to a long
groan.

"What I said," Ruger muttered. "More merciful—"

"Ryan," Lyn said, struggling to get the words out
through the stranglehold of emotion in her throat,
"Ruger can help you. But he needs power."

"It's not an Internet shopping cart, Lyn," Ruger said,
though his hands never stopped moving, never stopped
assessing. "It doesn't work that way."

"You don't know him." She held him as he twisted
against her, his breath harsh and panting, fresh trickles
of blood replacing the ones she'd so recently wiped
away. One of her tears joined it, escaped despite her
best efforts to blink it back. "You don't know what he
can do. Ryan, *listen. Ruger needs*—"

That was all she got out before Ruger, too, stiffened.
Before he swore copiously and creatively, yet never
hesitating to work with the new power he suddenly
had. He went in fast and deep, his trace thickening per-
ceptibly—musky to her taste, a sharp burr to her inner
sense, underlaid with a vibration so low in tone as to
be nearly subsonic.

It left her alone with Ryan, helpless to do anything but stroke his face and croon, kissing his temple and the strong angle of his cheek. His breathing came ragged; his torso trembled with tension. She wasn't even sure he knew she was there…at least, not until his hand crept up, hunting hers. She took it, then, though her eyes widened with the desperation behind his grip. But she held it close; she tightened her hold on him through her shields, knowing he'd feel that embrace if he could feel anything at all.

It might have gone on forever, there in the hot afternoon sun. It went on long enough for Maks and Michael to return; they sat on the porch bench. It went on long enough for Annorah to reemerge from the house and sit beside them, while Shea sat on the ground and dozed against the house. Lyn stroked back the dark, short hairs at Ryan's temple and realized they were naturally short— that the same went for the hair behind his ears and at his nape, and that his brows were more like that short dark hair than the tawny strands so wont to scatter over his forehead. She realized that the strength of his hand went right through to his fingers, that even his blunt-cut nails reflected the cougar with their sturdy thickness. She understood, then, that his body held strength she hadn't yet imagined, beyond the lean muscle and sinew all flowing so gracefully one to another, long legs to defined flanks to flexible torso broadening to those straight shoulders. Because then, finally, Ruger lifted his head—and although his eyes were dazed with fatigue and sweat glistened on his skin, his face held hope. It held expectation.

"Tell me," she said, and though it was meant to be a demand, it came out in a whisper.

He nodded, sitting back to swipe a forearm over his brow. "Yeah," he told her. "It's good. Still needs some clean-up healing, the sort his body needs to do on its own—but it's good." He shook his head. "Good holy hell, woman. Do you know what he did? Do you have any idea how impossible that was, a dying man plucking out power and handing it over all nice and neat? *Any* man handing over power like that? Brevis had no idea, I can tell you that much. This is one Sentinel who's never been used to full potential. Nick is going to shit bricks when I—"

"No!" Lyn lifted her head, horrified. "You can't tell him!"

It took him by surprise. "Lyn, he has to know."

She shook her head, more emphatically than she'd intended. "They'll never leave him alone. And if they decide they don't trust him? Think about it, Ruger. He's known what he could do. Yet he took what brevis dished out, he lived by their rules, he was *still* living by their rules when we came crashing in to blame him all over again."

"You don't *know* that he wasn't involved in that Vegas thing," Ruger pointed out.

"I do," she said, and realized she believed it. "I do, and I'm working on proving it. And meanwhile, he deserves the benefit of the doubt. Say something, and you ruin the rest of his life. Wait, and…all you've done is wait. For now." She hesitated—saw the doubt on his face. "Please," she said. "You know I like Nick. I trust him. But this…" She shook her head again, glancing over at the team at the bench. "*No one* needs to know this. Not yet. Please."

Ruger looked away. "Damn," he grumbled, and she knew she'd at least bought some time.

Ryan took a sudden deep breath, and Lyn realized what she hadn't before—that his body had relaxed, that while small spasms of pain sometimes took him, he no longer trembled with it. His color, once pale beneath the natural tan-to-gold hue, flushed to normal. "Hell," he said, half rolling over to sit up and getting only that far before falling back—Lyn caught him, and held him perhaps a little more tightly than she might have. "Now *that* was a wild ride." He frowned. "I'm not even sure what…" He stopped, shook his head; a hand went to his chest. "Did that—did she *shoot* me?"

"Trank," Ruger said matter-of-factly.

"Son of a bitch," Ryan muttered. "She let the cats out *and* she shot me? She is *so* out of here."

"I've got the trank pistol," Ruger told him. "But she stays, because she's what we have."

"Don't worry," Lyn said. "She takes a step wrong, I'll shred her." Good God, she even meant that, her voice fierce and edged with a little growl. Just like an untamed teenager, feeling Sentinel strength for the first time. She might have blushed—but Ryan was grinning. Ryan *liked* it. "You fool," she muttered, and bent down to kiss him—to kiss him long and hard, so fast caught up in it that Ruger had to clear his throat to get her attention again. She lifted her head and glared at the interruption, at which he laughed out loud.

"Okay," he said. "I get it. But we've got Core to find and tie up into little knots."

"Yeah, let's talk about that going after the Core thing," Ryan said. "Because I still think the key is up on the mountain. And I'm kinda wondering how long this thing with my eyes will last."

Lyn drew back to look at him—to look at clear, beautiful dusky hazel eyes, open to the sunshine…and not quite looking at her.

Not quite looking at anything.

She shot Ruger a glare, full of accusation. Ruger

himself started, and took Ryan's head between his hands, dropping into a quick but obvious inner sight and coming out of it with a sigh of equally obvious relief. "Can't tell you that, exactly," he said. "But it'll clear. You bled everywhere, man. Some places clear faster than others. Eyes aren't one of the fast ones."

Ryan stared off into his murky view of not quite anything. "Fix it?" he suggested.

Ruger snorted, clapping him on the leg. "You don't half want, do you? Sorry, man. This one is what it is. I saved your sight and your life. Let's stick with that. And here—you're going to want some of this restorative…" He reached for his backpack.

The team on the bench came immediately to life. "No, Ryan, don't do it!" "Run while you can!" "Save yourself!"

Ruger cast them an annoyed look. "He doesn't have to—I've already done that. But I've got a new formula I need to try out on a few volunteers, if I should hear of any."

Immediate silence.

"Impressive," Ryan noted. "But seriously, the eyes—"

Maybe Lyn was the only one to notice the little furrow of worry between his brows, or the extra tension flaring his nostrils. Or maybe not, because Ruger said, "They'll get better. Now come on. Let's talk about grabbing us up some Core."

Chapter 18

Joe stood on the deck with dusk all around him and shook a cat treat can, calling out with a short, deep purr—or as close as he could get, here in this human form. Maybe this was what it was like for most people come dusk and nighttime, this diffuse and murky vision, everything ill-defined and sometimes barely there at all.

Though he doubted any normal person saw through the dark bloodred hue now tinging his vision.

They'll get better.

Okay. When? Because Joe had things to do.

Or maybe not.

Maybe he'd been left behind in poorly disguised house arrest that would probably have disintegrated into handcuffs had it not been for these eyes of his.

Even by Lyn.

He shook the treats, called out into the woods. "C'mon, cats! You think I don't know you're right there?" But his coaxing tone belied his words, and he added another little purr right there at the end. After that he was silent, listening...hoping for the rustle of movement.

Utter silence.

On the other hand, that meant the birds were in hiding, too. Yeah, the cats were out there all right. He scattered a few treats across the deck and made his way back inside, setting the can just inside the door and feeling his way to the stairs.

Not that he blamed Ruger for this mess. The man had been exhausted, even with the trickle of power Joe had fed him. No, Joe knew who to blame.

She with the trank gun. She with the attitude. She with no field experience and too much fear and no damned business being anywhere near this mountain. *Son of a bitch.*

She who now played the role of jailer.

Annorah kept her silence, but he heard her moving around—keeping track of him, never quite letting him out of sight. But this was *his* home. He headed down the stairs with an easy step, one that defied the remaining fatigue and the aches threading through his body, the occasional jolt of lingering pain. *They'll get better.* At the bottom of the stairs he hesitated...not through uncertainty, but struck again by the feel of Lyn's hands on his face, in his hair, on his chest. Her tears on his skin. Her desperation in his ears. All things to which he had clung only an hour or so earlier.

Right. Before they'd left him here. *With Annorah.* Not because they didn't need him, and not because a power wrangler needed eyes to go to work. But because Ruger had seen too much, knew too much. Because they didn't trust him.

With Annorah, who had killed Mrs. Rosado.

He found that he'd sat on the bottom step somewhere in the middle of those thoughts, his forearms resting over his knees and his head tipped. Without his clear vision, the whispers and rustles of power seemed louder…or maybe it was just his imagination. Maybe it was simply his attention going undivided.

I could have helped, *dammit.*

Instead, Lyn was out there without him, guarded by a man who was doing nothing more than his job. Not that he had any reason to doubt Maks. But no one would watch Lyn's back better than Joe.

He pushed to his feet, caught the brief sensation of movement against his calf, and leaned down just in time to snag himself a cat. A pretty little tortie girl, to judge by the soft nature of her fur and the slight heft of her body. "Hey, you," he said, and lifted her up to face level to present himself for greeting. She rubbed her face against his chin, and then just as abruptly changed her mind and nipped him. He laughed and set her lightly on the tile, heading to the kitchen.

There he did a quick inspection of the counters—it was no good assuming things were as he'd left them—but found them clear. At that he began the comforting ritual of making coffee, barely hesitating even though the coffeemaker was a mere gleam of a sleek shape and the cabinet interiors proved to be nothing more than dark mysteries. Almost meditative, it was.

But not so engrossing that he wasn't completely aware when Annorah came up beside him, watching his every move, as if he needed to be supervised in his own kitchen. She no longer had the trank, he knew that. But she had *something*—something she thought gave her the edge, a false confidence.

She'd not been working with field Sentinels long if she harbored such illusions.

He left the coffeemaker to hiss and gurgle to itself; he turned to the island counter, to rest his elbows there. To wait. After a moment she let out a long breath she probably had no idea was so perfectly audible and turned to go. He didn't see it; he didn't have to. He struck, all the speed of his cougar, driven by anger. Driven, even, by a cat's penchant for play. *Not a nice kind of play.* He snatched her wrist; he pulled her back. He felt the clench of her hand and slid his own up to it, where he wrested away a stun gun. Little fool. Classic Sentinel defense against the Core for urban encounters—quiet, nonlethal, and it didn't leave dead bodies scattered around. But even enhanced by their field ops techs, it was never meant for use against their own.

For good reason. It never had a chance.

She cried out as he jerked her closer, tossing the stun gun away on the counter. He growled under his breath, his lip lifting ever so slightly. A warning. And he said, as it struck him anew, "You killed her. *You killed my friend.*"

She tried to break away—but he quickly felt the defeat in her. "I didn't know."

Because she'd taken Joe down, and he'd lost his power wedge, and the power surge hadn't been split quite enough, hadn't diverged widely enough. While the bulk of it had missed his sturdy log home, one wing had swept directly over Mrs. Rosado's house.

She had been human, not Sentinel. But she had been a modest sensitive. And she had been aged and vulnerable.

And she had died.

Michael had reluctantly reported it as they'd regrouped in the late afternoon; they'd found her in the yard with the little dog when they'd done their circuit of the area. In the background, he'd heard Lyn gasp, her soft, "Oh, *no,*" genuine and grief-tinged. Ruger had cursed, with equal feeling. And Michael...he started to describe how the dog was protecting his mistress, and couldn't finish.

Annorah had said nothing, even as she made arrangements to notify authorities and distant next of kin. It hadn't been good enough then, and it wasn't good enough now.

"That's the way it is, out here in the field," he told her, his voice gravelly with both grief and anger. "You did more than take me down—you did more than nearly kill *me*. Jury, judge, and nearly my executioner—all on your first time out. Good for you, eh? But this isn't just between us, Annorah—this isn't just a Sentinel thing. That's the *whole fucking point*. We guard this earth against what our enemies do to it. We protect those who know nothing about the forces in play between us. And if you forget that, and you somehow think it's about *you* in the moment, then you damned well end up killing wonderful old ladies you should have died to save."

Silence. He thought maybe she'd stopped breathing, but then he heard her, fast and shallow; he heard her swallow hard.

"Do you know how lucky we are," he asked, tightening his grip hard, "that no one else in the way of that power was a sensitive?" And that it dissipated before it reached populated areas...that they'd been this remote to start with.

That Joe himself had absorbed this much of it.

She'd thought she was his jailer. She damned well

might think differently now. Not that it truly mattered. Not when Lyn was out there without him. But even with Shea to shield them, to ward them…none of them could sense the power coming. If it surged in flash flood mode…

They'd go down before they even knew it was on the way.

"Stay off my back," he told Annorah, his voice strained. He released her arm, but neither of them moved otherwise, not for a long, silent moment. And then she breathed out the merest sigh, a shaky sound. He eased back, lost in his red-tinged world where the coffee gurgled to completion and the power played newly along his senses in unexpected skittery caresses, constant frissons between his shoulders.

Where she went after that, he didn't know, didn't care. His thoughts went to Lyn…to the hurt at her willingness to leave him behind, to the understanding that she'd had no choice. But mostly to the awareness that she was out there without a warning system, in a world gone awry with power.

Out there without *him*.

The last time Lyn stood in this pool of darkness, she'd been in Joe Ryan's arms. Oh, true, she'd been threatening to take his head off if he followed through with that you-must-be-kidding kiss—but he hadn't. And he'd never intended to, as much as she'd seen the hunger in his eyes.

Honest, that Joe Ryan. Honest then, honest now… *honest in Vegas*. She couldn't believe anything else, not any longer. Not after what she'd seen. She'd prove it, too, with her suspicions about those on the list Nick had sent that afternoon.

So now the Sentinels had failed Ryan once…failed

him twice. She couldn't help but reach for him, even knowing she lacked the skill to break through her own mind's silence. *I'm sorry,* she thought at him. *If I'd had any idea, I never would have left them in the house. I would have watched your back.*

Michael stood at the doorway of Gausto's hotel room, one hand held to the door, fingers splayed—not quite touching. His head bowed in concentration, he was for the moment vulnerable in the light. Early-evening darkness covered the rest of them—Lyn and Maks farther down the sidewalk, Ruger lingering against the tree-lined parking lot, Shea by the corner of the building.

Michael shook his head, took a step back. He lifted his head and said quietly, "There's something going on here. I can't quite get a handle on it."

"Core blood magic?" Maks said, standing close behind Lyn. He, too, had been in the Sonoita house; he had seen the terrible power of the blood magic Gausto had put into play—forbidden power he'd used so horribly against Meghan Lawrence and Dolan Treviño.

Michael waited for a couple leaving the adjoining restaurant to reach their vehicle, the doors closing them off from any hint of the conversation. "Blood magic needs someone to draw on it."

From the parking lot, Ruger said quietly, "We took the ancient workings before sending him on his way."

"That's why he's *here,* isn't it?" Lyn said, the scowl clear in her voice. "He can't let the septs prince catch up with him until he's offset that whole disaster." There in Sonoita, letting the man go had made sense—between his use of blood magic, forbidden by both the Sentinels and the Core, and his failure to secure the *Liber Nex* manuscript, it had seemed a certainty that his unforgiving septs prince would deal with him in short, merciless order.

They'd clearly underestimated the devious layers of Gausto's game-playing mind.

Ruger said, "We won't let him go a second time."

Lyn discovered that, to her surprise, she'd grown bloodthirsty. But the Core and the Sentinels danced in too precarious a balance to do anything but capture Gausto and turn him over to his own septs prince—the Core prince of princes. *Unless,* she thought—a touch too fiercely—he happened to get in the way of his own mishandled machinations of the mountain's power.

A polite tone in her mind startled her out of the thought, but it was nothing more than Annorah's incoming message signal. Lyn growled and Maks's hand landed briefly on her shoulder; she cleared her throat, embarrassed at that instinctive reaction. Whatever Annorah had done at the house, she was now merely doing her job—and a conversation that Annorah created was one that Lyn could very well join.

Progress? Annorah asked, a broadcast to the group.

At the hotel, Ruger said shortly. *Working on it. What's up?*

Annorah's hesitation reached them all, and Lyn found herself impressed. Few could broadcast such subtleties to casual acquaintances, never mind to a group. *Ryan says now he can pick up the power trace even without a surge. He wants to follow it.*

"What do you mean?" Ruger demanded it right out loud.

After what happened this afternoon...he says it changed— She stopped, as if interrupted, and came back with, *sensitized his perception. He says he can follow the disturbance to its root—*

He can't see. The interjection came from Shea, blunt and impatient.

Lyn suddenly knew exactly why Annorah had contacted them. *He wants us to come back. He thinks we can stop them faster his way.*

He's got a point, if he's right, Michael said. *We can sort Gausto out later.*

Maks made a disgruntled noise. *That's the thinking that got us into this mess in the first place.*

Well, not exactly. They hadn't expected to have to "sort Gausto out" at all. They'd thought his own would get there first.

"We're *here*," Ruger said, an eerie echo in her ears and mind both. "When we get back, we'll organize a tracer party."

Ryan could well be in on this conversation, Lyn knew. That he wasn't—that he was speaking through Annorah instead of as one of the group—told her how he felt about them. How he felt about himself. *Outsider.*

It's quiet now, he says. It's safe. Later, who knows.

"Annorah, this isn't science fiction. We can't beam to and fro as we please." Ruger tugged at his beard and abruptly silenced his outer voice—he, too, had noticed the approaching couple, fumbling with their keys and hauling luggage. Late check-ins. *Look, if we were there, we'd follow through. But we're not, and we need to finish this. If we can get inside this hotel room, we might well find a whole lot of answers.*

Silent amulets, Lyn added, in spite of herself. *Disappearing trace.* Things they'd need to understand for the future. "Look," she said out loud as the arriving couple closed their room door behind them, "we've got two cars. We *could* split up—"

"If anyone on this team was disposable, you wouldn't be here in the first place," Ruger said shortly.

Ryan isn't disposable, she thought at him, *and you*

left him behind easily enough. But it wasn't a group communication, not instigated and maintained by Annorah, and so the words went nowhere.

"Tell him we'll be back as soon as we can," Ruger said. "Tell him I get it."

And Lyn thought no, you don't. She thought she did, after watching Ryan at work, sifting through the faint streams and breezes of power. For him to have initiated this contact through Annorah—*she who had struck him down*—the change must be profound. If he'd been able to perceive faint streams far below the threshold of anything anyone else here could even imagine, what could he do now?

Follow it while it was safe.

While it wouldn't trap him in that gray place. While it wouldn't turn into a scourge that came down upon them all. While they could deal with Gausto and his gimmicks and tricks from a position of strength.

While they could save the mountain.

"Lyn," Ruger said, the single word an admonishment.

She faced him across the parking lot, from her dark pool to his shadowed tree, both of them able to see perfectly well through the night. "You're wrong," she said. "Oh, I'm here, and I'll do this thing—but you're wrong. Ryan's given you a chance to make right everything that happened today, and you just missed it."

In the silence that followed her statement, no one disputed her words. And finally, Annorah, faint and regretful, said, *I'll let him know.*

After another silent moment, Shea said, "Right. Back to the hotel room, then."

Michael stepped up to the door and went back to work and Lyn couldn't help but turn away, into the darkness that would be no camouflage against the Sentinel vision around her. Maks stepped away, offering her at least the pretense of privacy.

Deep breaths, that's what she needed. Because even if she didn't agree, even if she wanted with all her heart to run back to the mountainside and stand by Ryan's side, right now she was here, and she was part of this team. And she was worse than no good if she couldn't put her heart into that, too.

Michael shook his head. "It reads clean," he said, and Maks moved up beside him, an impatient gesture. "They've cleared out. No amulets, no nasties waiting."

Shea eased in from the corner. "Let's have a look at the place anyway."

"Should I—?" Lyn asked.

Ruger, too, moved in from the parking lot; even Maks left Lyn's side to move up on the door. Ruger said, "I think we can assume there's trace from whatever they were doing. That's one thing housekeeping will never take care of."

Michael snorted. "We won't muddy it," he assured her. He'd pulled an electronic card gizmo from inside his thoroughly pocketed leather jacket and had the thin card inserted into the door's card reader; it only took a moment for the gizmo's blinking light to glow solid green. By then the others had moved up, leaving Lyn in her puddle of darkness—knowing her strengths, biding her time.

Until Michael put his hand on the latch, and a brief but intense stench filled Lyn's senses. "Michael—"

Michael, too, hesitated, cocking his head slightly. But Maks's hand was already flat against the door, already pushing it open—and though he jerked his head to look at Lyn, the push was in motion and Lyn cried,

"Michael—!" as warning to them all, instinctively flinging herself down to the sidewalk.

For an instant, the night was silent—for an instant, she had the chance to think about her stinging palms and bruised knees, hard cinders rolling beneath her.

For an instant.

And then the darkness exploded in compressed power, lighting up her mind in a green flare so repugnant, so piercing…mental napalm with flying shrapnel, it blew through the men at the door, singeing up along Lyn's leg. She cried out in the pain and shock of it, turning her face away, her mind filled with a shriek that came partly from the explosion, partly from the combined mental outcry of her team. As soon as she dared, she looked back—knowing that anyone watching would have seen nothing.

Nothing but a small group of men dropping in their tracks.

Power tickled at him, called to him…both taunted and enticed him. He drew on it to keep moving, fumbling through the night woods with a cougar's sensitive whiskers and several years of intensive patrolling to keep him out of trouble.

"I'm supposed to stop you," Annorah had said, once it became clear the others weren't going to respond—that they expected him to sit and wait and fidget as it became more clear by the moment that the day had sensitized him to the even faintest whisper of power flow.

"You're supposed to do what's right," he told her darkly.

To his surprise, she laughed—short and a little bitter, definitely tinged with self-recriminations. "No one's put it in quite those terms before."

"Doing what's right can get you in trouble," he noted.

"Did *you?*" she asked, astutely enough. She sat at his dining room table, a heavy table of interlaced woods that Leandro had made shortly before he'd died. She no longer prickled with the need to take him down.

"Do what's right? You tell me. My partner and I had a business where we took care of people. Little things, big things…huge things. Dean took a gig relocating someone who crossed a Vegas crime boss—new identity, new life. I was running a cover job. The client made it out safely…Dean didn't."

"*That's* why he was killed?" In the murk of his vision, Annorah drew back, aghast. "Why didn't you just *tell* us?"

Joe snorted. "At first? It never occurred to me that the Sentinels could think I would kill Dean. Under any circumstances."

"But later—"

"It was the right thing," he said, his tone gentling at her confusion. "Compromising the operation after the fact would only have betrayed Dean's memory, and ruined the lives of the people he died to save. No, brevis never needs to know. If they can't believe in me, then… that's the price I pay for not being there when Dean needed me."

"It sounds to me like your job was specifically to be elsewhere," she said, brisk now, as though that could cover the slight wobble in her voice. When he didn't respond—not that he could, with the grip of it all in his throat now—she added, "Anyway, it doesn't seem to have changed anything. However things played out earlier today…you had a part, too."

"I did what was right," he said. "What I needed to. That hasn't changed."

"But—"

"I do what's right, when it comes down to being a guardian." He gentled his tone, hoping she could hear him this time. "Those are the decisions a field agent faces."

After a silence, she said, "I'm not likely to get another chance at that sort of decision." She took a deep breath and made an ostentatious rustle of paperwork. "Whatever. I'm busy here. I'd appreciate it if you didn't interrupt me for a while."

And so he didn't. He left from the sliding door in his bedroom, the one already cracked in hopes that the two wayward cats would return on their own, still warded on the inside to keep the other two in. He left in silence, so she would be able to say she hadn't heard him— although it would fool no one, not when she was supposed to be actively watching him.

Still. They did what they had to.

He'd run the first mile or so, the trail completely familiar beneath big platter paws, his mind's eye in complete certainty of his course. Slowly, then, the pull of the power and the trail had diverged, until he couldn't resist any longer—even though going off-trail slowed him considerably.

Surely his eyes were improving. Surely he'd gotten a crisp edge there in the corner of his vision, ever so briefly. Surely he'd be able to charge back into speed soon.

He skirted a blot of darkness that memory labeled a jutting formation of rough cinder rock, clawing up the steep slope beside it—and there at the top, paused, looking back down the mountain into featureless darkness. Not sure why, one foot poised to take that next step, and yet—

Sudden power blossomed before him, distinct and distant—not only an impact in his mind, but a sharp, unusual yellow-green in his hindered vision. Shards and sharp edges and dagger spikes, unnaturally contained and unnaturally released and yet…the faintest taste of familiarity.

That's mountain power, boy-o. Energy that had started out within the Peaks.

Energy stolen by the Core.

He found himself crouching up there on his high perch, ears flattened, tail lashing. If they'd wondered what Gausto intended to do with some of his stolen power…

Lyn! It didn't matter that he knew she couldn't hear, knew she wouldn't answer. *LYN!* He realized dimly that he'd turned around, that he now poised ready to plunge back down the mountain, all the way back into town if necessary—

Right, boy-o. Blind cougar headed down into the thick of Flagstaff. That'll turn out really well for everyone.

And still he stood there, on the brink of it, while the sickly yellow-green faded into nothing but an afterimage and the hint of power from above resumed its tug on him. Because…

Lyn…

Had she been there? Had she been affected? Hurt? Even—

No. He wouldn't think of it.

He took a step closer to the juncture of rock and slope. To the way back down.

God, Lyn—

His tail lashed. The power tugged at him. Power important enough to draw him out of the house without backup. Power significant enough to bring him up here with his eyesight still elusive and unreliable. And his own words, words he'd said so easily, so recently— *you're supposed to do what's right.*

And after all this time, after all this pain, he was supposed to choose between what was right for him and what was right for this mountain?

He snarled there, crouched on the rock. His claws dug in, breaking off crumbling chunks of the friable volcanic formation; his tail lashed hard enough to smack carelessly into that same rock from behind. Into that dark night he snarled the very agony of decision— not indecision, because the answer was clear enough even to one partially blinded cat. He turned in sudden fury, attacking the tree beside him—shredding the bark, sending chips of green wood flying.

And then he turned and flung himself into the night. Uphill.

Chapter 19

This is what they can do with some of that new power. This, without even really trying.

Lyn scrambled to her feet, running for them—breathless even before she started to move. "Ruger! Maks!" She reached them, found them sprawled like dolls, hesitated to touch them. "Shea! Michael! C'mon—one of you—come *on!*" The corruption lingered here, as cutting as acid—but more as a memory of the amulet's effect than the amulet itself, and even that much faded fast. Dammit, right before her senses the trace was disappearing—

Later. Clearly, the Core was covering their tracks in some new way. For now, only her team mattered. Michael had fallen within the room; Lyn stood at the threshold and hunted any sign of active trace. She found nothing; she took a deep breath and looked again, even as she bent to shake Maks. "Come on, come *on*—I can't drag you all back to the cars—" For they had to get out of public sight, even if it was only to lick their wounds. She had to rouse them enough for that, somehow. Back to the cars and close this door behind them, with no one the wiser.

With not even a flicker of new trace in her senses, she finally worked up the nerve to step inside, grabbing Michael by the shoulders of his leather jacket and tugging—only to discover that the friction factor of a solid Sentinel field agent against hotel carpet meant she hadn't moved him an inch. She cursed, prepared herself for it, and let the ocelot flow into her, through her—and dragged his ass right out of there. She shoved Shea's foot out of the way, closed the hotel door and plucked the dangling electronic gizmo free even as she surveyed them, piled around her feet in a tumble of limb and muscle.

They could be dying for all she knew. Or even dead, from the gray, waxen look of Shea's features. But she had to get them out of there anyway. She nudged them, she pushed them…she called on the ocelot and hauled Michael to his feet, draping him over her shoulder. It didn't quite work—even as the leanest of them, he was still too tall, and his feet dragged badly. She found the team's SUV, tumbled him into the backseat and ran back to the others, all the while waiting for someone to take notice of them.

Glory be, there was Maks on his hands and knees. She should have known. Strong, scrappy…he'd come to Sentinel training late, with more determination than most. "Maks!" She helped him up—his back to the wall and hands braced against his thighs—but she found nothing of true thought or understanding on his face. She pointed him at the SUV and put command into her voice as she reached for Shea. "Get to the car. *Now.*"

Ruger was the last of them—the biggest, the heaviest, and nearly too much for even the ocelot to handle. She couldn't begin to get her shoulder under his; she hooked her elbows under his arms and dragged him. Halfway there she heard voices and veered off next to a tree, throwing herself into the nighttime shadows and forcing her panting into fast, shallow breaths until they passed.

There was no way to get him into a seat, either. She pulled down the tailgate and rolled him into the back, pushing and shoving and grunting without the least dignity.

It was as she latched the tailgate again that she stopped thinking *gotta get them out of here, gotta get them hidden* and started thinking *what the hell am I going to do now* and *is Shea even alive* and *oh my God, it's only me now*.

But it wasn't.

She still had Ryan.

Annorah's polite and pleasant chime sounded inside her head as she double-checked the tailgate; the other woman gasped in greeting. *What* happened?

Trap, Lyn said shortly. *It's just me for now. You can probably tell better than I what kind of shape they're in.*

A pause. *Not good,* Annorah said. *I'll IM Nick for an emergency response team—*

Right. The Sentinel version of FEMA. *Wait! Why did you—?*

It doesn't matter now. Nothing we can do. Annorah took a mental breath. *Ryan went to follow the power down.*

But he can't see!

Said he didn't need to. A shrug. *Though I think his*

eyes have improved over the evening, so maybe— She cut herself off. *It doesn't matter. There's nothing we can do.*

Oh, yes, there was.

Lyn looked at her wounded team, strong men shattered by insidious Core power—defenseless. Counting on her. *Talk to them,* she told Annorah. *Stay with them. And come for them. Find Ryan's keys and take his SUV and come for them.*

Because she wasn't going to wait. She hesitated long enough to touch each of them—on the arm, on the shoulder—and to speak a few words of encouragement.

And then she got into her little rental beside the team SUV, and she ran red lights on night-deserted roads, and she went back to the mountain to find Ryan.

Chapter 20

Lyn abused the hell out of the little rental car, slinging it over narrow, uneven roads and rattling over the last section of dirt to slew into Ryan's driveway—his car gone, Annorah gone, the empty house blazing with light.

She stood in the yawning entryway, the cathedral ceiling soaring above, the darkened loft bedroom mocking her. He'd done it…he'd truly gone up the hill. He'd gone to find the power tap he'd been so certain of all the time—the one he believed she'd missed, the implication she'd been too furious to contemplate.

Except now it seemed as though he'd been far too right. She'd caught only a whiff of trace at the hotel room before her entire team went down—Michael hadn't gotten any more than that, not nearly enough warning. And if she'd missed that…if she'd missed the scent of the amulet anchor at the Elden Pueblo site until it went active…if she'd missed the scent of the amulet buried in landscaping gravel at the side of Ryan's house…

Michael hadn't come to any conclusions about that amulet; things had moved too fast. But the afternoon had only served to cement Lyn's suspicions.

Two of Gausto's men come looking for Ryan, but never pay him any obvious visit; later an amulet is found. Ryan comes down sick with a summer cold from which he never quite recovers. The power surges start, bearing his trace…and exacting a near-deadly toll on him.

They'd used him somehow, the Core had. Taken his connection with this mountain and captured it, twisted it, turned it into a tap to the mountain's strength. And though the trail should have been blindingly obvious, she'd missed it. Even now, believing it, *knowing* it, she still couldn't taste any part of it. She had only the faint trace from the top of the world, and now…

Now she reckoned she'd been damned lucky to find that much.

So now she'd do it Ryan's way. Pretty much as she should have been doing all along.

That *trust* thing. Hard to come by.

And she'd start with that easiest of things…following him. Not his scent, but the trace she'd once taken into herself, even if she hadn't fully comprehended that doing so also meant letting go. Of her past, of her obsession…leaving her with clear-eyed drive, leaving her with all her intent…but leaving her free to accept when it didn't belong. Free to allow…

Right. The trust thing. Not just between her and a backup partner, or her and her teammates, but between her and the man she'd let into her heart.

She covered her face with her hands, taking a deep,

steadying breath—accepting the truth of it. *Our men,* Mrs. Rosado had said to her, seeing it with her wise eyes long before Lyn. "All right," Lyn said softly, dropping her hands. "Mrs. Rosado, you're right. It's time we worked together on this thing."

She only hoped it wasn't too late.

Joe's paws ached, stubbed more times than he could count. Once he'd misjudged memory and put a confident foot out onto thin air, scrabbling backward in shock. A few moments of crouching in safety to realign his memory of the terrain, and he set off again—the slopes becoming steeper, the air thinner, the trees fading away into gnarled bristlecone.

When he broke above the treeline, he stopped, flanks heaving, his breath lightly misting the brisk air. Here, the partial moon washed the high slopes with unimpeded light...or maybe, finally, his eyes were improving. Now he moved out with more confidence...and now he thought he knew. He rarely approached it from this direction—it was a hard way to come—but he very much suspected that the top of the world was waiting after all.

Except as he grew near, grew more confident, the power trail changed, buzzing into obscurity. He stopped, pacing back and forth on the edges of it, and finally, perplexed, retreated to think. For the power had never changed in nature, regardless of how it had surged and waned over the days. It was his luck that he hadn't been mowed down by another flash flood.

Because the Core had been busy laying the attack in Flagstaff?

That depended, didn't it? On whether they were truly triggering the surges, deliberately unleashing waves of power when they were ready to harvest—or whether the events were as random as they'd felt.

They'd gotten more profound, there was no denying that. Joe couldn't imagine the amulet that could capture the flash flood that had killed his friend and neighbor, that had pitted him against the Sentinels—effectively, against Lyn—for one final time.

Because he didn't fool himself. They wouldn't trust him after this. Not if this new sensitivity was permanent. Not when Ruger reported Joe's casual ability to tap into power—to hand it over to another.

His best bet was to run.

Except they'd probably send Lyn after him...and he couldn't do that to her. What worse betrayal for a woman still struggling with the damage done by her brother?

Getting ahead of yourself, boy-o.

Because she could have been right in the middle of that blast he'd seen. She could have been there, wounded, waiting for backup...waiting for him. She could be—

No. Not that.

Do this thing, and go find her.

Well. Supposing he made it through.

Just do this thing.

He headed into the power again—and ran smack into that unsettling buzz once more. A retreat, some tail lashing...he paced a careful arc, triangulating, more certain than ever that he headed for the top of the world. It was the place to which his gut instinct had first taken him; it was the place where Lyn had detected the first and only signs of Core presence here on the mountain. But whenever he crossed the line of the broad arc he'd created, the power trickle disintegrated into a low buzz that made his teeth ache.

Too close?

That hardly made sense. The closer he got, the sweeter it should turn, the purer.

One way to find out, really. *Just do this thing.* Stop the mountain from boiling over, stop the vulnerable from dying in the path of the power, stop the Core from harvesting it for their mysteriously silent amulets. Find his way back to Lyn.

Do you hear me? I'll be coming for you.

Of course she didn't. Not able, not willing.

Lyn wasn't as big as Ryan's cougar, but she was light and swift, and she followed the strongest of traces.

Not to mention that she could see perfectly in the light of the partial moon, especially as she approached the tree line. A clear view of the alpine meadows rose above her—including the incongruous round bubble of darkness with moonlight glinting off its rotors.

She hesitated behind a particularly gnarled tree, instinctively concealing herself. A helicopter? Here?

Ryan must have rubbed off on her; her first reaction was a quick wince for the damage being done to the delicate high-altitude plants and soil. And her second was a tangled bundle of *what the hell* and *it must be Gausto* and *does Ryan even know?*

She doubted it; this trail was upwind. And there was no way he would have seen it. The Core was here and he didn't know it—unless they already had him.

She lowered into a hunting crouch, contemplating the man within the machine. Pilot? If she took him out, she could cripple the rest of them—trap them here. Even a feral house cat could rip a man to shreds, and

Lyn's ocelot could do much worse. It wasn't the
Sentinel way; no, the Sentinels tried to downplay the
powers that had led to the original conflict a thousand
years earlier. Stun guns and clever ploys and the occasional truncheon, with most transgressors turned right
back to the Core for justice—which they usually got,
for the Core was not merciful with those who failed, or
with those who bumbled enough to draw attention to
their activities.

Gausto had plenty of reason to be wary of his own
people…plenty of reason to push this gambit to the
limit. But still she didn't move, aside from the twitch
at the very end of her long and graceful tail. Because
reason enough to restrain came with thought of Ryan,
who didn't know of this chopper, or of Gausto's
presence. Or else might already be in the hands of his
men. If only she could warn him…

She reached deep, pushing against her own boundaries. *Ryan! Ryan, beware! Gausto is here!*

Nothing. Nothing but the dull flat echo of her own
words within her own mind. She shook her head,
hard—small ears flipping, luxurious fur rippling. Tried
again. *RYAN! Watch your back! Gausto—*

Nothing. Trapped words, going nowhere, just as they
always had. She'd never cared; she'd never wanted to.
Team communications had always been enough.

Until now.

Ryan!

Joe lowered his head and pushed past the line he'd
paced, ears flattening as the power grated against him.
He clenched wicked big-cat carnassials, squinted eyes
that couldn't see much anyway, and felt his way toward
the top of the world, lichens and delicate ground cover

beneath his pads, summer grasses brushing his belly. Ahead loomed the rock formation; before it, the spring, burbling with winter snows and recent monsoon storms. The buzz shredded into feedback reverberations; he sank lower into the grasses, stalking the power... breathing only in the lightest, shallowest breaths, lest it disturb the tenuous hold he had on the power root. One step... another...

There came a moment when he realized he was no longer moving. That he hadn't taken that next step. That it was all he could do to hold his ground.

That he was no longer alone.

"So. The great Sentinel finally figured it out."

If he hadn't been already frozen in his internal struggle, the astonishment of hearing those sardonic tones— here where only the hardiest hikers managed the official trails during daylight hours—would have done it. He forced nigh useless eyes open in spite of the discordant feedback shivering its way along his bones, hunting them—how many, how well armed—and knew that he had, as Lyn was also wont, allowed himself to become buried too deeply in his power-tracking riddle. He might not be able to see them clearly—even now, just dark, man-shaped blots in the night—but he could smell them. He could hear them. He *should* have.

But he hadn't, and now he was surrounded.

One of the men dumped the dark form of a body beside the spring, straightening with evident relief in his posture and tone. "You really want to—?"

"I might not have the ancient texts any longer, but I remember enough." That voice held command and self-assurance—perhaps a little too much of both. Still flattened to the ground, Joe nonetheless tipped his head in that direction. Gausto himself? And surely he wasn't referring to blood magic. Not here. Not at the top of the world. Not to sully this spiritual place. He couldn't help but paw at his eyes, desperately wanting to see—to know the details. Who had died? And how? Surely not one of the Sentinels—surely these men couldn't have made it up here from the explosion he'd seen, not so quickly.

"Ah," said that same man he'd thought to be Gausto. "Is that the problem, then?" He circled Joe, long, measured steps—just out of reach, with Joe still hugging the ground, out of balance and battered by noisy power. Weakened by it, he realized—not as dramatically as with the power surges, but more insidiously. More consistently.

Gausto stopped in front of him again. Joe knew him from reports and photographs, could easily fill in his features—the olive-dark skin tones, black hair slicked back and caught in a silver clasp, bold silver earring, strong features. Not unhandsome features, were it not for the habitual expression riding them, arrogance stamped clear. It came through strongly in Gausto's sudden hard laugh. "You can't see worth a damn, can you?"

Figured that out all by yourself, did you?

Someone outside the circle said, "That last power surge—I told you someone interfered with it. We're lucky it killed only Arno. This thing has gotten out of hand, drozhar. We need to pull the tap and get out of here. We already have more amulets powered up than we ever imagined, and with the way this method allows us to tune to—"

"Shut up," Gausto said, flat and cold.

The other man shut up.

"You have the blanks?" Gausto asked, that same quiet, deadly voice.

"I have the blanks." Very careful now, oh yes. "The pilot informs me the chopper has passed high altitude pre-flights and is ready to go."

"Then you may continue to shut up. Unless you can offer suggestions about using this particular Sentinel to our advantage."

Hell with *that*. Joe pulled up a cautious thread of power. Not something he could form, because forming power wasn't something he'd ever done. But the right power, pushed at the right time, could interfere with whatever Gausto had planned. The right power, at the right time, could even plug the tap they'd made. All he had to do was find it—and the power itself could do that, sweeping out before him until it reacted.

All right, boy-o. It's not much of a plan, but it's a plan. And it was better than sitting here blind and stuck while they figured out how to *use* him. So Joe pulled up his wee thread of power, and he cast it out before him.

He expected it to snag on something, to tug forward. He expected an attraction of power to power, with his own thread as a dowser.

He didn't expect the area to erupt in a sparkling of inanimate fireflies, sharp slivers of power glowing sickly yellow-green. He didn't expect his senses to erupt harsh, roaring feedback, startling him into a yowl of pain and surprise. He instantly lost his grasp on the faint thread of power; it dissipated, leaving him panting against ground that no longer seemed solid, flanks heaving in a quick pattern of distress.

Gausto laughed again. "Didn't work, did it? You can rest assured—whatever you tried, whatever you try next, it's not going to work."

Joe snarled. This was *his* place, *his* turf. Not their playground, not their plunder.

Abruptly, Gausto walked away from him. "Onfroi, watch him. I will prepare the blanks—and we will bathe the amulets in his blood as they absorb the gift of power he has released for us."

There were so many things wrong with those words. Bathe amulets in his blood? The gift of power *he'd* released? No, no. No way.

Gausto crouched in shadows impenetrable to Joe's eyes, and added, "We need him alive until the last surge has been triggered, but don't take any chances. Shoot him if he moves. Just don't make it a killing shot."

Nothing right about that, either.

The dark blot that was Onfroi moved up closer. A squatter blot than Gausto, and not nearly as graceful; no doubt his finger was already on the trigger. Joe settled into place, trying to look as innocuous as a furious cougar could ever look. His tail betrayed him, lashing out his fury…revealing his intent, if the man could but read it.

Because Joe might be reeling and blind, but he could see one thing for sure—and he could see it more clearly than the Core goons, who were blind in an entirely different way. They hadn't seen the firefly shrapnel; they hadn't felt the distinct and startling results of two clashing powers. *Feedback,* he'd been thinking, in description of what he'd felt upon closing in the spring.

Feedback, here, in the power *he'd released*.

With the power surges that Lyn insisted tasted of his own trace.

And the amulet at his house, and the illness that never went away, and the power that built up to scour through his system. He understood it now…that it was *because* of the trace, because of the similarities to himself. It was himself but not himself…and so it had

triggered a reaction within, as if he'd suddenly contracted a bizarre autoimmune disease only a power-
wielding Sentinel could expect to face. Feedback,
indeed.

Throwing his power out there within range of the tap
had created the same manner of reaction…this time on
the exterior. And Gausto's men had absolutely no idea
how much he'd learned from it.

Not to extend any more power, that's for sure.

In fact…

If he made this possible, if he somehow fed this
power…

Then he'd have to stop doing it.

Somehow.

Easier to stop breathing.

Somehow.

They had him.

Lyn couldn't tell just how. She only knew he
crouched, immobile, while Gausto paced freely
around him, his gestures taunting and the barely
audible hints of his voice the same. Two men lingered
within range; a body lay off to the side, near the
spring—near where she'd once scented the mere hint
of amulet corruption. Beside that, a small day pack
and several flashlights, all of which they'd wisely
chosen to set aside. Smarter to let their human eyes
adjust to the partial moonlight as well as they might,
than blind themselves with flashlights that could only
cover a tiny area.

Damn. She'd been hoping they weren't smart.

They hadn't been smart enough to look up on this
tower of rocks above the spring, anyway. At least, not
yet. For although she'd come up on them on Ryan's

trail, she'd been too wary to come close; she'd circled around and settled in up here. Watching. Assessing. Trying to understand what held Ryan so thoroughly pinned, his ears flattened to his skull, his entire body flattened to the ground in misery.

One of the men stood over him now, gun in hand, ready to shoot at any wrong flick of that black-tipped tail. But Ryan offered no resistance, and only the steady, heartbeat presence of his trace reassured Lyn that he breathed at all.

Off to the side, Gausto crouched with the second man—Amulet Man—who had shaken out an array of metal disks strung on thick, broad ribbon. It was how they differentiated certain amulets, she knew—the type of cording.

She'd never seen one on this ribbon before.

"It's the last time," Gausto said, with the air of someone repeating himself. "Make it good."

"That's why we're doing this on-site again," the other man said—with the similar overly patient air of someone who'd like to be irritated at repeating himself, but who knew better.

On-site again. They'd been here once, then, to set it up—coming in by the trail as Lyn had tracked them. And now again, via the helicopter. But not between. No wonder Ryan hadn't found signs of them when he'd hunted earlier this very long day—but he'd been right. The key had been here all along.

Amulet Man arranged the medallions to his satisfaction, an equidistant array around the edges of the spring—and then made a second row, and a third. Enough to power a large city. *Or destroy it.* While Gausto watched, he dragged the man's body to the uphill side of the spring, wedging it head-down between two of the amulets. Finally, he looked up; his face was as hard-featured as any of them, but it showed reluctance clearly enough. "Are you sure—"

"I said it, didn't I?" Gausto snapped at him.

"Drozhar," Amulet Man said, evidently a creature of much courage, "Arno is dead because the last surge was so very strong. I cannot say what will happen here if you mix in the blood magic. I had no chance to study—"

Nor ever a chance to finish his thoughts, it seemed. Gausto interrupted him again, this time reassuring, all-knowing. "Arno is dead because he was careless and greedy. He thought he could take some of that power for his own. And *I* have studied the blood magic. Did I or did I not bring Meghan Lawrence back to life?"

Lyn's whiskers crimped. Right, *after* Meghan had sacrificed herself rather than let him use her to find the *Liber Nex*. And Gausto had had his little blood magic cookbook right by his side. *Blood magic.* Did he really intend to bleed the dead man straight into the pure, clean stream at the top of the world?

"Do it," Gausto said. He handed the man an object— glass, Lyn thought, but couldn't be sure.

Amulet Man took it as he stood, groping in his pocket to come out with a knife—nothing more than a pocketknife that he pulled open with a practiced flick of his fingers, but it was enough to do the job. He knelt beside his dead companion and flicked the blade precisely beneath the slack jaw.

Lyn smelled the blood before she saw it, nothing more than a sluggish dark trickle; it dripped slowly into the spring. She growled, deep within, and had to contain herself—they still didn't know she was here. She glanced at Ryan, expecting some reaction…but he hadn't moved. His layered, reassuring trace surrounded her, but Ryan himself… *Are you in there?*

But of course he couldn't hear her.

The man at the spring stood, holding the glass out to Gausto. A vial of blood, for Gausto and his blood magic connection. Gausto sealed it with an expression of anticipation, his face turning into something just a little bit less than human. Lyn's tail puffed up without her permission. Even Amulet Man turned away, using the excuse of exchanging the knife for one final amulet. He let it dangle in the air from its cord, twisting back and forth, his hesitation evident.

"Do it," Gausto repeated.

Amulet Man closed a hand over the amulet. He might have squeezed it; he might have muttered something. Unlike the other, somehow silent amulets, the stench of this one immediately flooded the area.

But otherwise? Nothing.

Neither Amulet Man nor Gausto seemed surprised. Gausto, clutching his vial of dead blood, added a layer of thick, tarry essence to the spring. Lyn flicked her whiskers, trying to rid herself of the taste of it, her black-edged nose wrinkling, her snarl silent but too reflexive to quell entirely.

And then she thought she tasted it, that extra layer of Ryan's trace, that initial buzz of swelling power. For the first instant, she leaned into it. Almost instantly she realized that whatever she felt, Ryan must feel a hundredfold. Right here at the source, with the power welling up right beside him—and tainted, she could suddenly taste that, too, the blood magic oozing in, stinging her nose, singeing her whiskers. In an instant she pulled her shields into place, tight and close. Because she didn't dare extend them to Ryan, even if they could withstand the strain. Holding back her sneeze, blinking watering eyes…for the first time in her life, Lyn suddenly wasn't sure her shields would protect her.

Such concerns quickly went background as Ryan's guard stepped back, gun raised; he looked over his shoulder to Gausto, hunting guidance. For Ryan snarled, but at nothing in particular, his claws scraping long furrows into the earth, but he threatened no one; mingled, his blood touched the air. Still the guard tensed, his second hand coming up to steady the gun. "Should I—?"

That's when Ryan slammed his own head into the ground. Once, twice. The guard relaxed, laughing. "The Sentinel's lost his mind."

Gausto glanced over. "Not entirely surprising," he said, while Ryan stilled, apparently having dazed himself.

Lyn's claws flexed into rock; her eyes closed into slits of restraint. *Not yet.* Surely there would be a moment when she knew to act, when she knew just what to do…

Gausto took a few steps closer, looking down on Ryan—flanks heaving, lips drawn in a reflexive snarl, eyes glassy. "It's been quite satisfactory, watching him decline. For him to be so close to the power tap, even as it only just opens…" He looked over at Amulet Man. "Do tell me this is only the beginning for him."

Amulet Man cast a grim unto desperate look at his drozhar and indicated the amulets arrayed around the spring. "If you cannot feel it, watch them."

Lyn found her gaze drawn to the amulets—found herself staring in fascination at the first, faint hint of a glow. That same sickly yellow-green she'd seen at the hotel, this time tinged with a ruddy red. Ryan snarled again, a weaker sound; he slammed his head into the ground again, a weaker movement. *Oh God. Not yet.* Surely there would be a moment…

Right. Up here at the top of the world. Alone, aside from a man who had trusted her and who had asked for nothing but that trust in return—but whom she'd left, following protocol instead of his good instinct, following orders instead of fighting to back him up. How could she expect a *moment* of inspiration, of knowing what to do? She'd already missed that moment, and now Ryan lay dying here at the top of what had been his world.

Amulet Man gave an exclamation of surprise; Gausto cursed. Lyn tore her gaze away from Ryan to search the spring, hunting for the problem, not finding it. She saw nothing but the men at the spring—Amulet Man's desperation, Gausto's fury and the dead man's blood slowly dripping into the sullied water, swirling and slowly drifting toward the rocky little stream to soak into the earth…the flickering amulets…

The flickering amulets.

"No!" Gausto said, and he whirled away from the stream, stalking swiftly to Ryan, who lifted a weak and wobbly head to offer a token, soundless snarl. "Stop! Whatever you're doing—" Rather than finish the sentence, he turned back just enough to jerk the gun out of his own man's hands, startling the man back; he emptied two rounds in quick succession, into the earth beside Ryan's head—so close beside that one round furrowed through a golden cheek, adding new blood to Ryan's face.

Lyn found herself up in a stalking crouch, ready to leap. *And do what?* She was a tracker working alone, the rest of her team sorely wounded, the man who should have been the foundation piece to that team lying in the clearing before her....

Gausto must need him alive. It came to her suddenly, as he neatly sidestepped a slow-motion swipe of Ryan's claw without reacting to it. He wasn't afraid of what Ryan could do to *him,* not now. But he was afraid about something that Ryan could do...was doing.... He glanced over his shoulder, found those amulets still flickering. Lyn, too, could suddenly perceive the failing nature of the power surge—no longer building, no longer steady.

Gausto raised the gun again, sleek dark semiautomatic—pointed it, and then, with a sneer of disgust, let it fall aside. Instead of blowing off another useless round, he walked right to the cougar and with no hesitation in his stride, slammed his foot into those heaving ribs. Then another, behind a shoulder blade, and another, in the vulnerable flank. "Whatever," Gausto said, and punctuated his words each with another mighty kick. "You. Are. Doing. You. Will. *Stop!*"

Ryan managed to curl around, his hindquarters dragging, to wrap a long front limb around Gausto's leg. Gausto grunted in pain and peeled himself free, but his face bore satisfaction—for the amulets glowed more brightly than ever, and Ryan flopped back to the ground in battered defeat. The power rose, swelling around them—and quite suddenly the ground trembled.

"Fortun," Gausto said, leaving Ryan without a second glance, his voice a warning gone deep. "You said the volcano would not awaken with your methods."

"I don't know!" Amulet Man said, his eyes gone a little wild. "The blood magic changes things—this might not be the volcano at all!"

Above, Lyn clutched at rock; bits and pieces of her

perch broke away and rolled down, bouncing along the grassy slope below. The spring burped giant bubbles of air, spitting stained water and slopping over its banks. Lyn spat a feline curse, unable to stifle it—but no one heard her over the rumble of uneasy earth.

Only Ryan appeared not to notice the quaking. After several attempts, he rolled to his chest, couchant again, his head barely clearing the shaking ground. He coughed, spitting blood. His eyes slitted closed—not with defeat, but with concentration.

Lyn felt it this time. The withdrawal of his trace, the cessation of his interaction with the world. Not shields, not boundaries, but a siphoning off of everything that was Ryan—leaving her suddenly empty, quite suddenly bereft. The alarm at the instability of the earth beneath her abruptly turned to something deeper, something sharper. What the hell was he doing? Was it something he should even try? Was it something he could *survive?*

She realized, then, that the grumbling earth had tamed to mere shivers, that whatever he was doing… whyever he was doing it…

It was working.

The spring calmed…the top of the world seemed to take a deep breath into quiescence.

Gausto, for all he couldn't sense power or changing trace, knew well enough that the amulets dimmed, one of them flickering cold. He cursed, loud and sharp, and whirled back to Ryan, *ran* back to him, drawing his leg back to deliver a blow worthy of a field goal kicker. "A rock!" he shouted to the man who'd once held the gun. "Get me a rock!"

The man stared at him, blank-faced, until Gausto raised the gun, staring straight down the sights. "Get. Me. A. Rock."

As the man scrambled to obey, heading for the base of Lyn's perch, Gausto delivered another solid kick into Ryan; the earth trembled as if in response. "I need you alive," he said, his voice as cold as anything Lyn had ever heard, "but not for long. But I don't need you conscious. *Ever again.*" He looked over toward the man. "A *big* rock."

Lyn growled deep in her throat. *Ryan!* she cried, as the man found a rock, a *big* rock, and hefted it with both hands, returning to Gausto. *RYAN!*

If he'd made this possible, if he somehow fed this power...
Then he'd have to stop doing it.
Somehow.
Easier to stop breathing.
Somehow.

Gausto's blows made little impact, not the second time around. Not with the fiery power of the nearby tap scorching through his blood, slamming into his thoughts until there was room for only the one. *Got to stop doing it, boy-o.*

Or maybe for two. For overriding it all came regret, and sorrow, and the overwhelming need to send out an apology. *I'm sorry, Lyn, that I didn't do this better. That I didn't* Make It Happen *for us.* But if he did this thing, she would be safe. They would all be safe.

So he fought past the lingering pain of the latest blow, up close behind his shoulder blade and damned if he hadn't heard a rib crack. He fought past the encroaching gray edges at his mind, half enticing and half nothing but agony. He focused on the thing to be done—that which he'd never done, had never considered doing...had never believed could be done. He didn't shield himself from the outside…he shielded the outside from *himself*.

He pulled himself within, and since he knew no walls that would keep that power there, he simply kept pulling it into himself. He drew it smaller and tighter and deeper, and the top of the world settled beneath him, relaxing. Without Joe's trace—tagged and tainted—it had nothing to lure it from its deep lair within the Peaks.

Triumph was short-lived; the cougar trembled around him, a distant sensation that seemed far too remote. So now he knew. *Easier to stop breathing, boy-o.* The cougar's paws drew up in a spastic manner, posturing in a neurological cry for help…or maybe just an outward sign of damage already done while Joe hid deep within, still pulling at his own essence.

He barely felt it when Gausto came after him again— true insanity this time, to pistol-whip a cougar face-to-face.

Or not, because Joe did little more than lift cold lips in a partial snarl; couldn't afford to distract himself, couldn't afford to return to the place where he'd feel any of it. Stay deep within, hold himself bundled in tight… constantly, endlessly drawing himself in so he couldn't be used.

"The rock!" Gausto cried, all but incoherent. "Bring that damned rock!"

The rock. The damned rock. To slam on his head. He had to live only long enough for them to feed their amulets, a giant glut of power that would do more damage than Gausto seemed capable of understanding.

Because none of them would live long enough to see

that done. The top of the world had told him as much, with its furious tremblings and deep-rooted anger. Gausto had tapped too deeply, too strongly; had disrupted the stability of even this most beneficently stable place on earth.

Yeah, boy-o, ready to blow.

And here was Joe, stuck inside his own head, pulling in power for all he was worth, just to keep it from happening. None of which would do a bit of good if—

"The *rock*," Gausto demanded, as someone grunted in the background. An instant of panic seized Joe, the cougar's body tightly postured, his back arching, his head arching back. Nothing he could do, nothing from the outside with that damaged and wounded body, nothing from the inside without opening himself to a connection with the top of the world all over again...

More than an instant of panic. A big, fat, ham-handed glut of panic, forcing a weakened snarl from his throat, forcing his eyes open just enough to see the looming shapes above him—

Ryan!

His legs, he discovered, still worked. At least, in reaction to Lyn's never-heard voice in his mind, shocking him into action. Clumsy, flailing action, but enough to deal, momentarily, with men who'd come to take him for granted; caught in the sweep of his claws, they went down, a substantial rock thudding to the ground beside them. In the background, Fortun gave a cry of delight; the ground rumbled with fury; stones and pebbles clattered around them, tumbling from above.

Ryan! Lyn, fury in ocelot, sprinted straight down the side of the rock formation, a blur with a long, graceful tail. She tore through Gausto's setup, claws flashing and accurate; they didn't see her coming. Whirlwind Lyn, slashing and ripping, left them bleeding, left them cursing, left them crying out in surprise. She pounced at Fortun, twenty-five pounds taking him in the chest and clawing up and over even as he staggered backward; she dug in deep to launch from shoulders, twisted in midair to flip back at him, and ended up completely latched on the arm that had a gun at the end of it; she sank her teeth into his elbow.

Joe heard the crack of bone from where he lay, the thunk of the gun against ground, his vision just marginally clear enough to follow the action. For she hadn't yet hesitated, and she didn't now—she ignored Fortun's howl of pain and sprang away to the layered circles of amulets, flipping them into the air, disrupting their pattern. She darted to the dead man, trying to pull him from the spring—and, thwarted by his sheer bulk, bounded away again, flipping Fortun's gun away into the darkness on the way past.

She ended up at Ryan's side, panting lightly, standing with her head lowered in obvious protective threat. *That was it,* she said to him, as if they'd always spoken mind-to-mind. *That was the moment.*

He wanted to respond, but there was nothing in him left to do it. He wanted to tell her that it had been for nothing, because he'd lost his grip on the inward retreat. He wanted to tell her that without his ability to pull *within* and hide himself—even if it meant losing himself—the unleashed power had reached its tipping point. The *it's gonna blow* point.

But he thought she had the idea, from the way the ground heaved and half the rock formation came suddenly tumbling down toward them. Or from the way Gausto shouted some unintelligible phrase and scrambled to his bleeding legs, the way all of them fled without bothering to snag so much as a partially charged amulet in their wake.

He thought from the way she flung her smaller body over his, covering his head and shoulders as best she could, she had a pretty damned good idea at that. *Run,* he tried to tell her—as if she could get far enough away for her shields to withstand any part of this. As if anyone would.

Some of it must have gotten through. *I'm not going anywhere,* she told him. *You can fix this. I know you can.*

But he couldn't.

He had nowhere to go, not anymore—and it was his very presence that now inflamed the situation, the very call of the his own nature to the tap Gausto had put into the mountain.

Here.

It wasn't so much a voice as a feeling. An unfamiliar feeling, at that. Personalities he'd brushed against without actually meeting; essences he'd encountered simply by being here and being who he was.

Here.

No explanations. No details.

Here.

Joe shifted, moving toward that invitation.

Ryan? Ryan, my God, don't die—stay with me, please, stay with me!

Here.

While his very presence inflamed the mountain, the earth's roar growing around them, the displaced rocks growing bigger, bouncing farther, trees cracking, the amazing thunderous crash of a small helicopter in the distant background.

And so he went. He had no voice to say *I'm sorry, Lyn,* but he had just enough of a rasping purr, just enough movement in his head to offer the faintest indication of a loving head rub. With her cry of desolate dismay echoing in his mind, he went.

Chapter 21

Gausto…gone again, as if Lyn cared. The dead man hung over the stream, amulets strewn around him—blackened and smoking, melting into the ground with a stench that seared her nose and mind both.

Gausto and his men might live out the night; they might not. She'd shredded them fiercely. They had no transportation, no gear, nothing but their slick city suits and their slick city shoes.

And they were on a mountain that hated them.

She closed away the thoughts of them. She reached inside for the human—cautiously, because she wasn't sure how the mountain might react, or how the change itself might be affected by the mountain's power. But she saw the familiar flicker behind her eyelids, felt the surge of change—felt it come cleanly upon her, and gave herself up to it. In the next moment she stood on human feet—knees that felt loose, legs wobbling. No time for it. She ran to the dead man, wrapping her fingers around the lapels of his suit and hauling him away from the spring, his head higher than his feet.

But no more than that. Let Gausto run, let the debris of his passing scatter behind him, let the chopper smolder in its hard landing. Clean-up crews would get it all. Lyn barely noticed it—the backpack, the blood on the ground, the rock formation on which she'd so recently perched now half collapsed around its own base, some of it precariously close to where Ryan lay, every bit as still as she'd left him.

She couldn't taste him. She couldn't feel him. When she went searching for the mountain's power, she no longer found his trace lingering within it.

As though he was gone. As though the cougar somehow breathed on without him.

Ryan... She ran back to him, stumbling over a fragment of the rock formation and going down—but not particularly caring, as long as she ended up next to him. She crawled the last foot, put a tentative hand on his leg...moved closer yet and let her fingers sink into the thick, dense fur at his shoulder. *Ryan, come back.*

She knew her voice was going out—just as it had reached him the moment before she'd pounced from her high perch. Now, as then, that mental call reached out past the confines of her own mind; it felt *alive*.

But now, as then...no one answered.

She inched closer, pulling his heavy head into her lap. Blood from his nose, from his ears...from the furrow on his cheek where damned Gausto had come too close with his show-off warning shots. Lyn stretched out the hem of her shirt, wishing she'd worn something more substantial. A jacket and shoes might be nice, too; she shivered in the chill night breeze.

Didn't matter; she'd take the ocelot if she had to. For now...she cleaned Ryan's face as best she could, running trembling fingers over the black lines at the edges of his white muzzle, over the fine, short hair between his eyes and up his forehead. His head lolled; his jaws parted slightly. His eyelids were open just enough to see the glint of his eyes...and that they did not move, did not respond to her. She hunted for him again—hunted for him endlessly, for any sign of his trace.

She still couldn't taste him. Still couldn't feel him.

"Ryan," she said, and her voice broke, "what have you done?"

The breeze bit into her bare arms, but... The ocelot had warm fur and could curl up through this high summer night with ease, but the ocelot had no hands to stroke this wounded Sentinel, this lover of hers. The ocelot had no fingers to caress him, even if those fingers were still stained with the blood of the men she'd so recently attacked.

"Ryan," she said again, only a whisper this time, "what have you done?" She kissed that massive predator's head on the space between his eyes and settled onto the cold ground beside him, one heavy leg over her shoulder, as close as she could get to the pale fur of his chest. Face-to-face, curled up into his warmth, his shallow breath stirring the hair at her temple, his powerful jaw just touching her brow.

Down below, the Sentinel emergency response team had no doubt reached Annorah and the wounded, choppering in as close as they could get, maybe even to the hotel parking lot itself. Nick himself might have come along, looking to sort things out. Flagstaff itself was safe; the Mrs. Rosados of the area were safe again—

the human sensitives, the vulnerables. The people who just happened to be at the wrong stoplight at the wrong time, without Joe Ryan there to put things to right before the accident happened.

Eventually, someone would come for him...for her. For now, she was in her lover's arms—whether or not he'd ever return to her. She relaxed, warm enough; she breathed in the distinct scent of him, for the first time perceiving only the scent and none of the trace. Her shields, drawn so tight, expanded to take him in.

And she fell asleep, surrounded by Joe Ryan and surrounding him, and barely aware of the tears on her cheeks.

Your people are coming. We cannot keep your Joe Ryan any longer. Call him back.

As Lyn slept, some part of her was aware of the cold ground, aware of the warm fur, aware of the weight of him where he'd slumped farther against her.

And yet deep within, she was simultaneously alert and aware and awake...and listening. Immersed in a cloud of featureless color—of white and blue and black and yellow, each aligned with its own cardinal direction—but otherwise lost.

Your people are coming. Call your Joe Ryan back.

She gave a mental blink, stymied by this dual state of being, scrambling to understand the voices. A chorus, a deep reverberation, children laughing at the same time old men muttered and young girls giggled.

We cannot keep him safe any longer. He must return to himself now, or go on his way.

Oh, *that* didn't sound good. But...

How—?

Laughter, then. *Find him.*

And *how?*

Only more laughter. *Are you a tracker?*

But I have no place to start! She wailed it at them, at all the voices…and the voices were silent. Gone. With her outer self safe and warm and tucked into the cougar's embrace… Oh, God, was he getting cooler?

Am I a tracker?

She had a place to start, all right.

I love him.

I know him.

So she went looking for what she knew, what she loved. She closed out all else, and she hunted Ryan's trace. She pulled out every bit of her focus, every bit of her skill, every bit of her determination, and she turned it on the most important trail in her entire life.

And she found nothing.

With the colors thinning around her, with her awareness of the cold increasing, her awareness of his shallow, stuttered breathing increasing, she found nothing.

She took a deep breath, her body reflecting silent effort, and into those thinning colors, she shouted, *Joe Ryan! I love you! I want you!* And then, after a hesitation in which she realized something felt unsaid, *Please…won't you trust me?*

Trust me…? The words seemed to echo back at her—until she quite abruptly realized they weren't *hers* at all.

Yes! she cried, wild with hope. *YES! Always!*

Always…? A little stronger, that echoed word, and with it…a mere hint of trace. *Trust me…?*

Always, she said, as firmly as anyone ever could. *Always, Joe Ryan, and forever.*

Chapter 22

Joe woke up naked.

No, nearly naked.

In his own bed, surrounded by his own cats—all *four* of them at that—and wearing his own boxers. Pillows everywhere, quilts piled around, the overhead fan on a lazy middle speed and a midafternoon monsoon storm beating against closed sliding-glass doors.

On a hunch, he rolled over just enough to rest his face on the pillow beside him, breathing it in.

Definitely Lyn.

Definitely holy cow *ow,* too. *Someone's been using your back as a dance floor, boy-o.*

"Ryan!" Lyn came out of the bathroom in a set of casual yoga pants and sleeveless tee, her face flushed, her hair curled and shower damp. "You're not supposed to be awake yet. I meant to have coffee ready for you."

"Ah," he said. "Just as well, then. *I'll* make the coffee." But he didn't move. He thought about how much it had hurt to do that very thing and he decided maybe he didn't need to be awake yet after all. Still…

"I have a first name, you know," he said. "It's Joe. My mother was kind of fond of it."

She shrugged, pressing a towel around the ends of her hair and then tossing it over the railing. Without hesitation, she crawled onto the bed beside him, ignoring disgruntled cats, her movement as unconsciously sinuous as her ocelot. "Ryan," she said, and purred it, her voice throaty.

"Oh hell," he said instantly. "Ryan it is."

"Uh-huh," she agreed. Her hand landed on his chest, settled there. It seemed restless. Mischievous, even.

"Careful," he said. "I think someone was using me for a soccer ball." Come to think of it— "Hey. What happened? And where is everyone?"

"You don't *know* what happened?" she asked, surprised. Her hand did indeed wander—over the flat planes of his chest, over the strong lines of his collarbones.

"Up to a point. Details…not so much." He blinked, held his hand up for his own inspection. "Aah, I can see every one of 'em. Ruger was right at that." He looked at her, then. "The team? Ruger? I saw the explosion…"

"At brevis medical." She wrinkled her nose. "But they'll recover. Shea and Michael took the worst of it, but we got word today—they'll live." She resumed her explorations, finding the side of his neck.

He sucked in a breath. *Definitely waking up, boy-o.* "We?"

"You. Me. Annorah. She's here until we finish sorting this out. Nick wanted instant communication."

"She's *here?*"

"Take a breath. She's in town right now. Your pantry didn't suit her. Besides, she's…changed."

Joe grumbled expressively. She moved her hand, quite deliberately, and he grumbled in an entirely different way. His hand closed over her wrist, there under the covers. Under the boxers. "You know," he said, "I can barely move."

"No problem." She smiled at him, a totally Cheshire-ocelot kind of smile. "I can move just fine. See?"

"Now that you mention it." His words might have been a little strangled, as she so swiftly straddled him. He caught her hips, stilled her. "Lyn…last thing I remember, I was up at the top of the world, severing the connection Gausto had forged between me and that power tap. And Gausto kept—" His hand went to his cheek; he found a stiff scab there, a long furrow tracing his cheekbone. *"Gausto."*

"We don't know. His chopper went down, but his blood trail veered away from the landing site. We don't think he ever reached it—the pilot panicked and left without him.

"I have some of Ruger's salve," she said. "The response team doesn't think it'll scar too badly."

Joe frowned, but not in concern about any scar. "And then I couldn't…and I went…somewhere else…?"

Lyn shrugged. "My invitation came without instructions or explanations. I was only there long enough to find you."

"I remember that part," he said, and tightened his hands on her hips, shifting against her so she sighed and let her head tip back. "I remember being found." And for a few moments he enjoyed those memories— *they* enjoyed those memories. Sighs and gentle pressure and soft touch. Until, of course, he had to frown and add, "But I haven't the faintest idea how I got *here*."

"The response team that came for Ruger's crew," she said, somewhat distantly. "You think no one noticed that ruckus on the mountain? They got up there plenty fast, got us down just as fast—had their own chopper. And healer, which is why you're able to do—yes, that—"

Barely. But barely enough, stretching carefully, yearning carefully, touching carefully. Until she brought him to another stop, her eyes coming open and her hands stilling on his torso. "How could I forget?"

He narrowed his eyes. "Is that a trick question? Or am I supposed to guess something I'm not supposed to have forgotten but don't have a clue? Because I mean to tell you, there's a *lot* I haven't put together yet—"

She stopped him with an expedient lick and nibble, precisely placed. "Hush. No. This isn't something you know. This is about me clearing your name."

"Say what?" He sat straight up—or tried to, but every part of his back from butt to shoulders seized and dropped him back down again.

"For one thing, we've pretty much confirmed it— that amulet buried beside the house is how Gausto tied your trace into the mountain. Mrs. Rosado's visitors left it, no doubt—and right after that, you got sick with the cold that wasn't a cold. For another thing, I asked Nick for a roster of Sentinels in the Vegas area during the time of Dean's killing. Before, after, etcetera. And then with what Annorah told me— Don't look at me like that. She said *it was the right thing* to say something. She said you'd understand. Anyway, I found a clerical, a non-shifter who was working cover in the Martin family casino. He requested a transfer about six months after you moved out. To *Alaska*. When Nick had someone in brevis Alaska approach him for questioning, the guy pretty much melted down. Turns out he'd leaked information about you and Dean and Make It Happen—had no idea it would turn out as it did, just trying to make some extra cash."

"Ah," Joe said, trying to decide how he felt. Vindicated or betrayed all over again or suddenly free. Later, that's what he'd decide. "So you got your dark Sentinel after all."

"More like the color of white underwear that goes in the wash with black jeans." She wrinkled her nose at him, which damned well tickled, and he couldn't help but squirm a little, so she did it again and laughed, and they lost themselves in that for a little while.

"How long," Joe asked breathlessly, so very much wishing he could do more than lie on his back and reach for her. "How long?"

"Annorah?" she guessed. "Oh, easily all afternoon."

He grinned. And then didn't. "What has she told them? What has Ruger told them? Or…you?" Because if the Sentinels knew of his true abilities, of his renewed sensitivities…this sudden new sense of freedom he had could disappear in short order.

She didn't have to guess his concern. And she didn't make him wait, although her hands crept back under the covers and back under the boxers that, truly, could barely be called being worn at this point anyway. "I don't believe Ruger will remember much. Even if he does, he won't. Annorah seems somewhat confused— events happened so quickly, you know. As for me…I never really did understand what was happening on that mountaintop."

"It wasn't just me," he said, closing his eyes, savoring

her touch—but not for long, not when she was within reach and he could pull her atop him again. "Up on the mountain? I told you it wasn't just about us—the Sentinels, the Core. When I needed help, I had it. The Navajo mountain spirit, the Hopi Kachina spirits, the Apache soul…they saved the mountain, and they gave me a place to hide. And then you came along, and you…" He opened his eyes, found her big, dark gaze, the smudged edges that spoke of her ocelot. "*You* saved me."

"No," she told him, and did what he'd been waiting for all this time, settling over him, so they both gasped and wiggled in suddenly trembling, anticipating, readiness. "We saved each other."

"Okay," he said, his voice gone ragged and needy. "Let's do it again."

"Always," she agreed, and bent close to his lips. *Always and forever.*

* * * * *

Look for Doranna Durgin's next
SENTINELS *paranormal romance*
SENTINELS: WOLF HUNT
Coming soon
Only from Silhouette Nocturne!

GLOSSARY

Adjutant—A consul's executive officer.

Aeternus Contego—The strongest possible ward, tied to the life force of the one who sets it and broken only at that person's death.

Atrum Core—An ethnic group founded by and sired by the Roman's son, their basic goal is to acquire power in as many forms as possible, none of which is natively their own; they claim to monitor and control the "nefarious" activities of the Sentinels.

Brevis Regional—Headquarters for each of the Sentinel regions.

Consul—The leader of a brevis region.

Drozhar—An Atrum Core regional prince.

Monitio—A Sentinel warning call.

Sceleratus Vis—Forbidden ancient workings based on power drawn from blood, once used by the Atrum Core.

Sentinels—An organization of power-linked individuals whose driving purpose is to protect and nurture the earth—as befitting their Druid origins—while also keeping watch on the activities of the Atrum Core. Many Sentinels can shape-shift.

Septs Prince—The Atrum Core prince of princes.

Vigilia—The original Latin name for the Sentinels, discarded in recent centuries under Western influence.

Vigilia Adveho—A Sentinel telepathic long-distance call for help.

In 2009 Harlequin celebrates
60 years of pure reading pleasure!

We're marking this occasion by offering
16 **FREE** full books to download and read.

Visit

www.HarlequinCelebrates.com

to choose from a variety of
great romance stories
that are absolutely **FREE!**

(Total approximate retail value of $60)

We invite you to visit and share the Web site
with your friends, family
and anyone who enjoys reading.

REQUEST YOUR FREE BOOKS!

2 FREE NOVELS PLUS 2 FREE GIFTS!

Silhouette®

nocturne™

Dramatic and Sensual Tales of Paranormal Romance.

YES! Please send me 2 FREE Silhouette® Nocturne™ novels and my 2 FREE gifts (gifts are worth about $10). After receiving them, if I don't wish to receive any more books, I can return the shipping statement marked "cancel." If I don't cancel, I will receive 4 brand-new novels every other month and be billed just $4.47 per book in the U.S. or $4.99 per book in Canada. That's a savings of about 15% off the cover price! It's quite a bargain! Shipping and handling is just 25¢ per book*. I understand that accepting the 2 free books and gifts places me under no obligation to buy anything. I can always return a shipment and cancel at any time. Even if I never buy another book from Silhouette, the two free books and gifts are mine to keep forever.

238 SDN ELS4   338 SDN ELXG

Name	(PLEASE PRINT)

Address	Apt. #

City	State/Prov.	Zip/Postal Code

Signature (if under 18, a parent or guardian must sign)

Mail to the **Silhouette Reader Service:**
IN U.S.A.: P.O. Box 1867, Buffalo, NY 14240-1867
IN CANADA: P.O. Box 609, Fort Erie, Ontario L2A 5X3

Not valid to current subscribers of Silhouette Nocturne books.

Want to try two free books from another line?
Call 1-800-873-8635 or visit www.morefreebooks.com.

* Terms and prices subject to change without notice. Prices do not include applicable taxes. Sales tax applicable in N.Y. Canadian residents will be charged applicable provincial taxes and GST. Offer not valid in Quebec. This offer is limited to one order per household. All orders subject to approval. Credit or debit balances in a customer's account(s) may be offset by any other outstanding balance owed by or to the customer. Please allow 4 to 6 weeks for delivery. Offer available while quantities last.

Your Privacy: Silhouette is committed to protecting your privacy. Our Privacy Policy is available online at www.eHarlequin.com or upon request from the Reader Service. From time to time we make our lists of customers available to reputable third parties who may have a product or service of interest to you. If you would prefer we not share your name and address, please check here. ☐

SN09

Silhouette®

n o c t u r n e™

COMING NEXT MONTH

Available August 25, 2009

#71 TIME RAIDERS: THE SLAYER • Cindy Dees
Time Raiders

Army captain and time traveler Tessa Marconi can locate
any lost object, even if it's a medallion hidden in ancient
Persia. But before she can do so, she encounters the
gorgeous Rutam of Halicarnassus—a sorcerer whose very
presence robs her of breath *and* the powers she needs
to complete her mission. Now Tessa must get them back
before he manages to capture anything else....

#72 MOON KISSED • Michele Hauf
Wicked Games

Loner Stephen Sevaro never thought he would find his
mate, since female werewolves are rare...and there's no
way she would be human! But there is something about
the beautiful Belladonna Reynolds that calls to him and
rouses all his alpha senses. But how will the delicate
dancer react to his wolf when the moon is full?

SNCNMBPA0809